A MALIGNANT HOUSE

A MALIGNANT
HOUSE

Fay Sampson

This first world edition published 2009
in Great Britain and 2010 in the USA by
SEVERN HOUSE PUBLISHERS LTD of
9–15 High Street, Sutton, Surrey, England, SM1 1DF.
Trade paperback edition published
in Great Britain and the USA 2010 by
SEVERN HOUSE PUBLISHERS LTD

British Library Cataloguing in Publication Data

Sampson, Fay.
   A Malignant House.
   1. Women genealogists–Fiction. 2. West Country
   (England)–Fiction. 3. Detective and mystery stories.
   I. Title
   823.9'14-dc22

ISBN-13: 978-0-7278-6827-5   (cased)
ISBN-13: 978-1-84751-197-3   (trade paper)

All Severn House titles are printed on acid-free paper.

Severn House Publishers support The Forest Stewardship Council [FSC],
the leading international forest certification organisation. All our titles that
are printed on Greenpeace-approved FSC-certified paper carry the FSC logo.

 Mixed Sources
Product group from well-managed
forests and other controlled sources
FSC www.fsc.org Cert no. SA-COC-1565
© 1996 Forest Stewardship Council

Typeset by Palimpsest Book Production Ltd.,
Grangemouth, Stirlingshire, Scotland.
Printed and bound in Great Britain by
MPG Books Ltd., Bodmin, Cornwall.

Malignant: a name applied to Royalists by Parliamentarians during the English Civil War

ONE

'Look at this.' Nick turned his boyish grin on Suzie with the enthusiasm in his deep-blue eyes which still made her heart turn over after eighteen years of marriage.

She squeezed her way through the press of people to join him in front of a display board. There were pictures of early farm machinery: steam tractors, harvesters, cider presses. Nick was gesturing to the story printed alongside a photograph of a threshing machine.

'"Fatal Accident at Eastcott St George,"' Suzie read. "An inquest into the unfortunate boy Peter Marchant, who was killed by becoming entangled in a threshing machine, was held on Saturday last before G.E. Tupper, the county coroner. John Moore . . .'"

Suzie caught her breath. 'John Moore. That was my great-great-grandfather's name.' She read on. '"Who was working with the deceased at the time of the accident, and Mr Watkins, his employer, gave evidence. They stated that they were obliged to take the machine to pieces and cut the bag before they could extricate the body." That's gruesome. Fancy having to pick your friend's remains out of that. It doesn't bear thinking about.'

'Health and safety gets a bad press nowadays, but you can see their point.'

'Hang on.' She studied the press cutting. '1867. So John Moore couldn't be great-great-grandaddy. He'd gone for a soldier before then. But it must have been his cousin.'

'No wonder your John decided to pack in farm labouring and join the army. It was probably safer.'

Suzie looked around the crowded village hall. Eastcott St George had put on an exhibition of local history and she had been drawn here in search of her ancestors. Nick didn't share her passion for family history, but she was glad that he was finding plenty to interest him.

The next stand was quieter. It seemed to be extracts from various censuses. It didn't have the same pulling power for overgrown schoolboys as the farm machinery. She ran her eye

over the lists of names, addresses, occupations, birthplaces.
Much of it was already familiar to her. She had traced her
own family's connection with the village through the micro-
filmed census records at the local studies library in town. The
Moores had last appeared in Eastcott in 1881. She looked
higher up the display. 1871, 61, 51, 41. The contents were
familiar to her. John Moore had just scraped into that first
complete census as a child of one year old.

There were more sheets at the top of the board. They seemed
to show an older generation. Her eye was caught by another
familiar name. 'Walter Moore, ag. lab.' and his family at
Duck's Cottage. She stared at it in surprise. She knew about
Walter, but only through the parish registers of baptisms,
marriages and burials. He was John Moore's grandfather.
Walter had died in 1839, two years before the earliest census
records of 1841. Yet here he was, with wife Martha and some
of the younger children still living at home.

Her eyes went back to the heading on this sheet. 1821
CENSUS. EASTCOTT ST GEORGE.

'1821!'

Surprise forced the words out loud. People turned to look
at her. She smiled absent-mindedly, her heart still beating fast
with excitement.

1821. It wasn't possible. You never found census returns
before 1841.

Correction, a little voice in her mind rebuked her. The
government had begun to take censuses in 1801 and had
repeated the exercise every ten years. But on the first four
occasions, they had only been interested in collecting the
statistics – how many men, women and children, the spread
of ages and occupations, shifts of population from one place
to another. Afterwards, the enumerators' books with all the
personal details had been thrown away.

Or had they? Here, at least, in Eastcott St George, one such
notebook must have survived, crammed full of all the details
of jobs, homes and relationships that were a gold mine for
family historians.

She pushed her way back to Nick and grabbed his arm.
'Come and look at what I've found.'

It took some patient explanation before she could get him
to see why she was so excited.

'1821 censuses are rarer than hens' teeth. It's brilliant. Look, it tells me that John Moore's father Francis had left home by the time he was fifteen. See, there he is. Farm apprentice to Mr Mark Hereward of Hereward Court.'

'Sounds like he was working for the big nobs.'

'You can say that again.'

Suzie turned to find a young man with long, greasy hair and paint-stained jeans behind her.

He threw her a grin that released a breath of garlic. 'Eastcott's Hereward country. You can't even fart here without their say-so.'

Suzie was aware of a hush in the conversation around them. A stiffening of bodies. Hostile stares.

'Oops! Me and my big mouth.' A mischievous eye winked at her before he slipped away through the crowd.

'No respect, these dratted incomers,' muttered the farmer beside Suzie.

The tension eased and the chatter resumed. Suzie turned back to Nick.

'But why wasn't this in the local studies library, with all the other censuses?'

'Perhaps they don't know about it.'

'Well, they should. In fact, it ought to be on the Internet, so that anybody can access it, even if they live in Australia or America.'

Nick's blue eyes were amused. 'Why don't you do it then? Ask if you can take a copy and put it on one of those websites you spend so much of your time on.'

'Me?' Then doubt gave way to resolution. 'I could, couldn't I? I'd have to get permission, of course. Find out who did this transcript, who owns the original – if it still exists.'

'You'd better start asking questions then, while you've got the chance. There must be half the village here today.'

Suzie looked around. As well as the crowds jostling in front of the exhibition stands, there were women and men standing beside them, or seated behind tables, answering questions. She found one of these, a woman with a red-veined face, in a padded waistcoat, who looked as though she would be more at home on a horse than in a crowded village hall on a Saturday afternoon. Her exhibition was about Land Girls in the war.

'Excuse me. I've been looking at your display of censuses. You've got a really rare one for 1821. I wonder if you can tell me who transcribed it.'

'Censuses? Oh, that'll be Arthur, I expect. Arthur Beaman. That's him over there with the tithe maps.'

Suzie peered across the room, past the WI stall, the red and white display of the local football club, the colourful stand of the village school's history, staffed mainly by eager children. Between shoulders and heads she glimpsed an array of maps, their field boundaries carefully marked. There was writing in the white spaces which would tell her the ancient names of pastures and orchards. The stand was, as she might have expected, next to the census exhibition. As she edged back towards it, through the throng, she could make out a smallish man in a tweed jacket, holding a laughing conversation with a couple across the table. The woman was writing busily in a notebook.

Suzie waited her turn. The man turned his bespectacled grey eyes towards her with an encouraging smile.

'Arthur Beaman?'

'That's me. Can I help you?'

She gestured at the adjacent census display. 'That 1821 census for Eastcott St George. Someone told me you were probably the one who transcribed it.'

'That's right.'

'They're very rare. How did you get it?'

His eyes grew brighter and his smile widened. 'I can see you're an enthusiast like me. Done a lot of family history, have you? It's not everyone realizes what a treasure that is.'

'Hardly any of them have survived – not the personal details anyway. Where did you find it?'

'Well, strictly speaking, it wasn't me. The wife does some work for the Herewards, over at Hereward Court.'

That name again. The local 'big nobs'.

'I've just found out that one of my ancestors was a farm apprentice there.'

'He wouldn't be the only one from round here, by a long way. They're the biggest landowners hereabouts. Well, like I said, my wife helps out in the estate office and she was looking for some old rent books when Mr Hereward tells her they might be in the document chest in the great hall. He shows her where it is, and, blow me, it's crammed with papers going back to old King Henry the Eighth. She saw this notebook, with "Eastcott St George" on the cover, and told me about it, and when she said it had "1821 census" written underneath, I didn't believe her. But she went back next week and asked Mr Hereward if she could check, and when she said how my eyes had lit up, he told her she could borrow it and copy it out if she wanted.'

'He let her take it *home*?'

'Looks like he didn't know how valuable it was. Not money-wise, like, but the stuff in it. So I set to and typed it all out.'

'On a computer?'

'No. I didn't possess such a thing in those days. I'm catching up with the times now, though. Well, you've got to, haven't you, now they're putting so much stuff on this here Internet? Wonderful what you can find with the touch of a button. I'd never have known about some of these old maps without it.' He waved his hand at prints of estate maps far older than the nineteenth-century tithe maps. Curling hedges surrounded the fields and a mansion house was grandly depicted.

Suzie persisted. 'Does anyone else know about your tran-script? Have you lodged a copy with the Record Office? Is it on the Internet?'

A small frown creased his brow. 'No. I just did it for my own interest. And to put up at shows like this. If anyone in the village asks me about their family history, I let them look at it, of course. But putting it on the Internet, well, that's a bit beyond where I've got to.'

'Could I . . .? Do you think I could make a copy of your transcript? I've got a computer. I could run off copies for the Record Office and the local studies library and the family history society's collection. I'm sure they'd love to have it. And I could email it to the guy who does the Genuki web pages for the county. Then everyone who's got ancestors in this parish could read it, from California to Calcutta. It would be great. I'd have to get the owner's permission, of course.'

'Old Floridus Hereward. Well, he's not so old as me.'

'Floridus? That's not his real name, is it?'

'Goes back centuries, that name. They say there've been Floridus Herewards at Hereward Court since the Normans. This one has a name for being a bit of a character, but I've

always found him a reasonable enough chap, if you keep on
the right side of him. What do you think of this hunting ban?'

She flushed. 'I . . . I was in favour of it. I don't object to
shooting animals for food, if it's done quickly and cleanly,
but chasing terrified animals for sport . . . well, I don't think
that's right.'

'I'd keep quiet about that, then, if I were you. I often say
our Mr Hereward must have been born with a hunting crop
in his hand or a gun over his arm. Otherwise, there's no harm
in you asking him. Like I said, he let my Mary take the book
home with her to copy.'

She thought of what it would be like to hold that rare
enumerator's book in her hands, to see the information
almost no one else knew about. She could make her own
original contribution to the wealth of knowledge she so
enthusiastically searched on the web.

If only she could persuade Floridus Hereward to agree. If
she could avoid saying or doing anything to rub him up the
wrong way. What did Arthur Beaman mean by 'a bit of a
character'? There was nothing unusual about a country
landowner being passionately pro-hunting. Was it anything
more alarming than that?

TWO

Suzie worded her letter to Floridus Hereward carefully.
Lodging copies of the census transcript with the County
Record Office and the local studies library sounded
safely respectable. Publishing it on the Internet might be more
of a problem. How computer-literate was the supposedly
eccentric landowner of Hereward Court? Could she persuade
him how important this was? Or would a low-key reference
to 'the county page of the Genuki website' be better just tacked
on at the end of a list of more traditional archives. She could
hope that he wouldn't study that too closely.

To make it easy for him, she typed out a consent form,
which he would only need to sign, enclosed a stamped
addressed envelope, then sealed up the packet. It gave her a

certain pleasure to write 'Mr F. Hereward, Hereward Court, Eastcott St George' on the outer envelope. Snobbery?

She came out of the study with the letter in her hand, intending to leave it on the hall table to be posted in the morning. There were leaping footsteps on the stairs. Swinging round the banisters came her teenage son Tom. The same shock of black hair as Nick, the same astonishingly deep-blue eyes. The same constriction of her heart that she, Suzie Fewings, should have these two. But the laughter in Tom's eyes was more mischievous, the intelligence behind his smile more unpredictable.

'Hi. Are you on your way out?' she asked, surveying his Saturday-night gear. Black from head to ankles, then dazzling white trainers, a silver earring flashing in his left lobe.

'No, I just dressed up like this to give Millie a thrill if she's staying in.' He dropped an unexpected kiss on the top of her head. 'Course I'm going out, Mum. It's Saturday night. Meeting Paul down on the quay.'

'What time are you back?'

'Before one. They close the club at midnight. Got to be careful of us under-eighteens.'

'If you're going past the postbox, could you drop this in?'

Tom took her letter, weighed it in his hand and glanced at the address. 'Hey, cool. Hereward Court. Didn't know you were on corresponding terms with the aristocracy.'

'They're not aristocrats. Just landed gentry.'

He had taken a swift stride towards the door before he stopped. He looked at the envelope in his hand again. The dancing smile puckered into a frown. 'Hereward Court? That rings a bell. Someone said something to me about it not long ago.' He thought for a moment, then shook his head. 'No, it's gone. But I think Paul was there. Whatever it was, I seem to remember he got pretty steamed up about it. So, something to do with racism maybe? Yes, that's right. He said his family hadn't escaped from Matoposa to be victimized by white thugs here.'

'What would Hereward Court have to do with that?'

Tom shrugged. 'Search me. I'll ask Paul if he remembers.'

He was gone, with a rush of the front door closing that rustled the dried flowers on the hall table.

'You got a boyfriend, Mum?' asked Millie over her cornflakes.

Startled, Suzie looked up from the letters in her hand to

her thirteen-year-old daughter. 'What on earth are you talking about?'

Millie waved a spoon at the envelopes Suzie had been checking. 'The post. Every day this past week you've been belting to the door as soon as it comes, like a dog that's just seen next-door's cat. You can't wait to see what there is for you, and then you sort of sigh and give Dad his, as though you still haven't got the one from the bloke you were hoping for.'

'Millie!' Nick had been listening to this exchange with his mouth open.

'Only joking, Dad.' Her thin face creased into a wicked smile.

'Well, if you must know,' said Suzie, 'I'm still waiting for an answer from Floridus Hereward. It's two weeks since I wrote to him to see if he'd let me publish a transcript of that 1821 census on the Internet. It's beginning to look as if he's not going to reply.'

'Probably doesn't correspond with the plebs.' Tom gave her his lazy grin. 'Gives them ideas above their station.'

'Don't be silly. I've told you before, the Herewards aren't really aristocracy.'

'White elitist, though. I asked Paul. You know what he says? The word on the street is they use the Hereward estate as a training camp for fascist thugs.'

'Hearsay. There are always people who will spread malicious stories about someone who's got more money than they have. Arthur Beaman said Mr Hereward is perfectly easy to get on with, if you keep off hunting.'

'So why hasn't he answered you?' Tom challenged her.

'Perhaps he can't write,' Millie suggested. 'You know, like those medieval kings who thought it was beneath them to learn to read and write, because you paid clerk-thingies to do that sort of work for you.'

'I think Arthur Beaman's wife does some office work for him, but she hasn't written to me either.'

'He's probably just dropped your letter into the waste-paper basket,' Nick said, getting to his feet. 'It's what people do if they don't like to say no to somebody, but don't want to say yes, either. Or they push it to the bottom of their in-tray and forget about it. Hey, kids, it's twenty past eight. You'd better get your skates on or you'll be late for school.'

'Pity, though,' said Suzie, collecting the crockery and tidying the table. 'Just for a moment it seemed like a really exciting idea.'

She was unlocking the front door after a morning in the charity-shop office when she heard the phone ring inside. She dropped her bag in the hall and sped to answer it.

'Hello. Suzie Fewings.'

'Ah, so glad I caught you, m'dear,' said a woman's brisk voice. 'I rang this morning, but you were out. Terribly sorry not to have answered your letter before. I'm Alianor Hereward, by the way.'

Suzie's heart leaped.

'You wrote to my husband,' the woman continued.

'Yes, that's right.' It was hard to keep the eagerness out of her voice. 'I found a copy of this 1821 census. It's really rare, you know, and . . .'

'Yes, I know all that. Read your letter. I seem to remember the Beamans were quite excited about it too.'

'And I wondered if . . .'

'Quite all right. Should have replied before. Had a death in the family, you know. Funeral to arrange, and all that.'

'Oh, I'm terribly sorry. Look, if this is a bad time . . .'

'All in the past now. Funeral last Friday. Where was I . . .? Ah, yes. Thought you might like to come over and take a look at the original. See if there's anything else we've got that might interest you.'

'Come over . . . to Hereward Court?' Sounding like a fool, she was so taken by surprise.

'Where else?'

'When would it be convenient?'

'This afternoon? Have to be about two o'clock. Got to pick up the brats from school at three thirty.'

'Today?'

'That all right with you? Got a car?'

'No. At least, my husband's using it.'

'Hmm. I seem to remember there's a bus to Eastcott St George about twenty to two. We're a ten-minute walk from the village. Turn up the lane opposite the war memorial, then after a couple of hundred yards, look for a row of four wheelie bins by the gateposts. Follow your nose along the drive to the Court. Don't wear your best shoes.'

The phone clicked. Suzie was left looking at the receiver in her hand with a mixture of excitement and consternation.

The twenty to two bus from town? It was nearly twenty past one already.

THREE

She grabbed her handbag from the hall floor and a sheaf of writing paper from the study and ran down the road to the bus stop. To her joy, a bus was heading down the main road towards her. She shot out an arm.

The journey back into town had never seemed so slow. She would never make it. At the first opportunity she jumped off the bus and darted through the traffic towards the bus station.

She arrived at a run. She didn't even know what number the Eastcott St George bus would be. She threw a breathless question at a group of chatting drivers.

'Over there, love. Stand six.'

A queue of people was snaking on board. On the way in, Suzie had cursed the delays while passengers bought tickets before the driver could set off. Now she blessed the system. She paid her fare and collapsed into a seat. It was a pity, she realized, she had not had time to go the bathroom. She had had no lunch, either.

Her head was still whirling as the door hissed shut and the bus drew out of the houses into the countryside. This expedition was far more than she had expected. She would have been delighted enough to make Arthur Beaman's copy of the census available across the world. What else might she find now?

She was jolted out of her speculations as the bus passed a row of thatched cottages and drew up in the village centre. Suzie stumbled to the door and stepped down.

Eastcott St George might once have had a green, but road-widening had cut a swathe through the village centre. The houses and the shop on the far side were some distance away from her, but all that stood between them and the road was a small half moon of grass with a stone cross. There would be names carved on it from two world wars. She made a mental note that she must take a closer look at it, to see if any of her family were commemorated there. Then she remembered that the Moores had left Eastcott in the 1880s. There was, in any case, no time now. She checked her watch. It was already almost two.

There was a lane behind her, just as Alianor Hereward had said. She started along it.

Quite quickly, she left the cottages behind. To her right, there were pastures with sheep. On her left, as she hurried through the rustling autumn leaves, ran an unbroken red brick wall. Trees rose above it, still leafy enough to screen her view. This must be the Hereward estate. She startled a covey of half-grown pheasants who darted across the road at a zigzag run. Was 'covey' the right collective noun for pheasants? People like the Herewards would know.

She rounded a bend and the wall bellied outwards. It had scattered its bricks on the grass verge. Through the gap, she glimpsed parkland dipping downwards. No sign of the house.

Mrs Hereward's 'two hundred yards' had been an under-estimate. It was well after two before she reached the gates.

Even though she had been warned about the wheelie bins, the entrance was not what Suzie had expected. The precarious wall was interrupted by a pair of stone pillars. They might once have been painted, but now the plaster was peeling from them. The top of the left hand one was bare; the right still bore a stump of a carving which, at a quick inspection, she decided was the lower part of an eagle's legs. There were no wrought-iron gates between the pillars. The most eye-catching feature was indeed the row of green and black bins.

She had expected a sweeping drive, through an avenue of trees leading to a vista of the house. Instead, it looked like a weed-grown cart track. Now she saw why Alianor Hereward had warned her not to wear her best shoes. She hadn't had time to think about changing, but luckily she had worn flat-heeled casuals to the office.

The track curved past rhododendron bushes. When she turned her head, she had lost sight of the road.

It occurred to her for the first time that she had not told anyone where she was going. She thought about digging out her mobile and phoning Nick, but she was already going to

be late. Anyway, don't be ridiculous, she scolded herself.
The Herewards are Eastcott St George's squire and his lady.
One or both of them is probably a JP, sitting in the local
magistrates' court.

As the bend straightened out and the rhododendrons fell
behind her, the view opened out. There below her lay her
first sight of Hereward Court. It was disconcerting. She had
imagined the house set on an eminence, overlooking its park.
Instead, it lay in a hollow, surrounded on all sides by slopes
of fields and woods. Great shooting country, she thought,
remembering the pheasants.

She had no time to stop and study it, but as she hurried on
down she could see that the house was built around a square.
From each of its four corners rose a battlemented tower. That
must be a romantic whim of a past owner, she thought. No
one would build a real castle on such an indefensible site,
overlooked by hills on every side. She wished she knew more
about architecture. She could not date the façade.

She was walking faster downhill. Belatedly, she became
aware that the surface under her feet was now concrete, not
rutted earth. When had it changed? Was the rundown entrance
just a deception, to preserve the secret of the house which lay
round the bend? Then she thought of the collapsing wall and
could not make up her mind.

She was on the level now, passing between a large pool,
with a canoe drawn up among the irises, and the entrance to
the house. At the last moment, she realized that what she had
taken for a stone barn beside it was actually a chapel. There
was a skateboard abandoned in the long grass in front of it.

The drive led on past the house, but a narrower approach
turned off towards it. There was no visible front door, only a
stone arch leading into the courtyard she had seen from above.
She stood beneath the arch and looked for a bell pull. There
was none.

More nervous now, she stepped into the courtyard. A Land
Rover was parked there, a BMW and a small Polo. Suzie
looked around her. There were windows on every side and
doors in all four walls. There was nothing to show which one
she should go to. She felt uncomfortably vulnerable to
watching eyes.

Daunted by the size of the house which surrounded her,

and its silence, she seized on a small, familiar object on one of the ground-floor windowsills. A bottle of washing-up liquid. No matter that the Herewards had battlemented turrets that looked as if they ought to be flying heraldic flags, they also had a kitchen with the everyday problem of dirty crockery. She started across the yard to the door nearest that window.

There was a roar of barking behind her. As Suzie turned in alarm, she met two black Labradors hurling themselves towards her. One leaped for her chest, the other barged into her knees, sending her staggering backwards.

'Dizzy! Gladstone! Down!' A human voice roared almost as loud as the dogs.

As the Labradors subsided into a pair of quivering hindquarters and slobbering jaws, Suzie found herself facing an open door, near the corner of the range of rooms through which she had passed under the arch. On the threshold stood a short, square-built woman, with short, black, square-cut hair. She was wearing wellington boots, though the day was dry and she was indoors. Now she advanced across the courtyard, her hand stuck out in greeting.

'You must be Susan Fewings. You found us, then. Good-oh.'

Suzie's hand was crushed in a strong grip.

'Yes, thank you, though I nearly missed the bus.'

'Sorry about the dogs. Flo spoils them rotten. Still, better than a burglar alarm, don't you think? So, you want to look at our document chest, do you?'

'I . . . it's very generous of you. I only wrote to you to see if your husband would let me make copies of the 1821 census available to researchers. But if I *could* look at other things too . . .'

'Come this way. Should have told you to wear a thick jersey. It's the sort of house that feels colder on the inside than the outside, and we can't afford central heating.'

'My jacket's quite warm, thank you.'

As she followed Mrs Hereward, she looked around her, wide-eyed, at the carved, and probably medieval, door through which she was being led, at the age-darkened oil paintings of ancestors frowning down on the staircase, at the suit of armour that rattled precariously as the dogs rushed past. Everybody she knew had central heating. Could the squires of Hereward Court really not manage it? Then she thought of the four-sided building that had surrounded her as she stood in the courtyard, of the vast number of rooms it must contain, of how many pipes and radiators that would have to be installed and heated. She remembered the sagging boundary wall and was glad that the upkeep of all this was not her responsibility.

Alianor Hereward was stumping her way down a stone-flagged corridor. She threw open another arched oak door. 'There we are. Great hall. Bit of a mess, I'm afraid.'

Suzie gasped. The high-raftered hall was panelled in wood, and there were coats of arms at the top of every panel. Between them, ragged velvet curtains framed the windows and made a soft green twilight. Facing her was an enormous fireplace that could have held a double bed. More astonishingly, almost the whole of the floor was occupied by a train set, whose track ran in elaborate curves and loops, through tunnels under wooded hills, past stations crowded with passengers and uniformed staff, into sidings where goods vans waited. There was even a lake, which seemed to contain real water.

'Out!' roared Alianor Hereward, slamming the door on the dogs.

Something crunched under Suzie's foot. She drew back in dismay. 'I'm so sorry!'

Mrs Hereward cut her apology short, kicking the blue coach out of the way. 'Hornby 1930s. Don't worry, m'dear. Freddie'll mend it. My daughter says we should sell it on eBay, whatever that is. Make a fortune. But Flo won't part with it.'

'Is Flo another of your daughters?'

'Floridus. My husband. Ridiculous name, isn't it? The Herewards have always been called that, right back to Hastings. Alternate generations. Lords of Hereward manor have always been Floridus, Mark, Floridus, Mark. I got the wrong generation. Next one should have been Mark. Won't be, though. We buried him last week.'

Suzie stood stunned. Mrs Hereward had told her on the phone that there had been a family funeral. She had imagined an elderly relative.

'Your son? I'm so terribly sorry. I shouldn't be intruding.'

The woman's grey eyes glinted brightly. 'Nonsense. Over and done with. Life's got to go on.'

'Was it an accident? How old was he?' Suzie did not know

whether so brief an acquaintance entitled her to ask such questions, but it seemed impossibly insensitive to carry on as though it did not matter.

'Fourteen. Playing rugger at Harrow. Nobody's fault. Clot on the brain. Could have happened any time. Hard on Flo, though. Son and heir. There won't be a Mark to be lord of the manor this time. It's down to Freddie now. Better in a way. Mark was the arty type. Freddie's got a feel for the land. That's what you need. Look, here's the chest.'

Mrs Hereward had picked her way across the relatively clear space within the train circuit and stepped over a station to reach the fireplace. Suzie followed cautiously.

To the left of the hearth stood an iron-bound wooden chest with an arched lid. Alianor Hereward flung it open. It was piled high with papers.

'Here's where Mary Beaman found your census.' She rummaged around in what Suzie feared was a reckless way with a potential treasure trove. 'There we are.'

She drew out a notebook with a mottled blue cover. As she opened it up, Suzie saw pages of neat, copperplate handwriting. Her heartbeat quickened at the sight of this first-hand evidence. All the details of people's lives nearly two centuries ago, which Arthur Beaman had so faithfully copied.

'Could be more of them. Anyway, see what you can find. Help yourself. If you'll excuse me, I need to weed the onions.'

Footing it neatly through the train set, in spite of her wellingtons, she was gone.

Suzie knelt before the chest, wondering how to begin. Was there a dating order in these bundles of papers, which she ought to preserve? Then she remembered the casual way Alianor Hereward had rummaged through them and decided it was probably too late for that.

She began to lift out papers from the top layer. A smaller black notebook. She turned the pages. It seemed to record the trees felled and planted on the estate from the mid-nineteenth century. The next was a bundle of small sheets tied with ribbon. Love letters between a squire and his lady? She undid the knot carefully. It was a collection of butcher's bills. Why would anyone keep them? But still a mine of information for some social historian. Beneath them was a larger book than

either of the first two. A scuffed buff cover. Inside was page
after page of details about the tenants of the Hereward estate.
Against each property there were three names.

Something tugged at her memory. Wasn't there a system
of leases for three lives? A tenant could nominate someone,
perhaps a son or a daughter, to take over the tenancy after he
died, and someone else after that. It must have been a gamble
in those days, when life was more precarious. Suppose the
second person died before the first? Could you name someone
else in their place, or would the property go straight to number
three?

Like Freddie.

She read some of the rents.

Monthill

Ja^s. Newcombe	Ja^s. Newcombe	48		13.0)
	Mary Newcombe	26	Capon or 2.0)	32.12.6
	George Flood	18	H. Day 2.0)	

Wonderful stuff. So a fat cockerel could be substituted for a
rent of two shillings. But what was 'H. Day'? She puzzled
over it. Work at harvest time? Mary Newcombe was probably
James's daughter, but who was George Flood?

She read the heading at the top of the column. *Lives and
Ages in 1793*. She turned more pages. List after list of names,
all living in Eastcott St George, in the manor of Hereward.
This was older than the 1821 census by nearly 30 years.

She put the book down with a hand that was trembling
with excitement. The census had seemed like treasure
enough. This was gold dust. The eighteenth century. With
the help of this book, she could tell people where their ancestors lived, the rent they paid, the yearly value of their land.
And Alison Hereward had told her she could copy anything
she wanted.

She felt in her handbag for the sheaf of paper she had
grabbed before she left home. She was torn between the desire
to start right now, getting these precious facts copied, while
she had the chance, and the curiosity to know what else might
lie beneath her hands.

She looked in frustration at her watch. It was half past two
already. Mrs Hereward had to pick up the children from school

at 3.30. Not Harrow for the younger ones yet, obviously. What
could she do in just one hour?

Better a bird in the hand. She picked up the rent book
again and looked around for somewhere to write. There
was only one small table in this vast room, and it held an
enormous marble clock. She did not want to risk lifting it
off. She went out into the silent corridor. A door to her left
was a little ajar. She pushed it tentatively open and peered
inside.

It was a lavatory. Wonderful. She'd been too embarrassed
to ask for one.

The next door she tried opened on a library. Bookshelves
climbed to the high ceiling on every wall. They were crowded
with mostly leather-bound volumes that spoke of age. There
was a mahogany table so large that it filled most of the floor
space. There was nothing on it except a stoneware bowl of
potpourri. The room felt uninhabited, unlike the great hall
with its train set.

She laid the book and her paper on the polished wood and
settled down to write.

As the hour wore on, Suzie was increasingly aware that Mrs
Hereward had been right about the temperature. Though the
day was sunny, no warmth penetrated the tall windows. This
room must face north. She could see the small lake at the front
of the house. Her blouse was thin. At work, she had taken off
her light woollen jacket, but now it felt inadequate. She was
conscious that she had missed lunch, and her last hot drink
had been mid-morning.

Her cramped fingers gripped her pen, trying to race over
the pages and yet preserve the accuracy of names and figures.

She heard a movement behind her. She turned, expecting
to find Mrs Hereward apologizing that it was time for her to
leave. She was only a quarter of the way through the rent
book. She felt a wave of frustration, knowing how many such
finds must be waiting to be discovered in the document chest.
What good was one hour?

It was not the stocky figure of Alianor Hereward in the
doorway. A tall man in a tweed jacket and plus fours stood
watching her. His rosy tanned face seemed to have been chiselled into planes and angles, rather than grown from flesh and

bone. Even his dark-gold hair was crimped into precisely sculpted waves.

She knew at once who this must be. Either something about him or what she had heard of him made her get to her feet in a hurry. Whatever she had said to Tom, this man looked quintessentially aristocratic, arrogantly handsome. Except, she realized after a moment, for his grey-blue eyes. They looked, not only startled to find her there, but almost, strange though that sounded, alarmed.

'I'm sorry.' A high, clipped voice, as precise as the waves of his hair, not the earthy half sentences of his wife, which were not unlike the bark of her dogs. 'I didn't know there was anyone here. What I mean is, I thought I heard something.' His tan flushed deeper.

Suzie had started to gather her papers together. She held out her hand. 'I'm Suzie Fewings. You must be Floridus Hereward. I'm so grateful to you and your wife for letting me see your family documents. And for agreeing to make copies available to other people.'

He did not take her offered hand. She let it fall, feeling her own face flush, and gestured to the book on the table. 'I've found this wonderful rent book from 1793. It's full of details about all the Hereward tenants.'

Her voice died away as she found him staring at her blankly.

Then he gave a small shake of his shoulders. 'That must be Allie. She's into all that sort of thing. Family history. She's a writer, you know.'

'Didn't she tell you she'd invited me?'

'She might have done.' He stood staring at her for a while. Then he collected himself, as though making an effort at polite conversation. 'You must be cold in here. This is a morgue of a house. Won't you come to the kitchen for a cup of tea? It's the only place we can keep warm. We couldn't survive without the old Aga.'

'I'm afraid I'll have to go. Your wife said she had to pick up the children from school at half past three. I've outstayed my time. There's just so much I wanted to copy.'

'There's no need to go. She'll be back soon. Earl Grey or Darjeeling?'

'Earl Grey, please.' She remembered the consent form she had carefully drafted for him to sign, giving her permission

to disseminate copies of her transcriptions. Alianor hadn't
mentioned it.

Shouldering her handbag, she picked up the rent book. 'Shall
I put this back in the document chest where I found it?'

'You've finished copying it, have you?'

'No. I'm afraid I've only done a quarter of it. There's such
a lot of valuable stuff in it.'

'Why don't you take it, then?'

'Take it home?'

'It would be easier, don't you think?'

Delight flooded her.

'Yes. Yes, *thank you*. I could type it straight on to my
computer. But are you sure? I mean, you've never met me
before.'

He turned to lead the way down the corridor. His voice
came muffled over his shoulder. 'You don't look like a member
of the criminal classes.'

She stood in the kitchen with him, her hands wrapped round
the mug of Earl Grey tea. The room and the drink were both
blessedly warm. Floridus Hereward seemed to have run out
of conversation. He twisted his own mug in his fingers.

Belatedly, Suzie remembered that this was a man who had
just suffered a family tragedy. The death of his teenage son.
Mark had been three years younger than her Tom. She could
not imagine sufficiently the pain. Would it be indelicate to
raise the subject of bereavement with a man she had only
just met?

'I'm so sorry about your son,' she said. 'Mrs Hereward told
me. It must be a terrible loss to both of you.'

Floridus Hereward did not brush it aside with the brisk
common sense with which his wife disguised her grief. He
stood with his head bowed, staring down at his tea in silence.

Had she made a mistake? She tried to steer the conversation
back to safer ground.

'When I wrote to you, I enclosed a consent form, so you
could say you were willing for me to put transcripts in various
libraries and record offices, and on the Genuki website. Is that
all right?'

'I presume that's what you're here for.'

She was nervous about making a nuisance of herself, but

she needed his signature. 'If you haven't got the form, I could write out another one.'

He took out a fountain pen. She wondered how long it was since she had last seen someone use anything other than a ballpoint.

Quickly, she spread out a clean sheet of paper on the kitchen table and wrote, as well as she could remember, the words she needed.

'There. You just have to sign at the bottom.'

He came to stand beside her. Without appearing to read her words he wrote *Floridus Hereward* in a flourishing hand and put the pen away. Again he was silent.

'I ought to go. I don't know how often the buses run.'

'You should have asked Allie to give you a lift. The school's in the village.'

'It's quite all right. It wasn't such a very long walk. The exercise will do me good, and it's a beautiful afternoon.'

'Keep to the drive. It's not a good idea to wander off into the woods. It's the shooting season.'

'I wouldn't dream of trespassing. I just need to get to the bus stop.'

'Good.'

A car roared into the courtyard outside. The Labradors, Dizzy and Gladstone, appeared from nowhere in a frenzy of barking. Mrs Hereward climbed out of the Polo, followed by an avalanche of children. All of them erupted into the kitchen, including the dogs. Suzie was suddenly overwhelmed with figures all talking loudly, cake tins rattling, drinks being poured. The dogs were leaping on to the table, noses thrusting for the cake. It was several minutes before Suzie established that there were only three children: a ruddy-faced boy with his mother's black hair – Freddie, she assumed – a younger girl with golden-brown pigtails, and a still smaller boy, already showing the sculptured, handsome face of his father.

Alianor Hereward was shouting at her. 'Had a good afternoon? Get what you wanted?'

'Yes, thank you. It was wonderful. I found this rent book from 1793.' She could hardly make herself heard.

'Good-oh.'

'Your husband very kindly said I could take it home with me and make the transcription there. Is that all right?'

She looked around and discovered that Floridus Hereward had gone.

'If Flo says so. It's his. Bring it back next week, why don't you? Then you can have another rummage and see what else you fancy. Same time? Monday, two o'clock?'

Next time, she could take a sandwich to work and go straight to the bus station.

Incredulously, Suzie saw the weeks stretching out in front of her. Who knew how many more treasures she might uncover, what gems she could share with the family history community?

'Thank you so much.' It seemed inadequate.

The courtyard struck oddly silent as she closed the oak door on the clamour in the kitchen. As she started to climb the drive to the clumps of rhododendrons before the gate-posts, she saw Floridus Hereward striding in the opposite direction across a field towards the wood. He carried a gun over his arm.

FOUR

She had to wait nearly an hour at the village bus stop. The timetable in the shelter showed her that she had just missed one. At first she was buoyed up with the excitement of the day. She hugged her shoulder bag against her side, with the old rent book safely enclosed. As the autumn sun sank lower, and a chill breeze lifted the fallen leaves, some of her euphoria faded. She wandered over to the war memorial. As she had guessed, there were no Moores inscribed on it.

At last the bus arrived. It made its unhurried way back into the city and then she had to catch another one home. It was nearly six before she turned the key in the lock.

Nick met her in the hall. 'Where have you *been*? I get home and you're not there, the kids say they haven't seen you. There's no note, no phone call, nothing.'

Suzie stared at him blankly. She was aware of Millie's pale face in the kitchen doorway, sharp with curiosity, of Tom hanging over the banisters to listen.

'I'm sorry. I didn't think. I left home in such a rush there wasn't time to write a note. I've had an amazing day. Out of the blue, Mrs Hereward rang up and invited me over to Hereward Court this afternoon. I only just had time to catch the bus. I had to run for it.'

'Didn't you have your phone with you?'

'I . . . yes. I'm sorry. My mind's in such a whirl. It was fantastic. They've got this huge chest, simply stuffed with papers. Just like that man in the village hall told us. And she said I could help myself to anything I wanted. I didn't know where to begin. Only then I saw this rent book. 1793, would you believe? And it's crammed full of information about who was renting what property, how old they were, how much rent they were paying, what the farm or the cottage was worth. And then I had to wait ages for a bus home. I should have phoned then, shouldn't I? I just didn't think. My head was so full of it all.'

Nick's face softened into an affectionate grin. 'Family history. I should have known. There's nothing like it for driving everything else out of an otherwise sane woman's mind.'

'But that's not all,' she exclaimed, unzipping her bag. 'Look at this. He actually let me bring the book home with me, so I can go on transcribing it on my computer. And Mrs Hereward said I can go back next week and take something else to work on, and keep on doing it for as long as I like. There's so much stuff there, you wouldn't believe.'

'You've been to Hereward Court?' Millie's eyes grew rounder. 'Was it, like, really posh?'

'Very rundown, actually.' Suzie laughed. 'The eagles have fallen off the gateposts, the boundary wall is collapsing, and the house is freezing because they can't afford central heating.'

'That's the trouble with these big properties,' Nick said. 'I always warn clients when they want me to design a particularly grandiose house for them. It's not just the money you need to build it; it'll cost a fortune to maintain it, unless you think green.'

'I don't think building a new house features in the Herewards' thinking. From what I gathered, they've been at Hereward Court since William the Conqueror.'

'You said "he" just now. You met him?' Tom's voice came

down the stairwell. 'The notorious Floridus Hereward? The one everyone says is a fascist?'

'He's not.' Suzie's reply came short and sharp. 'He was perfectly nice to me. A real country gentleman. He made me a cup of tea.'

'What's he like?' Millie came closer. 'I bet if this was a Mills and Boon novel, he'd be tall and ramrod straight, like a Guards officer. And he'd have this blond hair, cut short, but with a wave in it, and blue eyes and a sort of lean, chiselled face. And this girl from the village would come to the hall and fall head over heels in love with him, only he wouldn't really notice her at first, because there'd be this really glamorous society girl. Only in the end, of course, she'd turn out to be a wrong 'un and our humble heroine would get her man.'

Suzie felt the blood mounting in her cheeks. 'As it happens, that wasn't a bad description of Mr Hereward.'

'Watch out, Dad.' Millie nudged Nick. 'I think she's smitten.'

'Don't be ridiculous.' She crinkled her eyes for Nick and Tom. 'I prefer my men with black hair. Anyway, he's married, with three children . . .' She stopped short. 'That was the really ghastly thing. Only a couple of weeks ago, their eldest son died. He was only fourteen.' She looked from Millie up to Tom on the landing. 'Younger than you, Tom. Just imagine.'

Her heart ached at the thought of what the loss of her own son would mean to her.

Tom came down the stairs, a grin teasing the corners of his mouth. 'How about demonstrating your maternal love in the kitchen then? I'm starving. What's for tea?'

The doorbell rang that evening. Suzie left the computer to answer it. Her smile widened irresistibly at the sight of the grin which greeted her.

'Hi, Suzie. How are you doin'?'

The broad black face shone with sweat. His ample figure was clad in a green tracksuit, with white trainers. For all his bulk, Paul looked as though he had run from his house to theirs.

'I'm fine, Paul. How are you?' She let him in. 'Tom's in his room.'

'I'm on my way, ma'am.'

She watched him go affectionately. You would never guess, she thought, from Paul's sunny disposition, what he had been through. His father had been a political prisoner in Matoposa for much of Paul's childhood. The family had gone hungry. After his release, all the family had received death threats. Men in cars with darkened windows had watched the house. The family had slipped over the border by a dangerous river crossing and made their way to England, where Mr Shino had been accepted as a temporary refugee. Yet Paul always had a smile for her like sunshine.

She was on her way back to the study to resume her interrupted transcription when Tom's voice on the landing arrested her.

'Cheers, mate. Hey, you'll never guess what. My mum's actually been inside the dreaded Hereward Court.'

The bedroom door closed. She could not hear Paul's reply.

Suzie sat with the rent book on her knee, turning its pages one last time. The bus was rolling her towards Eastcott to return it. She had been disappointed to get to the end of transcribing it and find no mention of the Moores in her family. Apparently they were not manorial tenants. How many families in the parish would that apply to? Might the Moores have been craftsmen then, only slipping down the scale to agricultural labourers in the nineteenth century?

She almost failed to notice the bus slowing in the village centre.

The travel had been so much easier this time, she thought, setting off down the leaf-strewn lane. When she had finished work at one, there had been time to eat her packed lunch in the office, and still make it to the bus station without running. She was wearing sensible shoes and a warm sweater. Even this final walk seemed shorter, now that she knew where she was going.

There were fewer red and yellow leaves on the branches today. The sky was greyer than last week. She had not thought to bring an umbrella. If it rained, the distance to Hereward Court was still long enough for her to get considerably wet.

A burst of gunfire startled her. She stopped short, her heart racing.

'Stupid,' she told herself, relaxing into a smile several

moments later. 'They said it's the pheasant season. Time for shooting other things, too, probably.'

She turned between the damaged gateposts and started down the drive. A little of her confidence dropped away. She knew so little of these people's way of life. And she must seem alien to them, despite their kindness.

A breeze ruffled the surface of the grey lake. Suzie passed under the archway into the courtyard. The Land Rover had gone. This time, she headed straight for the stout oak door in the corner. There was a bell pull. She listened to the sound jangling down stone corridors. She waited for the outburst of frenzied barking.

The door in front of her opened almost silently. Unprepared by the heralding of the Labradors, Suzie jumped. Alianor Hereward stood alone.

'You came back, then.'

'Of course.' Suzie produced the rent book. 'I said I'd return this. I can't thank you enough. Look, I've run off a copy of my transcript for your own records. If you'd like it in electronic form, I could email it to you as an attachment.'

'Thanks. Most kind.' Alianor took the printed sheets from her without looking at them.

Did they, Suzie wondered, have a computer? Were they on email? Hadn't Floridus Hereward said something about his wife being a writer? What would a woman like this write? Articles for *Country Life*?

'I suppose you'd like something else.' The woman's manner seemed less enthusiastic than the week before. Have I got it wrong? thought Suzie. Have they changed their minds about giving me the run of their document chest?

'If that's still all right. I don't want to be a nuisance, but you've got so much wonderful stuff there.'

Mrs Hereward was already leading the way towards the great hall.

'Glad somebody appreciates it. Mark was the one who was keen on the history of this place. Can't say Freddie's interested. Just give him a gun or a tractor.'

Mark. The son they had lost. Suzie felt increasingly awkward and out of place.

'Where are your Labradors today?' She tried a smile, to move the conversation on to safer ground.

'Out with Floridus. Killing something. Flo, I mean, not the dogs.'

Did that mean that Mrs Hereward was not a fan of blood sports? With her tweed skirt and her clumping gait, she looked the sort of no-nonsense woman whom Suzie could imagine riding bravely to hounds. But that might just be a lazy stereotype.

'Here you are. What are you thinking of taking next?' The invitation, if more grudging than last week, was still there. She must seize it. It was too good an opportunity to let slip.

'Could I have another look first?'

She knelt down and began to lift out the top layer of papers and notebooks. Some of them she had seen last week. There were more rent books, some even older.

'1760!' A whole generation back from 1793.

'You want that one?'

'I'd certainly like to do it sometime.'

She was hesitating about whether she could undo some of the packets of letters tied with ribbon. Mrs Hereward forestalled her by untying one.

'How about this? Answers to invitations to a ball here in 1920. The County Sheriff. General Sir John Hittisburn and Lady Monica. The Ottermores. The family are still our neighbours, four miles over that way.'

But Suzie had found something else, nestling under the letters. She caught her breath. It looked like . . .

It was. Another 1821 census, this time for the neighbouring village of Lambsforde, and under that a third one, for Quinton Bishop.

'I know the Beamans took the Eastcott St George census away to transcribe. Has anyone ever copied these?'

'Not as far as I know. Why? Are you interested?'

'Interested! There's so much treasure here, I don't know where to begin. Yes, maybe these censuses, if I could? The more different families I can help, the better.'

'Suit yourself. It's the letters that interest me. Got some from the First World War. Heartbreaking. Officers were twice as likely to get killed as other ranks, you know.'

'I didn't. But I suppose they had to be out in front.'

She thought of the last *Blackadder* episode, where comedy turned to tragedy as they went over the top.

'Still, all good fodder for the writing.' Alianor dropped the invitation replies back in the chest.

'You mean you're writing the history of Hereward Court?'

There was an explosive snort. 'Good heavens, no. Slush. Romantic fiction, they call it. Don't worry, you won't have heard of me. Use a pen name. Used to do doctors and nurses, but nowadays they expect you to be up-to-date on all the medical stuff. So I switched to colonials. You know, officers in pith helmets and khaki shorts, and plucky young women with rifles.'

Suzie tried to disguise her gulp of surprise. Anything less like a romantic novelist than this stocky woman with straight black hair, which looked as if it might have been hacked short with the aid of a pudding basin, was hard to imagine. Another stereotype shot to pieces.

She got to her feet, holding the census books. 'That sounds like fun. Yes, I think these will do for this week's homework. They'll make a lot of happy bunnies . . . I don't think I've met a novelist before.'

'Somebody's got to pay the bills to keep a roof on this place. Well, part of it, anyway. Floridus is hardly going to. Does a few house parties for Americans to shoot pheasants. Flo can spin a good story, and they love all the medieval stuff, of course. Insist on calling me Lady Hereward. Still, they're a bit shocked when he lets the Labradors jump on the table and lick their plates. Put it down to British eccentricity and dine out on it afterwards, I shouldn't wonder. Tea?'

Suzie glanced at her watch. Today, there would be plenty of time to catch the quarter to four bus.

'Yes, thank you.'

They sat at the table in the warm kitchen, which overlooked the courtyard on one side and wooded slopes on the other.

'I take it your family are from round here. Any names we know?' Mrs Hereward questioned her.

'I had Moores here in the nineteenth century, but I couldn't find them in your 1793 rent book.'

'Not mine. It's the Herewards'.'

'Yes, of course. My husband's family are from Lancashire and the east coast, but all my people seem to be in this county. My maiden name was Loosemore and the furthest I've traced them back is in Southcombe during the Civil War.'

'Southcombe!' Mrs Hereward snorted. 'They'll be Parliamentarians, then. That was a notorious Roundhead hot spot. It was villagers from there who sacked this house in the Civil War after Fairfax captured it.'

'I . . . I didn't know that.' It was hard to know how to answer. Alianor Hereward's brusque voice made it sound like a personal accusation.

'It wasn't Eastcott men. They were loyal to the king, and to us. You know what the Roundheads called the Herewards? Malignants. That's the name they gave to Royalists. Hereward Court was a "malignant house". So it was fair game. They threw that Floridus Hereward into prison and let the mob loot this place.'

'I'm sorry.'

Was she? Which side would she have been on? It was probably better not to mention that one of her ancestors had ejected the Royalist clergyman from Southcombe so violently that he'd died later.

The gap between them was widening uncomfortably. Yet they were drinking tea together. The newly discovered census books were in her shoulder bag.

She put down her mug. 'I shouldn't be taking up any more of your time. I expect you want to be writing your novel. Shall I bring them back next week?'

'Do that. Monday again. No, don't worry, by lunchtime my brain's addled. Glad to have someone sane to talk to.'

What could she mean by that?

A few drops of rain struck Suzie's face as she walked across the courtyard. She really should have brought an umbrella. But the shower blew away on the breeze. As she started to climb the drive she heard gunfire again, more distant. Floridus Hereward had been right to warn her to keep clear of the wood. Not that she would have gone in there, of course.

She turned and scanned the hollow in which the house stood beside its little lake and the ring of hills which shielded it from view. What had it been like when General Fairfax's cannons had come over that ridge to threaten it? Had her ancestors really come looting here after the Herewards had surrendered? What trophies had they carried away from this 'malignant house'?

But were there other ancestors, loyal tenants of the Herewards perhaps, defending it?

Tom straddled a kitchen chair, his vivid blue eyes intent upon her. 'Tell me about it, Mum, this Hereward Court place.'

'I've already told you. What else is there to say? It's a big country house, built around a courtyard. None of those classical pillars and porticoes. It's not that grand. It doesn't look Elizabethan, with mullioned windows and tall chimneys. More . . . I don't know . . . early-eighteenth century? Maybe they had to rebuild it after Fairfax's cannons bombarded it in the Civil War. And it's got these four rather silly towers at the corners, as though someone was trying to pretend it was a castle. I half expected a portcullis in the archway leading to the courtyard.'

'Skip the architecture lesson,' he interrupted. 'What's it like *now*?'

'What do you mean?'

'Well, who's there, besides the Herewards?'

'I've no idea. I've only met Mr and Mrs Hereward and the three children. Their eldest son was at public school, but this lot go to the village primary school.'

'Staff? Gamekeepers?'

'How would I know? I suppose they must have help. They couldn't run a place that big all by themselves, even if it is falling apart. I didn't see anyone. Now I come to think of it, there were some farm buildings off to one side of the drive. Barns and so on. There could be another house there.'

'No lodge at the gate you had to get past?'

'No. Now that you mention it, that's odd, isn't it? You'd have expected one for a house that size, even if there was no one living in it now. In fact, it wasn't a very grand entrance at all. Maybe . . .' She thought of the drive going on past the house across the fields opposite, to where the woods started to climb again. 'Maybe that wasn't the main entrance, after all. I haven't seen the whole estate, by a long way.'

'And you didn't see any signs of people camping in the woods? No urban types who looked as if they didn't belong there?'

'Certainly not. Look, what is this?'

'Nothing. Just checking.'

'Tom. It's that ridiculous rumour Paul told you about, isn't it? That Floridus Hereward is part of some kind of fascist plot? Well, I can tell you I've seen absolutely nothing like that. The Herewards have been perfectly charming to me. They've let me, a total stranger, into their house, given me the run of their priceless document chest. Even let me take stuff home with me. And all this at a time when they're mourning the loss of their eldest son. It's not just ridiculous; it's unfair.'

He held up both arms. 'All right. Keep your hair on. Still, what's it you're always telling me? Absence of evidence isn't evidence of absence. It could still be true. Just because you haven't *seen* anything doesn't mean it's not there to see.'

'You want to believe this, don't you? Whether there's evidence or not?'

Tom coloured. '*Touché*. Yeah, I guess it does make a good story. Brighten up our boring little lives.'

'I don't think yours will ever be boring, Tom.'

He grinned and swung his leg over the chair seat to stand up. 'Yeah, well. Keep your eyes open next time you go. You never know.'

FIVE

The following Monday the wind threw rain and wet leaves against the patio windows. Suzie looked up from spreading honey on her toast and pulled a rueful face. 'Looks like I'm going to get wet today. It's the sort of weather when an umbrella's not a lot of good, and it's quite a walk.'

'You're going to Hereward Court again?' Nick asked.

'Of course. It's the chance of a lifetime. I'm not going to pass it up. I've made some great discoveries already, and I've only just started.'

'Would you like the car?'

'Don't you need it?'

Nick was an architect. It was not uncommon for him to be driving to a site or liaising with a client or contractor.

He consulted his diary. 'Nope. Only one out-of-office

appointment. And that's in town. No problem. Drop me off by the shopping precinct and I'll get the bus home.'

'Thanks. It'll save me arriving looking like a dripping spaniel. And I'd be mortified if I got those notebooks wet.'

It was strange how different it felt, swinging the car into the Herewards' drive. Suzie had a sense of added status, as though this time she were a little closer to their social level. Is this, she reflected, why men don't like using buses?

She slowed for the potholed track, which was all that could be seen of the drive from the road. Then, when it straightened out after the rhododendrons, she felt the hard concrete under her wheels. A little smile twitched her lips. She was entering the Herewards' hidden kingdom. A well-kept secret.

This Monday she looked around her with a keener eye. Yes, there was definitely a farmhouse down that turning. She had not paid it much attention before. The concrete track that led to it was plastered with wet straw. A blue tractor was parked outside a barn. She did not think it had been there last week.

So there were other people living and working on this estate. Hardly surprising. She peered through the rain at the grey smudge of meadows and the brown blur of woods. How many people did you need nowadays to farm this land, to manage the coverts so that the shooting would be good enough to attract paying guests? She had no idea.

She steered carefully under the narrow archway and parked alongside Mrs Hereward's Polo.

She had hardly got out before she knew that the Labradors were back. They slammed their large wet paws against her raincoat.

'Down, Dizzy! Down, Gladstone!' Alianor Hereward's roar sounded less formidable now that Suzie knew more of the woman behind the mannish exterior.

'Hang your raincoat by the Aga,' she ordered Suzie, when the dogs had herded her indoors.

'It's hardly wet. I borrowed the car today.'

'Mud. Brushes off better when it's dry. Dratted dogs. And it'll be warm when you put it on again. Thought you might like to see this.'

She had led the way into the kitchen and was waving her hand at the table. Suzie saw a family tree spread out on it.

It was large enough to need several sheets, Sellotaped together. She hung her coat as directed and leaned over the table.

'First Floridus Hereward is on the Battle Roll for Hastings, 1066. Course, that's not Bible proof. The Roll was drawn up much later. Lots of families wanted to claim their ancestors fought at Hastings. Only half a dozen names can be verified independently. I think myself it's more of an Anglo-Saxon name. Remember Hereward the Wake? Some English families did that, you know. Married a Norman girl, started speaking French and giving their children French names, like Mark. Assimilation to the ruling class. What do you think?'

'Me? Er . . .' Suzie had been following a more selfish line of thought, scanning the list of Hereward marriages to see if there was a surname she recognized from her own family tree. 'I'm still a bit vague about Normans and Plantagenets. I'm afraid I haven't got that far back in my own family history.'

'Well, you won't, of course, unless you've got someone who married the daughter of a lord of the manor. Then you're away. Herald's Visitations. Burke's *Landed Gentry*. County genealogists. Manorial Rolls. Not all accurate, mind you, but good fun. You end up related to half the landed families in the country, and royalty as well, if you're lucky.'

'I'm not sure that sounds like my family.'

'You never know. Found anything hopeful?' Her shrewd eyes watched Suzie scan the Hereward pedigree.

'Yes. Here's one. Douce Doble, married 1325. What a lovely name.'

'Dulcia in the Latin deeds. Got Dobles on your tree, have you? That *is* an old French name.'

'Yes, but only yeoman farmers in the early-eighteenth century. I haven't gone any further back on that line yet.'

'Worth following up. If it's the same family, and they're marrying one of their girls to a leading Hereward, they were almost certainly gentry themselves.'

'It's a long way further back. Four centuries.'

'If you can tap into one of these pedigrees, it's all done for you.'

Suzie straightened up and smiled. 'Here are your census notebooks. And copies of my transcripts. Would you believe, I've already had comeback from the rent book I did the first week? I had Genuki put it on their website under Eastcott

St George, and I had this wonderful email from a guy in New Zealand who's thrilled because it tells him where his ancestor was farming in 1793.'

'Flo'll be pleased. All good publicity for the place. Now, we'll put these back and you can help yourself to the next one. Come back to the kitchen when you've finished. The Labs will let me know.'

Again, she left Suzie alone by the document chest in the great hall. *She's amazingly trusting*, thought Suzie.

Without Alianor Hereward's scrutiny, she felt freer to delve deep into the papers. The top layer seemed mostly from the nineteenth and late-eighteenth centuries. As she lifted them out, older documents came into view. There were scrolls with wax seals attached to them by ribbons. She gasped as she deciphered the name of King Henry VIII. Arthur Beaman had been right. With a feeling of daring, she slipped off the tape that bound the scroll and unrolled the parchment.

Disappointment met her eager eyes. The elegant script baffled her. Where she could puzzle out the letters, the words themselves were unfamiliar. Latin. She sighed. Whatever the deed contained, it would be beyond her ability even to transcribe it, let alone understand what it said. Regretfully, she rolled it up and replaced the tape. She laid the document back in the chest, taking care that the weighty wax seal hanging from it was safely stored.

She sat back on her heels. How much time had passed? Mrs Hereward would be expecting her back in the kitchen. She replaced the upper layers of papers, reserving the 1760 rent book for this week's transcription. She closed the curved lid of the box and slipped the iron hasp in place.

There was the usual problem of negotiating the train set to reach the corridor.

As she passed the door to the courtyard, it swung open with such force that she had to leap back to avoid being hit. A burly man in dripping black leather overcoat stopped in mid-stride as he burst into the house. Rain glistened on his bare, shaved head, darkened by black stubble.

He stood for a few moments glaring at her with small eyes narrowed between folds of puckered flesh. Then he gave a sudden high laugh. 'Sorry, darling. Wasn't expecting to see anybody here.'

He swung off down the corridor in the opposite direction to the great hall. Suzie felt strangely relieved to see the back of him.

She heard a distant barking, as if muffled behind a door. By the time the dogs appeared, skidding on the flagstones, with Alianor Hereward in their wake, the man had turned the corner out of sight.

The family tree had disappeared too. Belatedly Suzie realized that she should have made notes. While Alianor boiled the kettle, Suzie drew out a sheet of paper and scribbled what she could remember. Douce Doble, m. ? Hereward 1325. Something for her next research trip to the local studies library.

Alianor did not mention the man in the black leather coat. But why should she? He must have been on his way to see Floridus Hereward. Yet he had looked oddly out of place in Hereward Court.

The wind was tearing the clouds apart as Suzie drove out of the archway. A vivid shaft of sunlight transformed the grassland to emerald and raced on over ruby and amber woods. When she met the drive by the lake, where she should have turned left, she paused. As the engine idled, she looked where the ribbon of concrete stretched away on her right up the further slope into the trees. Had Tom been right? Was that once the main approach to the house? Was there a more ornate gateway up there? A lodge-keeper's cottage? In the clearer air she thought she could make out a line of telegraph poles along the ridge. There was probably a road up there.

For a moment, she was tempted to turn the car that way and find out. But she was quickly overcome with nervousness. Alianor Hereward would probably see her from the window, maybe Floridus as well. She was trespassing so much on their generosity already. She must not risk fouling it up by impertinent curiosity. Perhaps she could ask Alianor about it next week.

Dutifully, she turned the wheel the other way and headed back up the drive towards Eastcott.

Emerging on to the lane, she signalled right towards the village centre and the main road. Unnecessary, really. There was no other car in sight. She was already swinging the nose of the car round when she put her foot on the brake. Where *did* this lane go?

She reversed off the tarmac and reached for the road atlas on the back seat. Her finger traced the yellow thread of the lane. Hereward Court was marked to the left of it, in a Gothic script that denoted an historic building. She followed the line on the map to a crossroads. Yes, she was right about the tele-graph poles. The left fork showed a minor road in white running along the ridge she had seen from below. If there was another entrance to Hereward Court, it must lie along there.

Enjoying the freedom to explore more widely that the car gave her, she turned away from the village.

The brick wall stretched on, still backed by its screen of trees. On the other side, field gates made breaks in the hedge bank, giving her occasional glimpses of high farmland, of distant moors still streaked with rain clouds.

She reached the crossroads. The lane to her left was even narrower than this one. Hedges crowded close on her right, the wall on her left. There was no grass verge. She hoped she wouldn't meet another vehicle.

She drove slowly along it. The brick wall frustrated her curiosity. Seated in the car, it was impossible for her to see over it. In the hollow below, Hereward Court kept its secret.

Then she rounded a bend and was caught by surprise. She was almost on it. A square, grey house, darkened by rain, with black woodwork. It stood beside a gateway far more splendid than the one by the wheelie bins. Two massive square pillars still bore their huge stone eagles. A pair of heavy wrought-iron gates was fastened between them. The drive beyond was incongruously grass-grown, unsurfaced, until she remembered the deceptively neglected entrance she usually used. Here, too, were towering rhododendron bushes, and that curve in the drive which hid the vista below.

Opposite, a cart track headed down towards the next village.

She stopped the car and studied the gatehouse. Was it occu-pied? Nothing ornamented the windowsills facing the road, but she thought she glimpsed curtains through the reflected light of their glass. She got out and walked up to the gate. It was padlocked. She had the uneasy feeling that if anyone was in the house they might be watching her.

She was turning away guiltily when a movement in the

wind caught her eye. Behind the house two black shirts were flapping damply on a clothes line half overhung by trees.

It was an odd sense of relief to climb back into the shelter of the car. Of course the Herewards would want a house like that to be occupied, whether it was by estate staff or an income-generating tenant.

She picked up the atlas again to trace her route from here to the main road.

Sunshine lay ahead as the tall hedge on her right gave way to open fencing. At the next crossroads she would leave the Hereward estate behind. She had satisfied her curiosity, found what had once been the principal entrance. It must, she thought, lead out, not to Eastcott St George, but towards the neighbouring village of Quinton Bishop, whose census returns she had also transcribed. Perhaps that was where the former Herewards went to church, driving their carriages out through those grander gateposts.

She almost missed it. A corner of her brain registered a greater lightness on her left. She slammed on the brakes, and skidded a little on the wet road.

Another collapse of the wall. Not fresh. Someone had cleared the bricks from the road and piled them by the footings of the wall. She got out again and walked around the car. Carefully she mounted the pile of tumbled bricks.

Sunlit grass showed between her and the silver trunks of beech trees. She was looking down at Hereward Court from the other side. The little towers at its four corners, the glint of the lake, the family chapel. She could see the part of the drive she had walked threading its way up the further hill.

The upper slopes that surrounded the parkland were clothed with trees. The leaves were falling, beginning to reveal their winter skeletons. Over to her right, a flash of something bright. She narrowed her eyes, trying to focus. The reflection of sunlight on a vehicle in a clearing? No, two . . . three cars. Something long and brown. A wooden hut, perhaps. And what could those small green and greyish white shapes be? Tents?

Alianor had talked about moneymaking house parties. But a campsite? She could imagine Floridus might well let a scout troop use his land, but it wasn't half-term. It was too late in the year for the holiday trade. She shook her head, trying to think of a logical explanation.

She clambered down from the bricks, baffled, and started up the engine again.

Something Tom had said flickered briefly through her mind. She pushed it away.

SIX

Suzie drove the car into the garage and switched off the ignition. She sat there for a while, thinking. She always came home from these forays on a high of excitement. It was such enormous good fortune to be allowed to see all those documents, let alone borrow them. Part of her mind told her they should be securely lodged in the Record Office, preserved under optimum conditions. Perhaps she should mention this, tactfully, to Alianor Hereward. Another, more selfish, part of her exulted that she, Suzie Fewings, was the only one given this privilege, apart from the Beamans with one 1821 census. She did not know how long she could continue her work without outstaying her welcome. There was such a huge amount still to be discovered and copied.

But today this mix of euphoria and anxiety was darkened by a more disturbing discovery. That man who had almost cannoned into her as he'd burst open the door. '*Sorry, darling.*' Those Estuary vowels had no origin here in the West Country. And they were out of place with the clipped accents of the Herewards. He had looked more like a bouncer from a nightclub than the tenant of the home farm or a tweedy gamekeeper. And then there had been that unexplained camp-site in the woods.

A small cold voice reminded her of Paul's story of an extremist group on the Hereward lands. Could he be right? Was this evidence?

Melodramatic rubbish. She gathered up her handbag, with the still older rent book for this week's transcription, and opened the door of the car. You've been hearing too many colourful stories from the past. General Fairfax besieging Hereward Court, an earlier Floridus flung into prison as a malignant, villagers, maybe even her own ancestors, looting

the house. She was being lured into imagining that her own
life was part of a conflict similarly violent and exciting. What
was it Tom had said about 'brightening up our boring little
lives'?

Tom. She stopped on the path to the front door. What should
she tell him? No matter how innocent the things she had seen,
if she told him about the camp, he would undoubtedly be
straight off to Paul's. Within moments, the two of them
would have worked it up into a far-right conspiracy to bring
down the government and put a racialist dictatorship in its
place. Two seventeen-year-olds out to save the world from
destruction.

She opened the door, still thinking. What would they do?
Tell the police? A wave of embarrassment burned her cheeks.
Of course the police wouldn't take them seriously, would they?
*'Someone's put up a few tents on a country estate and you
want us to raid the place? Do us a favour. Off home, sonny,
or we'll nick you for wasting police time.'*

But supposing, just supposing, the police did follow it up?
What if it came out that it was her son who was the cause of
it? That the report had come from Suzie herself? Her scalp
crawled at the thought. She saw coldness descend like a shutter
over Alianor Hereward's face, heard the Labradors' joyful
welcome turn menacing, felt Floridus Hereward's distant courtesy stiffen into contemptuous rejection. *'You've abused our
hospitality, Mrs Fewings. Under the circumstances, it would
be better if you didn't come back.'* She would have to creep
away like a whipped spaniel, leaving the treasures of that
document chest unexplored.

And it could not be anything but a wild right-wing
conspiracy theory, could it?

She started guiltily as the first person she met in the hall
was Tom.

'Hi, Mum. Had an exciting afternoon?'

'Yes, as a matter of fact, I have.' She felt the false bright-
ness of her smile. For a moment she wavered. In spite of
herself, it was on the tip of her tongue to reward his affectionate grin with the information he wanted. He would almost
certainly hug her. Then she steadied herself. 'Mrs Hereward
showed me this fabulous family tree, going right back to the
Battle of Hastings, or so it says – not that she believes they

were actually Normans. But a long way back, in the 1300s, one of the Herewards married a woman called Douce Doble. And we've got Dobles on our family tree. So we might even be related to the Herewards, some sort of cousin, goodness knows how many times removed.'

'Big deal.'

'Anyway, I'm going to the Record Office to see what I can find. I'm only back to the eighteenth century with them so far. I'll have to see if I can find a link. Of course –' she turned away as she hung up her raincoat – 'that's not the way you're supposed to do genealogical research – trying to prove a hypothesis that you're related to someone famous. You ought just to follow the lines back wherever they lead. No preconceptions. Otherwise, you can get tricked into believing something is true when you haven't really got enough evidence. Look at all those people on *Who Do You Think You Are?* who look as though their world has come crashing down, because they've just been shown that some family legend was wrong all along.'

'Yeah, well, good luck with it. How long till tea? I need to see Paul.'

She dropped her papers in the study. The moment had passed safely. She could have told Tom what she had seen, and she had not.

What was there to get excited about, after all?

It gave her a feeling of pleasure to walk into the spacious calm of the Record Office search room. A treasure house of resources. She would have to begin with the obvious, the parish registers. She had traced the marriage of Walter Doble and Alice Frost to the village of Perry Ash in 1720. Alice's ancestry there went back long before that, but she had drawn a blank on Walter. There was nothing in the marriage register to indicate that he came from another parish, and he and Alice had raised their family in Perry Ash, but she could not find him, or any other Dobles, in the local parish registers before that. The IGI website had been no help, but a lot of the smaller parishes weren't on it.

For a while she trawled the microfiches of parishes around Perry Ash, without success. Neighbouring Romanswell was a dead end anyway. While the others had registers going back to the 1500s, when Henry VIII, bless him, had decreed that records be kept, Romanswell had lost all its early ones. Perhaps she would never know if Walter had been born there.

She sat back in her chair, discouraged. It looked as though she was not going to find the answer to her question. Sometimes you hit a brick wall. The evidence just wasn't there. In this case, Walter Doble's marriage in Perry Ash was the end of the line.

It occurred to her that there was just one more thing she could try. A long shot. She got up and searched the shelves until she found what she was looking for, the index of diocesan marriage licences. There had been nothing in the register to indicate that this was not a normal marriage by banns. But you never knew.

She ran her eye down the index. Yes! *Walter Doble, p. 93.* She found the right volume and opened it at the page. On the second of June 1720 a licence had been granted to Walter Doble, yeoman, *of Romanswell*, to marry Alice Frost, spinster, of Perry Ash. Witnessed by Henry Carter, blacksmith, and Roger Frost, tanner.

She was both elated that her hunch had proved right and frustrated further by the realization that she was back in that uncharted territory of Romanswell, with its missing registers.

She drummed her fists on the table. Surely there must be something she could do? She let her eyes roam along the shelves, hoping for inspiration. They came to rest on a row of thick volumes, their red cloth bindings long faded to pink. Abstracts of wills made nearly a century ago by a diligent researcher. It was worth looking. She carried the volume containing the Ds back to the table. There were several Dobles. A name leaped out. *Robert Doble, gent. of Romanswell, 1665.*

So Walter Doble, yeoman farmer of Perry Ash, *had* been descended from the gentry.

Robert had left money to his son, Robert junior, his grandson Andrew, and two daughters. Suzie did the sums. If Andrew had been a boy in 1665, then he could quite plausibly be the father of Walter, who had married in 1720.

Plausible was not proof.

If Andrew himself had left a will . . . She turned the pages back to the beginning of the Dobles. No Andrew. Yet, as she leafed forward again, his name leaped out at her. The will of another Robert Doble, gent. of Romanswell, 1675 this time, leaving a bequest to his son Andrew Doble of Maryswell.

Maryswell? The name of that village was unfamiliar to her. There was a map of the county, divided into parishes, displayed on the wall. She got up to study it and found Maryswell west of Romanswell. It was sufficiently far from Perry Ash that her trawl of the surrounding parishes had not included it.

Andrew Doble of Maryswell, would almost certainly be the father of Walter Doble of Perry Ash. Her vital link to the Doble gentry of the seventeenth century.

She stood, indecisive. There were no more wills that could help her.

Idiot! Just because Romanswell's early registers were missing, that didn't mean that Maryswell's were. She almost flew to back to the microfiches. Baptisms 1538-1718. She snatched the fiches from the drawer. Her fingers fumbled with the glass plate. The grey, dust-flecked screen flashed into life.

As she feared, the early pages were faded, almost illegible. She snarled with frustration. If the evidence was here, she was not going to be able to read it. She moved to the next row of images. Suddenly the writing changed. A firm, regular script in clear, black ink. The 1630s, 40s. Then a gap. Cromwell's Commonwealth. The records resumed in the 1660s. She sped on.

Christenings in the Year of our Lord 1695.
Walter, son of Andrew Doble and Thomasin his wife.
2nd Sept.

She stared at it, almost unable to believe her luck. Walter Doble might have brought up his family in Perry Ash, and been 'of Romanswell' before his marriage, but here he was, baptized in Maryswell. She had made the link.

Or had she? Might this not be another Walter Doble? Names were so often recycled within a family. She read on, changing to the second fiche, checking for a marriage, baptisms for the children of Walter, a burial. There was nothing. After his baptism, Walter had disappeared from the Maryswell records. He could therefore have moved back to Romanswell, where his grandfather and great-grandfather had lived. It made sense.

She rubbed her tired eyes and sighed. Robert Doble senior

had made his will in 1665. That still left three centuries between him and Douce Doble on the Hereward tree. But it was a start. She knew now that her Dobles had once been gentlemen.

She glanced at her watch and discovered with astonishment how far she had overstayed her usual time. Millie and Tom would be wondering where she was.

On the bus, she tried to adjust her imagination to her new discoveries. She had grown so used to seeing herself as the descendant of agricultural labourers, village craftsmen, at the most, yeomen farmers. This was the first time she had added the word 'gentleman' to her records.

Did it make such a difference? Could she hold her head a little higher with the Herewards, feeling herself closer to their station on the strength of one line of ancestors, very much down the female end of her tree?

Where had her Dobles stood in the Civil War? Had Robert of Romanswell been a Royalist Cavalier, with lace collar and plumed hat, like that older Floridus Hereward? Many of the county gentlemen were not. He could just as well have been a sober Puritan, earnest for the rights of Parliament against the king, keen to regulate the royal expenditure and safeguard the wool trade. The Dobles and the Herewards might have been on different sides when Fairfax and his Roundheads marched on Eastcott St George.

Why did it seem so important to know if they were on the same side?

'You don't think you're being just a touch obsessive?' Nick suggested gently as they walked up the churchyard path to the door of St Ruman's in Romanswell. 'Monday afternoons at Hereward Court, Tuesdays at the Record Office, Saturdays chasing up parishes on the ground – not that I'm complaining, mind. I enjoy this exploring – but then there's all the evenings you spend transcribing the stuff.'

'It's not all for myself,' Suzie protested. 'I hoped at first I'd find more about my own ancestors in the Hereward documents. I thought they'd be manorial tenants. But in fact, I haven't seen a mention of them. It's what I do in the Record Office that's for me. I'm trying to establish whether I'm ever so distantly related to the Herewards, by marriage at least.'

He gave her a crooked grin as he held the church door open for her. 'I hope you don't get too grand to live with a humble Fewings. As far as I know, my folk were Lancashire cotton workers or North Sea fishermen.'

'You ought to find out. You can never tell. My dad would have fallen off his chair if I'd told him he was descended from landed gentry.'

'Begging your pardon, missus, but oi knows moi place.'

She punched him.

'Shh, woman. That's not the right sort of behaviour when you're entering a church.'

'Actually, what I'm looking for probably isn't inside.'

'What's that? A gravestone?'

'Not much chance of finding one from the seventeenth century. There might be a grave slab inside, if I'm lucky.'

'So why aren't we going in?'

'I want to see the well.'

Nick looked blank.

'You know. Romanswell. St Ruman's well. There's got to be a holy well somewhere. He was a Celtic saint, back in the time of King Arthur, or not long after.'

'Ancestor of yours, was he?'

'Don't be silly. I do have wider historical interests, you know.'

She strolled around the outside of the church, threading the paths between the graves. A holy well should have some sort of stone structure. She could find nothing that looked like it.

She came back around the tower to find Nick sitting on the porch steps. He was looking intently at the wooden lychgate through which they had entered the churchyard. He held up his hand for her to be quiet. She halted.

After a few moments he relaxed and stood up. 'Nuthatch. Chestnut breast, blue back. Pecking for insects under the little roof of the gate. Did you find what you were looking for?'

'No. No well.'

'Shall we look inside?'

Suzie went ahead of him. A little cry of pleasure escaped her. 'Lovely. The dreaded Victorians haven't got to it, or not too badly. Look, it's still got its rood loft.'

Over the intricately carved wooden screen, which separated the nave from the chancel, reared a large wooden cross bearing the figure of the crucified Christ. Carvings of Mary and St John stood on either side.

She started to search the floor for engraved slabs, which might mark the burial of her ancestors. After a while, she paused in an unproductive trawl of the north aisle and straightened her back. Her eye was caught by a colourful memorial on the wall above her. Her delighted call rang across the nave to Nick.

'Look what I've found!'

As he came across to join her she pointed to the wall above them. In high relief, two kneeling figures faced each other across an heraldic shield. The woman wore a ruff and a flat, probably velvet, cap. The man, a gown with long, slashed sleeves. These were costumes older than the Civil War. She read the notice below.

'"Humphrey Doble, d. 1617, and his wife Anne, d. 1620." Brilliant! Another generation I didn't even know about. I think these must be the parents of Robert who made his will in 1665. Or . . .' She did some rapid calculations. 'Maybe his grandparents.'

'Uncle and aunt? Cousins twice removed? You're jumping to conclusions.'

'It's a pretty safe bet. They were obviously the leading gentry in the village to warrant a monument like this. And so was Robert fifty years later. I don't think there would have been room for two branches of the family here.'

She got out her camera and photographed the monument. 'Wonderful.'

'Did you pick up the booklet about the church and its history? It says here that your Dobles up there were bene-factors of the church. When the tower was hit by lightning in 1595 they paid for restoring it . . . Oh, and there's something else in the early stuff. That saint's well you couldn't find. Apparently it's round the back, on the outside of the church-yard wall.'

'Of course! I should have thought of that. Where the common people could get their water.'

Feeling she was floating above the grass with the joy of discovery, she followed Nick around the church again and they headed for another gate at the end of one of the paths. Sure enough, in the lane outside, overhung by an oak tree still fringed with golden leaves, a stone basin jutted from the wall. There was water in it, surprisingly clear.

Suzie dipped her hand into its coldness.

'You're not going to drink that, are you?' Nick asked, alarmed.

She tasted it on her fingers. 'It's holy water. It's probably still OK. But perhaps not.'

'So, you found it, in the end.'

'Yes . . . It's a bit like Hereward Court, actually.'

'How do you mean?'

'Well, you know before I went there, Tom was coming out with all that alarmist rubbish about the Herewards, how Paul had told him it was a training base for right-wing extremists?'

'Yes, well. There's no shortage of conspiracy theories, if you want to go looking for them. And you can understand why Paul would be jittery about that sort of thing, after what his family's been through.'

'His father was fleeing from a *black* government.'

'Out of the frying pan into the fire? You have to make allowances for a bit of paranoia. What's it got to do with St Ruman's well?'

'I didn't find this when I was on the inside. I had to come outside to see it.'

'And your point is?'

'Hereward Court. I'd been there three times, and I hadn't seen a sign of what Tom was talking about. The Herewards have been perfectly sweet to me. Not that I've seen Floridus since the first day, or not to speak to. Only this week you lent me the car, and I thought it would be interesting to drive further round the estate, find where the main entrance used to be. I found it OK. A massive stone affair with eagles, and a gatekeeper's lodge. But that wasn't all. As I drove on, I got to a bit where the wall that goes round the estate had fallen down. I could look down over the park and the woods from a different angle. And there was a clearing among the trees, with vehicles and tents.'

Nick looked hard at her under lowered brows. 'And you think that that's got something to do with Paul's theory?'

'Well, no. Not really. I mean, it's a bit far-fetched, isn't it? There'll be a perfectly innocent explanation.'

'It's not exactly illegal to put up a few tents, is it?'

'Of course not.'

'Have you mentioned this to Tom?'

'No. I was afraid he'd . . .' She looked at Nick for approval.

'So would I be. You did absolutely the right thing. The last thing we need is for those two to be getting some mad idea into their heads about saving democracy from an extremist coup. They need to be concentrating on their A levels and composing their CVs for university applications.'

'That's what I thought.'

'Right. As you said, there'll be a perfectly simple explanation. People like us don't have a clue about how that sort of estate works, what normally goes on there.'

People like us. As they walked away down the lane, Suzie looked back at the church with its Jacobean memorial. In spite of Nick's teasing, it gave her pleasure to think that she might be closer to the Herewards than she had thought.

A sudden, unexpected image crossed her mind. A burly man with a shaved head and a leather coat, whose voice was harsh with Estuary vowels. Nothing about him signalled '*people like us*', compared to the Herewards. Yet he had let himself into Hereward Court and glared at her as though she were the intruder.

She hadn't told Nick about him yet. Should she?

SEVEN

Alianor Hereward's eyes were bright with encouragement as she ushered Suzie out into the courtyard after another rewarding raid on the document chest.

'How are you getting on with your Dobles? Any luck yet?'

She sounded as though she were genuinely interested that Suzie might trace her ancestry back to the family of Douce Doble, who had married a Hereward in 1325.

Suzie eagerly explained the trail of evidence which had led her back to the gentlemen Dobles of Romanswell and the memorial to Humphrey Doble, who died in 1617.

'But I'm still looking for Humphrey's parents.'

Her hostess nodded. 'Good-oh. Let me know how you get on. Did I tell you I was a Doble?'

Suzie's mouth fell open. 'No, really?'

'Douce Doble's brother was one of my ancestors. Small world, isn't it?'

'So we could be related? Ever so distantly, of course.'

'Worth following it up, don't you think?'

'Yes! That would be so amazing.'

Suzie walked out under the archway, her mind whirling.

She was on foot again. The day was grey, colder than before, but dry. When the clocks went back, and the afternoons darkened early, she might try to wheedle the car from Nick more often.

Now, however, she was positively enjoying the walk back to Eastcott, past the chapel by the lake, up the unfenced drive through the meadows. Sheep, their fleeces turning from white to golden as they aged, browsed the grass. Was the cattle grid before the farm enough to keep them in? She was beginning to feel an affinity with this place, to care about its animals, its parkland, its buildings, as well as its family.

The Herewards? Her face creased in a surprised smile. Did Alianor's news make such a difference? She had been working for weeks on all the common people, the cottagers and tenants of the censuses and rent books, whose undistinguished histories she could illuminate for their descendants.

And yet . . . She might be closer to Mr and Mrs Hereward than she had dreamed when she began.

She smiled more broadly as she pushed herself up the hill. That would be a ridiculous coincidence, wouldn't it? Or would it? Her family were apparently deeply rooted in this county. And as the generations fanned out back over the centuries, was it so surprising that they should link with the ancestry of other people she knew, of landed gentry at one end of the scale, as well as paupers at the other?

Was this why Alianor had seemed surprisingly eager for Suzie to keep coming back?

Halfway up the slope, just short of the farm, Suzie stopped for breath. She turned to look down on the Court and its outbuildings, the little grey lake with its red canoe, then up to the fringe of woods that shielded this grassy hollow. It was becoming familiar to her. She felt an almost proprietary affection for it, as though she were at least one of its staff. Which in a way she was. Its chronicler for the digital age. More of her files were being added to the Genuki website weekly.

She was about to resume her climb when she remembered something. Up there, hidden by the trees opposite her, was the gatehouse, where once a road must have run down to Quinton Bishop in the next valley. And somewhere to the left of that . . .

She scanned the woods below the ridge more keenly. Visibility was poor, this grey afternoon. But she did not think that, from this angle, she could have seen that clearing with the tents, even in bright sunshine. Was the camp still there?

She had not heard it coming. There was a sudden rattle of the cattle grid behind her. Then a roar that seemed to be coming straight at her. She leaped for the grass at the side of the drive.

A small truck, with khaki canvas over its open back, flew past her. Men in camouflage overalls leaned out, grinning and jeering.

'Wotcher, darling!'

'Cor! Get 'em off!'

One whistled.

The truck careered on down the drive, sped past the house and shot up the slope beyond, into the trees.

Suzie stood shaken. It was ridiculous for a woman her age, even, she hoped, an attractive one, to feel threatened by the casual catcalls of a group of men. But she had. It had not been the words themselves. There had been about those men a sense of power, of invincibility, as though they could do anything they liked. As though they owned this place. That, she realized, was part of her outrage.

Still, the bus would not wait. She turned again, her cheeks still flaming, and started to walk rapidly.

As she passed the farmyard wall, a figure stepped out in front of her. Floridus Hereward was dressed as she had seen him before, in tweed jacket and plus fours. He managed to wear what might have seemed quaintly old-fashioned clothes with a military distinction. The precision of his jawbone, the crispness of the waves of his golden-brown hair, would make him, she reflected, a stereotypical hero of one of Alianor's romantic novels.

'I'm sorry about that,' he said, in those clipped accents she remembered from their first meeting. 'Townies, I'm afraid. They seem to have no idea these days how to behave to a lady.'

'It's all right,' she told him, not entirely truthfully. 'I've been whistled at before. But I was scared they were going to run me down.'

'Boys' games. Apparently it's all the rage these days. These executive types. Like to get out of the office. Can't say I blame them. I'd go mad myself, shut up in one of those skyscrapers. And they pay good money for frolicking about in our woods for a week or two.'

For all the lightness of his words, he fixed her with a stare whose directness she found disturbing.

Of course. A wave of embarrassment swept over Suzie. Tom and Paul, with their talk of white supremacist plots, had almost carried her away with their own feverish imaginings. Management team-building. Bonding exercises through war games, paintball sessions, commando courses. It all made sense now.

She managed a smile for Floridus. 'It's a good idea. I know it must cost you a fortune to keep up Hereward Court. Only isn't it a problem with the pheasant shooting?'

'They'll be gone by the end of the week. The pheasants will still be here. Most of them. I wouldn't be surprised if a few of them have ended up in their mess tins. A shot that just happened to go a bit wide.'

'They have real guns?'

A momentary tightening of the muscles of Floridus Hereward's face. 'Target practice. Good discipline. Strictly controlled, of course. No more dangerous than the Pony Club tetrathlon. As long as you stay on this drive, you're quite safe.'

As he said this, he did smile suddenly. He really had a most attractive smile, revealing impossibly white and regular teeth.

'Yes, I'm sure I am,' she said breathlessly. 'The only danger I'm in is of missing my bus. Thank you again for the documents.' She patted her shoulder bag. 'I've picked up a book which seems to be notes of court cases, taken by a nineteenth-century Hereward magistrate. I'm hoping they'll provide me with some colourful stories about your local villains.'

'Yes.' The smile had faded. He sounded more distant. 'I suppose there were criminal classes even then. Need to come down on them hard. None of this rehabilitation nonsense. Human rights, and all that. You need strong government.'

'Yes.' Her own smile was weaker. It was no place for a political argument. 'Right. I'd better be going.'

He stood aside, and she picked her way over the cattle grid. She would need to hurry.

The bus passed the end of the lane in a flash of blue and red, while she was still fifty yards from it. It would be a cold, cheerless wait.

As dusk fell, the occasional surge of a vehicle past the bus stop was interspersed with the distant staccato of gunfire.

Millie's angular form was hunched on the sofa before the television. She was eating a large sandwich. Jam dripped on to the plate.

'I thought you were dieting.'

'That was last week. It didn't work.'

'You still look as thin as a rake to me. Talking of which . . .'

A dark cloud seemed to be welling up from the back garden. Suzie stared through the patio windows. Two dark silhouettes, like magicians, seemed to be conjuring it.

'What's going on?'

'Just Tom and Paul fooling about. Paul said it would be cool if they swept up all the dead leaves to surprise Dad.'

'It would certainly do that. He has to practically break Tom's wrist to get him to help in the garden. But there doesn't seem to be an awful lot of tidying up going on. Quite the reverse.'

'Yes, well. You know what those two are like when they get together. Guess a leaf fight was more fun.'

Suzie stepped out into the dusk-filled garden. As she approached the boys they stopped hurling armfuls at each other, and stood panting. Leaves continued to patter down on to the paths and grass.

'Hiya, Suzie. How ya doin'?' Paul's face broke into an infectious grin.

Suzie was never quite sure where, in his passage from Matoposa to Britain, Paul had picked up an American accent. There were lots of things about Paul she didn't understand. How he could be so persistently cheerful, after the things his family had been through. Their house firebombed, death threats on the telephone, his father picked up at night in his pyjamas and dumped 200 miles away in the bush to walk home barefoot.

Her own face softened, as it always did for him.

'It was a nice thought to clear up the leaves for Nick,' she said, looking around her pointedly.

'No sweat, ma'am. We'll have it cleared in two ticks.'

Paul began racing round the lawn with a broom like a madman. Tom leaned on his rake and watched him. Then he turned his gaze on Suzie. His expression was hard to read in the twilight.

'You've been back again.' It was a statement, not a question.

'To Hereward Court? Yes.'

'Got anything for us yet?'

'What do you mean?' Though she knew.

'Look, Mum. You've got a priceless opportunity. Inside the place. Walking through the grounds. If anyone ought to be able to see what goes on there, it's you.'

'Nothing goes on there . . .' Her breath caught on the in-accuracy of what she was saying. 'Nothing except the sort of thing you'd expect on a country estate,' she added quickly. 'You know. Pheasant shooting, and so on. It's normal.'

'Nothing else? Nobody who looks as though they don't quite belong with the nobs? Mind you, some of these neo-Nazis are stockbroker types. They could probably pass in a tweed suit. But others are thugs. If you called them working class, you'd be insulting the proletariat. Nobody like that? It's just you and the Herewards, is it?'

Paul had stopped piling the leaves in the barrow. He hung on the edge of their conversation, serious now.

Suzie looked from one to the other. She threw up her hands helplessly. 'You two. You've cooked up this conspiracy theory. Dark doings in the woods. Local eccentric head of neo-Nazi gang. Secret training camps. You've got the whole thing completely wrong. Yes, I did see a camp in the woods. But it's not what you think. It's a perfectly innocent arrangement by some city firm who want to do corporate bonding. You know, commando exercises, living rough, competitive war games. These executives do it all the time. It's so normal, it's a cliché. And it's a way for the Herewards to make money. Goodness knows the house needs it.'

As soon as she broke off, she realized the extent of her mistake. Tom and Paul were looking at each other over her head, their shadowed faces made bright with excitement.

'Told you, man!' exulted Paul.

Tom high-fived him. 'Got them!'

'What do you mean?' said Suzie urgently. 'Haven't you been listening to me? It's not what you think. Somebody's seen one of these camps in the past, heard gunfire, and jumped to a wild conclusion. That's how rumours start. You haven't got a shred of evidence that it's anything out of the ordinary.'

'We know what we know, Suzie.' Paul shook his head, as though regretful for something he could see and she could not.

'I forbid you to say anything about this.' Suzie turned to Tom in sudden alarm. 'Not to the police, not to anyone. If you take some crazy, half-baked story to the police, sooner or later the Herewards will get to hear about it. They'll blame me. They'll probably stop me going there again.'

Tom leaned towards her over the rake. 'That's more important to you, is it? Your family history, copying those documents? It doesn't matter to you that, if that lot ever takes over the country, they'd throw out people like Paul? The only place he's ever been safe?'

She looked back helplessly at Paul's earnest face watching her. 'It's because you two are so concerned about that – and rightly so, don't get me wrong – that you want to see Nazis under every hedge. You *want* that rumour to be true, don't you? Never mind the evidence. It would be much more exciting for you to think you'd uncovered a fascist plot. You don't care if you make fools of yourselves, and me.'

'OK,' said Tom. She caught his quick warning look at Paul. 'Whatever you say. Can Paul stay to tea?'

'Of course he can.' Her smile was more relaxed now. 'He's always welcome.'

Paul grinned at her. He picked up the handles of the wheelbarrow and trundled it away to the compost heap.

'I mean it,' said Suzie to Tom.

'Yes, Mum. Understood.'

She could barely see his face now.

EIGHT

Suzie was enjoying herself. Beside her on the desk lay the latest notebook from Hereward Court. This one was difficult to read. The nineteenth-century Floridus Hereward had been a magistrate who evidently scribbled verbatim notes while he listened to court cases brought before him. Yet, as she patiently deciphered his scrawled words and typed them on to the computer, the colourful stories she had hoped for began to emerge.

In a seaside town, a drunken woman had pushed a policeman over and threatened to beat his brains out with a length of railing. A twelve-year-old girl had been waylaid crossing a meadow on her way home after dark. A ram had gone missing and been found in a neighbour's outhouse. The neighbour claimed he had found it terrorizing his ewes.

A familiar name caught her eye. *Thompson's Gardens*. She and Nick had heard that their house and its neighbours had been built on what had once been a horticultural nursery. Now she read that in 1852 a number of rare plants imported from South Africa had gone missing from here. Identical plants had been found in a collector's garden, though no other nursery in the country was selling them.

Nick would be interested in that one. Their garden was his creation. Perhaps its past history was why the soil was so rich and productive. Nick, of course, would say that it was his composting and hard work.

Her concentration was flagging. Time to pack up. Time, too, to suggest that Paul went home. Having boys in the sixth form required a delicate balancing act. They were no longer quite schoolchildren, yet not adults either.

She was about to close the exercise book when she noticed

the entry at the foot of the page. *West Quinton*. She had more ancestors there. The Arscotts of West Quinton had intermarried with the Moores of Eastcott St George.

She read the names of the accused. Muscles tightened in her throat.

> George Arscott 42 and William Pike 17.

It couldn't be him, could it? The father of Lily Arscott who had married John Moore? What had he done?

> Stealing as servants 3 pecks of wheat from John Wendover Farmer of West Quinton.

She turned over the page. Here was the farmer's testimony.

> Pris – presumably 'prisoners' – worked for me Arscott was in barn Pike ploughing I had lost corn before I there-fore watched barn between 5-6 afternoon saw Pike go to barn he could not see me took bag from barn & put it in wagon shed. He then went to barn & helped Arscott in work 1/4 hour after they went they went to wagon shed Arscott brought bag went to gate Pike opened it I was in hedge. I said that's far enough he said first time Pike said he had nothing to do with it

She struggled a bit with the lack of punctuation, but the story was clear. The scene was vivid before her eyes. The men stealthily filling the sack with corn. Maybe the older one keeping a lookout before the younger man hid it in the shed. According to the farmer they had done this before. Then the dangerous crossing of the yard at the end of the day's work. Dusk was probably falling. Reaching the gate; thinking themselves safe. Suddenly, retribution in the shape of the furious farmer jumping up from behind the hedge. The very words he said as he arrested them. *'That's far enough.'*

Why had they done it? Greed? Resentment at low wages? Did they have families at home on the edge of starvation? Could she excuse George Arscott? Or was he just a common felon?

People got transported for theft, didn't they? She read quickly on.

> George Arscott Whip 3 months
> William Pike 1 Whip 1 day

They had got away lightly. Floridus Hereward had evidently accepted that young Pike had been the tool of the middle-aged George Arscott. But she saw the shirt stripped from their bodies, the lash of the whip drawing blood. Heard the cell door slam on them in the city gaol.

Who had fed George Arscott's family while he was a prisoner for three months?

Her imagination came back to the courtroom. To Floridus Hereward sitting in judgement on the magistrates' bench. She could not help seeing his features as those of the only Floridus Hereward she knew.

And in the dock before him, George Arscott, her ancestor, guilty of theft. Could she tell this discovery to the Herewards and not feel diminished in their eyes by it?

The house was quiet. Tom had breezed in after school, changed into black polo-neck sweater and jeans, and swept briefly into the kitchen.

'I'm eating at Paul's. That OK?'

'Of course. Don't be late back.'

'Yeah, yeah.'

He dropped an unexpected kiss on her head. She stopped herself from asking, 'What was that for?'

He was gone, leaving a gust of air through the hall.

At tea, Millie had sat brooding over the table, crumbling a piece of bread.

'Anything wrong, kid?' Nick had asked. 'You're very quiet.'

Millie had shrugged her bony shoulders without replying.

Now Suzie sat, half watching a television drama, thinking about her children. Tom had had his own problems in the past, but he seemed to have got it together now. Nearing eighteen, he was handsome, cheerful, reasonably clever. He appeared to sail through life on an ebullient high that needed no artificial stimulants.

Paul was a good influence on him, mostly, she decided.

He had made Tom see how much he had to be thankful for. He had focused Tom's mind on the world beyond himself. You had to forgive Paul his occasional paranoia about persecution, under the circumstances. He was the right friend for Tom.

The memory of that swift, uncalled-for kiss in the kitchen warmed her heart.

It was Millie she was starting to worry about. Was it normal for thirteen-year-olds to swing so dramatically from almost hysterically shrill laughter over the phone with her school mates to uncommunicative silence around the house? Shouldn't daughters confide in their mothers? Could she be bipolar, manic-depressive? Or was this just the way teenage girls were?

Millie sidled into the room. Suzie had not drawn the curtains over the patio window. She did not hear Millie come, but saw a movement in the reflection against the darkness. A pale wraith hovering behind the sofa.

Suzie flicked off the television. Something in the body language of that mirrored figure told her that Millie was nerving herself to say something important. Thoughts raced through Suzie's mind. Uppermost, was she pregnant?

She turned slowly, giving herself time to compose her face into a welcoming smile, a warm maternal invitation to share a confidence.

'Hi, love. Can I help?'

Millie looked down, shuffling her feet, unwilling to meet her mother's eyes.

'Not sure if I should tell you.'

'Come and sit down,' Suzie invited, patting the sofa cushion beside her. 'I'm getting a crick in my neck turning to look at you.'

Millie came forward slowly, but chose a cane armchair at right angles to the sofa. She seemed to be studying the rug in front of the patio window.

'Go on. You can tell me. You never know, I may be able to help.'

'Yeah, well. It's probably a bit late now.'

'Late for what?' Suzie's heart was thundering.

'They'll have gone hours ago.'

'Who?'

'Tom and Paul.'

Her heart seemed to do a somersault. Tom? She struggled to reassemble her scrambled thoughts.

'Gone where? Why? I thought he was round at Paul's.'

Millie wriggled her shoulders uncomfortably. 'I wasn't going to tell you. It was, like, eavesdropping. I didn't mean to. Only yesterday he left his bedroom door a bit open, and I was coming back from the bathroom and I heard him talking on his mobile to Paul, and he was, like, getting really excited.'

'What about?'

'You.'

'Me?' Suzie stared at her daughter.

'Yeah. Apparently you'd told them some stuff about what you'd seen at that Hereward place.'

'That?' A cold fear was creeping over Suzie.

'And how neither of them believes it was what you said. I think it was stuff about some city types management-bonding, whatever that is.'

'And?' She was half out of her seat.

'And they'd have to go and see for themselves.'

'*Tonight?* How? It's miles out of town. It takes me twenty minutes on the bus, and it goes at quite a speed outside the city.'

'Tom told Paul to see if he could borrow his dad's car. Otherwise they'd have to use their bikes.'

Seventeen. Tom would be taking his own driving test soon. Paul had already passed his.

'They're going to Hereward Court in the dark? To spy on that camp?'

Millie nodded dumbly.

'You idiot! Why ever didn't you tell me?' All thoughts of maternal sympathy, or mother and daughter bonding, had vanished.

'Sorry,' Millie mumbled. 'I knew you'd be cross.'

Belatedly, Suzie ran across to hug her. 'Sorry, love. It's Tom I'm mad with, not you. How could he? I *told* him. He said he'd understood.'

Her mind was racing. It was hours since Tom had left. She remembered too vividly the black sweater and jeans, night gear. The farewell kiss. Idiot. Idiot. She was the fool, not seeing, not guessing what that pair would do.

Nick! She flew to the study next door.

He swung the desk chair to face her, with a surprised grin.

'What's the excitement? Someone won the lottery?'

'Nick, it's Tom.' She told him Millie's news.

'It's not fair. I'm the one who told you about it. I want to come too.'

Nick laid his hand on Millie's arm. 'Look, sweetheart, I wish we could take you, rather than leave you on your own. But Mum's the one who knows the layout. And somebody's got to stay home in case Tom gets back before us, or phones in. You'll have to let us know. That's really important.'

'Stupid git. Who does he think he is? Batman? Trust Tom to think he can save the world on his own. Well, him and Paul.'

'Don't worry. I shall have plenty to say to him myself on that score, when I see him.'

Suzie hovered in the hall. She was guiltily conscious how much she was copying Tom in her dark, warm clothing. Nick joined her, leaving a still resentful Millie to hold the fort.

The car slid smoothly into the road.

'We'll be far too late to stop him,' Suzie said. 'He left three hours ago.'

'It would still have been light then, more or less.' Nick swung the car out of their avenue and on to the ring road. 'If they had any sense, they'd wait till nightfall. My guess is that he went round to Paul's for a meal and then they set off afterwards in his dad's car, or failing that, on their bikes.'

'Was Tom's bike in the garage?'

'No, but he might just have gone as far as Paul's on it.'

'I should have phoned Paul's parents.'

'You still can.'

Suzie felt for her mobile. The little screen came to life. 'I haven't got their number. And what would I say? "Your son's gone trespassing at a stately home in the middle of the night, because he thinks a fascist group is about to take over the country"? That family's got enough problems, as it is. I just want to get the boys back, before they do any damage.'

Nick glanced at her in the harsh glow of the street lamps. 'It's not just the boys you're worried about, is it? It's yourself as well. What your Herewards will think of you if they're caught.'

'Of course I'll be embarrassed. Won't you?'

'I've got less to lose personally, haven't I? I've never met them. I can see how much those documents you've been transcribing mean to you.'

'You were keen enough to come out and try to stop Tom and Paul before anyone catches them.'

'Has it occurred to you that they might actually be in real danger?'

'Yes. I don't know if the Herewards employ a gamekeeper, but those sort of people are usually touchy about their game. If he mistook the boys for poachers . . .'

'You're not worried about the group in that camp? The ones you saw in the truck? They're the ones the boys are going spying on.'

'Some city firm doing boy-things in the woods.'

'With guns, you said.'

'Come on, Nick. This is England, not New York.'

'I hadn't noticed that we were a gun-free culture nowadays.'

They were out in the darkness of the countryside. She shivered. 'You don't really believe their theory, do you?'

'I'll just be happier when our son's safe home and I can give him the bollocking he deserves.'

They drove in silence for a while. Suzie quietly indicated the turn-off, some way short of the village of Eastcott St George. The headlights probed their way along the narrow lane. Suzie peered at the hedgerows, watching for the cross-roads where the brick wall of the Hereward estate would begin. Somewhere along that lane lay the tumbledown section of wall and the gatekeeper's lodge.

'Boy-things, was it?' Nick's voice came out of the dark beside her. 'No women on this firm's team-bonding course?'

'I didn't see any. It was hard to tell. They were all dressed up in camouflage gear, with black on their faces. The way they were shouting at me, it didn't sound like men do when there are women with them. You know how threatening it feels when you walk into a room and you're the only woman there? No, well, I suppose you wouldn't.'

'Case for the Equal Opportunities Commission, then?'

'It's not funny. But it's still not what the boys think it is.'

'Maybe not, but it's odd.'

'It's somewhere along here. Yes! Stop.'

The headlights picked out the tumbled bricks at the road-side, the gaping blackness framed by broken wings of red wall.

Nick stopped the car, with the engine still running. 'I can't park here. I'm blocking the lane.'

'I can't see Paul's car. We didn't pass anything parked did we? Perhaps they turned right at the last crossroads, instead of coming straight across like us. They could get over the wall that side and down into the woods.'

'Never mind about that. If they came on their bikes, they could have hidden them under a hedge. What do you want me to do now? Go on, or back? I can't say I fancy reversing in a lane this narrow in the dark.'

'If we go on, we'll get to the gatehouse. There's room to turn round there. Only there's someone living there. I'm not happy about drawing attention to ourselves.'

'And after that?'

'Another crossroads.'

Nick took a torch out of the glove compartment and opened the door. 'Drive on until you can turn the car safely. Then come back and keep going. I think we passed a field gate about a hundred yards back. You should have enough room to pull off the road. Wait for me there.'

'I'm coming with you.'

'No, you're not. Damage limitation. I'm not intending to get caught myself, but if I have to intervene on behalf of those two, it's better if you're not involved. Besides, two of us are more likely to give ourselves away than one.'

'Two of us could search a wider area.'

'I'd feel a lot happier if one of us kept out of trouble. And in contact with Millie.'

He was standing at the roadside now, out of range of the headlights.

'I'm scared for you.'

'I thought you said they were harmless office types? Do you want to change your mind? Go home?'

'No. Whatever the boys are up to, we've got to stop them before it goes wrong.'

'My thinking too.'

She stared into the darkness beyond the wall. It was only now, faced with the enormity of the Hereward estate at night, that she saw how hopeless it was, searching for two black-clad boys who would themselves be moving silently, stealthily.

'Hold on. I can see something.'

The excitement in Nick's voice brought her out of the car to join him, stumbling on the bricks. Nick reached in and switched off the headlights.

'There.'

Distances and angles were hard to judge in the darkness. But somewhere to their right and below them, lights burned. They were either too small or too far away to illuminate what lay around them. They were just tiny beacons in the night.

'That's where I saw the tents and a big hut, I'm fairly sure. They're still there.'

'It couldn't be some farm cottages?'

'I didn't see any. But it's thick woodland there.'

'If the boys have seen those lights, that's where they'll make for.'

She caught his arm, both wanting to stop him going and desperate for him to hurry. Nick seemed to understand.

'Don't worry. I won't do anything silly, and with luck I'll see that they don't, either.'

He kissed her and detached himself from her hand.

She saw him for a moment, silhouetted against the greyer sky as he scrambled over the debris. Then he was gone.

Suzie shivered in the chill of the night air. Her eyes probed the wider darkness. Those lights up there on the ridge opposite must be Eastcott St George, separated from her now by the Hereward parkland. By daylight, she had been able to see the house itself, the only glimpse she had had of it from any road. She peered down, where she thought it should be. There must be mist in the hollow. She could just make out a blur, which might be lights in the windows of Hereward Court. Knowing how short of money they were, by their own standards at least, she guessed they would probably not keep many bulbs burning. The camp lights were brighter, more conspicuous.

She turned away reluctantly, climbed into the driver's seat and switched on the headlights again. Immediately she was aware of herself as dangerously visible. If she could see their lights, they could see hers. Unable now to tell what lay around her, except for that inadequate cone of light ahead of the bonnet, she pressed the accelerator and eased the car forward.

The lodge-keeper's house loomed ahead. There were no lights in the front windows. She glimpsed a faint reflection from the ironwork of the closed gates. As she passed, she glanced over her shoulder. There was a hint of light in the garden, which must come from a room at the back of the house. She thought of those black shirts flapping on the clothes line. Would the owner notice her passing? There could not be many cars up here after dark.

She almost missed the next crossroads. The headlights caught the white column of the signpost and she stamped on the brake. She was straddling the road that led back to the village, past the other entrance to Hereward Court, with its row of wheelie bins. She felt a treacherous tug to turn right, to speed back to lights and houses, to the main road home.

But she could not just wish away Tom's folly, or leave Nick stumbling through the woods in the dark. Carefully she reversed around the corner with the signpost, using its white gleam to guide her and hoping there was not a ditch lying in wait for her wheels.

She would have to pass the gatehouse a second time. Guiltily, she considered switching off her lights. She kept her nerve. She was past. All she had to do now was locate the field gate Nick had remembered, where she could park.

She paused again by the broken wall and turned off the engine. She opened the door and listened for the sound of people returning. There was, of course, nothing. At last she drove on.

It was in one sense a relief that she had seen no other headlights coming towards her. She wasn't sure how she would negotiate another vehicle in the dark. On the other hand, it heightened her sense of how conspicuous her own car must be.

Nonsense. This was a public road. Why should anyone on the Hereward estate think it suspicious that a car should drive along it in the middle of the evening?

Was that the gate ahead? She had been imagining it on her left, another break in the wall. Silly. She should have realized that the fields lay on the right side of the road. She reversed a little way and manoeuvred the car on to the rutted earth and weeds. Now at last she could kill the lights, switch off the engine, merge with the night.

There was nothing to do but wait.

NINE

Suzie felt for her mobile and dialled home. Almost immediately Millie answered.

'*Yes?*'

Her breathless anticipation told Suzie at once what she feared.

'It's me. Tom isn't back, is he? Nobody's rung?'

'No. And no. It's so boring. Where are you? What's happening?'

'In a lane above the Hereward estate. And I wish I knew. Dad's gone off to search for Tom. We could see the lights of that camp, so he knows where they'll be heading.'

'Lucky pig. All I get to do is mind the phone and watch some crap sports quiz.'

'Haven't you got homework to do?'

'*Mum.* How do you expect me to concentrate, when the rest of you are about to be shot at or arrested or something?'

'Don't exaggerate. We're just trying to stop Tom getting us into an embarrassing situation.'

'Oh, yeah? Is that why Dad was looking so white and jittery?'

'Don't be silly. Mr Hereward spoke to me about those guys in the wood. They're just some city executives. All right, they're not our types, but they're quite harmless.'

'Sez you.'

'Look. I'd better get off the line in case Tom rings.'

The little screen of her mobile faded. Suzie sat there, her fingers aching to phone Nick, to know where he was, what he was doing. She knew she must not. The last thing he would want was a betraying ring tone.

From the roadside, they had been able to see the lights of the camp in the clearing. She knew that as he dropped lower the trees would rise up around him. He would lose the lights. Though he had a torch, he would not dare to use it. He would be feeling his way in the dark between the tree trunks. His feet would be rustling leaves, cracking twigs. It would be easy for him to lose his sense of direction, except what was up and down the slope. She thought of those wide autumn woods she had seen in the daylight, clothing the hillside. Nick could get hopelessly lost. He might miss even the brightly lit camp, never mind two boys in black, creeping as silently as they could. It had been mad to think they could stop them.

Tom and Paul might be hot-headed teenagers, but they were not complete idiots. They might actually succeed in stealing up on the camp, listening long enough to satisfy themselves about what was going on there, and making it back to the road undetected. It was not as if that sort of campers would have posted sentries, would they? Like the boys, though for a different reason, she had been panicking about nothing.

So why had Nick been so alarmed?

She tried to open the window to listen, and realized she had switched the ignition off. There was a time, she recalled, when you could just wind the window down manually. She changed her mind and got out of the car.

The field gate where she was parked gave her a view back towards the city. The glow from thousands of street lamps stained the sky above it. When she turned round, the lights of Eastcott St George twinkled like a small constellation. Isolated house lights sparkled in the distance. Occasional travelling headlights showed the progress of vehicles along the main road.

Her ears were less finely tuned to the darkness. She tried to listen more attentively. Behind her, the car gave out creaks and groans as it cooled. An owl's cry startled her. It was so like the stereotypical 'tu-whit, tu-whoo' that she thought it must be someone imitating an owl. A sentry's signal? It came again, or another bird answered it, further away. She listened for it to be followed by more alarming sounds. There was nothing.

Would she know if anything happened to the boys, or to Nick? She walked across to the gap in the wall. She could see the lights of the camp. They seemed unnecessarily bright. Not the glow of oil lamps or firelight. But she could hear nothing at that distance. No music, no laughter. Anything could happen there. She wouldn't know.

The owl called again, quite close. It must, she thought, be real, after all. What kind of owl made that classic call? A barn owl, a tawny owl? Presumably not a screech owl. She felt out of place, ignorant, an alien townie.

A shot rang out, shattering the silence. A clatter of birds rose shrieking from the wood. She was almost sure she heard the shout of human voices. A fist of fear was gripping her chest.

It seemed to take for ever for the echoes to die away. Still the blood was pounding in her ears. *What had happened?*

There were smaller lights now moving around the camp. Disappearing among the trees.

Tom? Nick?

Every nerve wanted to send her racing down the slope after Nick, to find what was going on. She had taken a few unsteady steps across the grass before she checked. She did not remember climbing the loose bricks, but her ankles were grazed and sore.

What did she think she could do? That gunshot had echoed all along the hillside. She had no idea where it came from.

Why didn't Nick ring her? Where was he?

Careless of added danger now, she raced back to the car and rang his mobile. She must talk to him. Nothing. Tom's. No answer. They must both have been careful to switch them off. She pounded her fists on the dashboard. What could she *do*?

Wait till Nick came back. The gunshot might have nothing to do with him or the boys. Did people like the Herewards or their workers go out shooting at night? They would hardly think it sporting to shoot a sleeping pheasant. But a thieving fox?

Common sense was no match for terror.

She hesitated. Then she got out of the car and crossed the wall again. An insistent voice reminded her that Nick had not wanted the two of them to plunge into the trees separately. She knew she was rationalizing the fear which stood like a barrier between her and these woods.

The shot had changed things. She had to know.

She had only taken a few uncertain steps down the slope

when the lights of the village were cut off. She was in amongst the trees, all landmarks lost.

She paused to listen. Was it only her imagination that she could still hear distant shouting? Was it just the night wind in the leaves?

Slowly, she felt her way on. With every step, the fear grew that she would not be able to find her way back. She remembered hearing that the pygmies of the Congo are the only people who do not have a primeval fear of forests, because they alone never cut trees down.

It was the twenty-first century danger she must concentrate on, not the age-old atavistic terror of trees.

Her probing hand passed her from tree trunk to tree trunk. Suddenly, there was nothing to hold. She stopped. Had she reached a track? Those men must have driven their vehicle through this wood to their camp. There was no strip of stars overhead to tell her, but she thought the darkness was thinner as she looked up.

She stepped out, stumbled down into a ditch, and then felt a harder surface underfoot.

She caught her breath. There was light, glimpsed through the sparse foliage to her right. Its source was hidden from her by the trees, but surely it must be the camp.

Again that inner war, the desire to go on, when every nerve was screaming at her to flee.

She drew back to the trees at the edge of the track and crept forward in their shelter. It was a little easier now, each tree trunk silhouetted before she reached it. She was making faster progress. She was beginning to hear men's voices.

Suddenly the ground under her feet exploded. For a wild moment, she thought she had trodden on a mine. Then the storm of feathers around her face told her she had stepped on a sleeping pheasant. It went clattering away, shrieking its indignation.

She stopped, rigid with shock, terrified by the bird, until she realized what it was. Gradually her senses steadied. As the wider world around her swung into focus again, she was struck by a new and more rational terror. Those faintly heard voices had erupted into masculine shouts. There was the sound of an engine roaring into life. Headlights lit the track ahead.

Suzie threw herself further back under the trees. She crouched there, trembling, while the blaze of lights advanced. It was coming slowly. Powerful torches probed the woods on either side. She could imagine vividly that truck which had passed her on the drive, the men in camouflage overalls, the shouts and jeers. However harmless their antics in the Herewards' woods, she did not want to be caught by them, alone, in the dark.

She hid her face, and the torchlight passed over her. Between her fingers, she saw its gleam on the fallen leaves. When she peeped up, the red tail lights were passing slowly. A little way on, they stopped. She heard the sound of men climbing down, calling orders to each other.

Under cover of their noise, she scrambled back. Higher and higher up the slope. She could hear them crashing through the undergrowth now, searching for her. Another pheasant broke out into shrill scolding. One of the men laughed.

Her heart was hammering in terror, but the sounds were retreating now. After a while, she realized she was safe.

Guided only by the slope of the ground, she felt her way back uphill. It seemed to be hours before she broke out of the trees and the blessed city lights lit the sky ahead.

She stumbled along the wall until she found the car and sat there, shaking uncontrollably.

She rang Millie again. There was still no news. Suzie was trying to keep the waves of panic out of her voice, not entirely successfully.

'Mum? Has something happened? Are you all right?'

'I'm fine, love. Just waiting.'

'Come home, Mum. It's starting to get scary.'

'As soon as we can.'

She cut the call before she could betray herself further. As she nursed the mobile in her lap, she wondered if she was betraying Millie.

Time crawled on. Surely Nick should be back by now? It had never occurred to them to discuss how long she should wait. The idea that Nick might not return had been unthinkable.

And Tom? Would Tom be coming back?

She must not let herself think that a boys' adventure game

played by grown men could metamorphose into something sinister, lethal. There would be a harmless explanation.

The chill of the night was creeping into her bones. The lane was dark, silent. It was uncanny that not a single car had passed this way.

Millie was at home alone, getting more and more scared as the hours crept on.

At last she could bear the inaction no longer. She started the engine. The headlights sprang to life. The enveloping darkness was pushed back to the sides of the lane. It was no less threatening. She drove on slowly, scanning for a dark figure in the lee of the wall. At the next crossroads she turned left.

She had never been along this lane before. It must lead back to Eastcott St George by a more circuitous route. Still the brick wall accompanied her on her left. She had seen from the map that Tom and Paul might have chosen to enter the woods from this side. Had they left Paul's father's car parked at the side of the road? Would she recognize it? But they might not have even come by car.

She passed the occasional farmhouse on the other side of the narrow lane. Their entrances yawned darkly, their house lights set back beyond a farmyard. She saw no glint of a parked car on the splay in front of their gates. And they would have hidden their bicycles too well for her to see.

At last the wall gave way to hedges. There were cottages ahead. She was on the edge of the village, the Hereward estate behind her.

The main road tempted her. She could be home quickly from here. But she thought of Nick stumbling back up the slope, perhaps hurt, to find her missing. Of Tom . . .

No. She had been given one job to do. To wait with the car until Nick returned. She made her way, still carefully searching, back along the lanes she had come by.

No longed-for figure stepped out into the headlights from the broken wall, demanding to know where on earth she had been. She would have welcomed Nick's anger.

Millie had no more news.

'Mum, what's *happening*?'

Suzie made a painful decision.

'I'm coming home.'

She slammed the shutters of her mind on the scenario that would make such a choice the only possible one.

All the members of her family were screaming out their need to her. She could not be everywhere at once.

Reversing in a narrow lane, with an inadequate field gateway behind her, would not have been easy in daylight, and with her nerves firmly under control. She felt the rear of the car hit the gate. Then she was away.

Was it a sense of disaster or relief to reach the crossroads again and drive straight on? Almost immediately she was back on the main road, having to cope with the bewilderment of oncoming headlights and fast-moving vehicles, after the darkness and slow progress of unfamiliar country lanes. In her overwrought state, she needed to be extra vigilant about her driving.

She was home at last, Millie flying into the hall, hugging her.

'Where's Dad? Didn't you find them? Did they get caught by those men?'

'I don't know.' She agonized over how much to tell Millie. 'There was a noise. And then some sort of upset down in their camp. Lights and people shouting. I don't know if it was anything to do with Tom and Paul, or Dad. I waited and waited, but nobody came.'

Millie was no fool. She raised her pale, sharp face to Suzie. 'What sort of noise?'

'It sounded like a gunshot.'

Over Millie's shoulder Suzie stared at the phone in the hall, willing it to ring. Tom? Nick? She no longer knew what she feared, or for whom. Fear was a nightmare creature that possessed her. It was beyond reason.

'Do you think . . . one of them's dead?'

Suzie was startled out of her own terror by her daughter's sharp voice so close to her. She shook herself back into the role of sensible mother and drew back a little to smile at Millie.

'Don't be silly. This is rural England, not some inner city gangland. The only things that get shot at are pheasants and foxes.'

'So why hasn't either of them come back?'

'Well . . . it means there was somebody else in the woods. Dad and the boys may be lying low till the coast is clear.'

'But you *knew* there was somebody else in the woods. That's why Tom went. That camp you saw.'

'Ye–es. Only . . . after the gunshot there was shouting from there. Lights moving, as if they were searching for somebody. I *think* they may have been as surprised as I was.'

'Somebody *else* with a gun?'

'I know. It sounds surprisingly busy for an October evening, doesn't it?' She was talking almost gaily. She must at all costs avoid telling Millie how she had felt, crouching at the edge of the track with the headlights coming towards her. Men, possibly armed, shouting, crashing through the undergrowth, searching for her. She did not want to revive that feeling of being a rabbit facing the barrel of a shotgun, paralysed.

It was all right. The torchlight had passed over her, as she crouched, hiding her face. She had got away. She was safe.

But she might not have done. What would have happened if she had been caught, at night, by those loud, macho men playing at soldiers? No doubt in their offices by daylight they would be suave, neatly suited, professionally courteous. In the woods, free from those constraints, from their inhibitions, they had become different animals.

She steered Millie towards the kitchen. 'I could use some hot chocolate. It was freezing standing around. I might even add a tot of whisky.'

Perhaps not. Some time that phone is going to ring, she thought. I'll have to get in the car again and drive to pick Nick up. Unless he's made contact with Tom and Paul and they come home together in Paul's dad's car.

That's it. She seized on the solution to her worries with delight. That's why he didn't come back to the car. They're all together, the three of them. Once the alarm went up, they'll have kept well away from the camp. Gone back to where Paul parked his dad's car. They'll have driven to Paul's house first, and then Tom and Nick will come home together.

'Mum?'

'Sorry. I was just thinking. I bet Dad's found the boys. That was what he set out to do, to keep them out of trouble. They'll have taken a long way round the camp to avoid being caught. Paul will bring them to his house. Perhaps I should ring the Shinos.'

'So why hasn't Dad rung you?'

A guilty silence. 'Men. I expect he just forgot. It's been an exciting evening. And he was closer to that gunshot than I was. It'll have driven everything else out of his head.'

She took the steaming mug Millie handed her. Her daughter looked at her shrewdly.

'You look a mess. Shall I get the whisky?'

'Better not. Just in case I'm wrong and I have to pick Dad up.'

They sat at the kitchen table in silence, sipping hot chocolate. Suzie sensed the tension in Millie. They were both listening.

The noise that startled them was not the telephone. There was a rattle of the lock and then the front door burst open. Millie and Suzie collided in the kitchen doorway as they raced into the hall.

Tom stood leaning back against the closed door as though it was an enormous relief to be back in his own home. He straightened up when he saw them. He looked taller than ever in his night black clothes. There were still smudges of dirt on his face, which he had not quite washed away. Suzie saw fragments of twig and leaves caught in his wavy black hair.

His blue eyes tried to assume their usual merriment and smile at Suzie, but did not quite succeed.

'Hi, Mum.'

'Where have you *been*? What happened?'

Tom looked startled and wary. 'At Paul's. I told you.'

'You didn't stay there, did you? The two of you borrowed Paul's father's car. Or else you biked. You went to Hereward Court.'

His gaze shot from her to Millie and back. He was robbed of words. He had not expected her to know.

'I . . .'

'Don't lie. Just tell me what happened. Have you seen Dad?'

'Dad? Where? Why?'

'Because when we heard what you idiots were planning, we set out to try and stop you . . .'

'You did *what*?'

'Tom, the Herewards are friends of mine, well, almost. They've been terribly kind. They were just trying to make a bit of money by letting people use their grounds for an adventure camp. Think how I'd have felt if they'd caught you trespassing.'

'They didn't. They were never going to. Do you think we're complete morons? And Dad has to go blundering around, giving all of us away. We couldn't think what had set the alarm off.' He started, as the force of what she said struck him. 'You said he's not back? Well, where is he, then?'

'I hoped he was with you.'

'Never saw him. So what were you doing?'

'I waited by the car while Dad went down into the woods. We expected he'd find you somewhere on the outskirts of the camp, trying to get evidence for your preposterous theory. Only then I heard the gunshot.'

'So did we.'

'And I haven't seen him since.'

'Oh, crikey.' Tom passed his hands over his face.

'I really hoped he'd found you. I thought the three of you might be lying low until the excitement died down, and then you'd all come home in Paul's dad's car.'

Tom shook his head. 'We biked. You're partly right. It took us quite a time to find the place. From the little lane where we stopped, we could see the lights. Only once we got into the woods, we lost them. And never having seen the place by daylight, we were just blundering around and trying not to make a noise. We had to cross a ravine once, with a stream at the bottom. We'd just started to hear voices, but we hadn't even got close when that gun went off. And after that it was pandemonium. Lights all over the place, people shouting. We were scared, but it never in a million Sundays occurred to us it might be Dad. We crouched down for a bit, waiting for things to go quiet. Then just when it seemed safe to go on, it all started up again.'

That was me, Suzie thought. She kept this information to herself.

'They came pretty close to finding us, that time. Well, after that, we decided our luck was going to run out if we hung around any longer. Those guys were jittery, and if they'd got guns . . .'

'It wasn't them,' Suzie said. 'I think the gunshot came from somewhere else.'

Tom checked in surprise. 'You could have fooled me. And they were all done up in military gear, camouflage uniforms.'

'What else would you wear for playing commando games in the woods?'

They stared at each other, on the edge of hostility.

'Suit yourself. If Dad hadn't messed things up, we'd have got the evidence. Got in close and heard what they were talking about in that camp. I bet it wasn't price movements on the Japanese Stock Exchange.'

His eyes travelled over her, newly aware. 'You said you were waiting by the car. So how come there's mud down the front of your jersey, and a big tear in your sock and blood on your ankle?'

Suzie looked down at herself. She had not noticed until now. 'When Dad didn't come back, I went down a little way to see if I could find him. But it was stupid, of course. I fell over. And I didn't know which way he'd gone.'

'Have you rung Hereward Court?'

She was shocked out of contemplation of her ruined clothes. 'No. Why?'

'Because it's their place. Because there was someone firing a gun on their land.'

'People do shoot foxes at night. It's normal. And how would I explain what we were doing there?'

Tom shrugged. 'That's your problem. But if Dad's missing and somebody's shot him, I'd have thought you'd want to find out.'

TEN

Suzie stared at the telephone, not with hope now but with dread. Should she?

'It's late,' she said. 'They'll be in bed.'

'Ten o'clock's not late,' said Millie. 'Go on, Mum.'

Suzie checked her watch and was astonished to find that Millie was right. 'It feels like at least midnight.' She took a reluctant step towards the phone. 'All the same, they're country people. They're probably the sort of folk who go to bed early and are out of doors at the crack of dawn.'

'So is etiquette more important than the fact that Dad may be bleeding to death somewhere?' Tom's smile was more uneasy than mocking.

'I don't know what to say.'

'Tell them the truth, if you like. It's no skin off my nose. You and Dad were trying to be responsible citizens. Blame it on me. But leave Paul out of it. Please, Mum. He's got a lot more to lose than I have.'

Suzie restrained herself from saying, 'He should have thought of that before.'

She was just reaching her hand out to the receiver when the phone rang. She jumped as violently as if it had been another gunshot. The phone rang on.

'Answer it, Mum,' urged Millie.

Suzie picked it up. 'It'll be one of your friends,' she said, covering the mouthpiece. But she knew Millie's mates would ring her mobile.

'Hello?'

'Mrs Fewings?' A woman's voice, not quite recognizable.

'Yes.'

'Alianor Hereward. We've got your husband. I think you'd better come over here.'

The line went dead.

Suzie stood staring at the display panel on the phone. DIAL NUMBER. She was struggling to connect the words she had heard with reality.

'What's up? Is it Dad? Is he hurt? He's not . . .?' Tom's mask of insouciance had dropped. He looked terrified.

'No,' she said, collecting her wits. She put the receiver back carefully. 'That was Mrs Hereward. Apparently Dad's at Hereward Court. She wants me to fetch him.'

'But did they shoot him?' begged Millie. 'What have they done to him?'

'I don't know. She didn't say. I don't think she's very pleased.' It occurred to her that this brusque manner was Alianor Hereward's normal way of speaking. Perhaps it meant nothing. 'I'll have to go.'

'Don't you think you'd better change first?' Millie said.

Suzie looked down curiously at her stained and dishevelled clothes. 'Right.'

She should be racing to find Nick, but she walked slowly up the stairs, as though sleepwalking. In the bedroom, it was hard to choose what to wear.

Millie appeared in the doorway. She took charge of the situation. She opened the wardrobe, threw a pair of grey trousers on the bed, rummaged on the shelves and produced a clean, pale-blue sweater. Socks and shoes followed.

'Get a move on, Mum. Dad's waiting.'

She ushered Suzie to the bathroom and made her wash her face.

Tom stood in the hall with the spare car keys in his hand. 'I'm coming with you.'

'No.' More sharply than she had intended. 'Stay with Millie. I've already left her alone all evening. It's too late for you to do any good now.'

He flushed. 'If you hadn't come interfering . . .'

She took up the handbag she had dropped and found her own keys. 'I'll be back as soon as I can.' She hesitated and kissed them both. 'Don't do anything else stupid.'

The night was cold, still, no wind to break the clouds. She pulled her padded jacket closer and hurried to the car.

The roads seemed strangely empty of traffic. It heightened Suzie's sense of unreality. This could not be happening to her. She had been offered the chance of a lifetime, the free run of a chest full of documents dating back centuries, records which existed nowhere else. And now she . . . Nick . . . Tom had thrown it away. She would never be able to go back to Hereward Court after this.

A small part of her brain told her that she was concentrating on this long-term grief to stop herself thinking about the immediate trauma which lay in front of her. Meeting the Herewards. What could she say? What had Nick said?

Nick. He couldn't be hurt, could he? Conscience gnawed at her. Alianor Hereward would surely have said. They'd have taken him to hospital, not called for her to come.

I think you'd better come over here. How urgent had that summons been? Was the doctor there now? Could Nick not be moved? No, that's nonsense. An ambulance with paramedics would have rushed him to hospital if he were gravely injured. Unless . . . He couldn't be . . .?

If only that gate beside the lodge-keeper's house was open. It would have been quicker that way. Instead, she drove on to the village of Eastcott and turned off there.

The lane seemed longer in the dark. The Herewards' entrance was unlit. Her lights picked up the faint gleam of wheelie bins.

She had been right about the lack of lights in Hereward Court too. There was barely a glimmer from its windows as she steered her way cautiously down the unfenced drive. It would be easy to stray off course.

From this angle, there was no sign of the camp in the woods. It seemed impossible now that there should be those bright lights, that roaring truck, those shouting men. She could imagine the bland, blank faces of the well-bred Herewards. 'What camp?'

But Floridus had been there when that truck full of jeering men had passed her. He had told her they needed the camp to make money. She was not making it up. She had changed her clothes, but the graze on her ankle from this evening was still sore.

A ragged edge of cloud drifted away from a half moon. Light silvered the pond by the chapel. With sinking heart, Suzie guided the car in under the archway and stopped.

If they had heard her, they were not making it easy for her. She had to walk alone across the courtyard to the dark door.

Suzie had a sudden, shaming memory of her ancestor, George Arscott, carrying a sack of stolen corn across the farm-yard, and then the farmer himself rearing up from behind the hedge. '*That's far enough.*' Of an older Floridus Hereward sitting in judgement on the magistrates' bench. '*Whip. Three months.*' As she stood on the doorstep, her cheeks flamed with humiliation.

The bell clanged mournfully. At least the instant frenzy of the dogs barking was familiar.

Alianor herself opened the door. There was the usual rush of Labradors, quelled by a commanding bark not too unlike their own. Mrs Hereward looked Suzie up and down without smiling.

'You'd better come in.'

She turned right along the corridor away from the great hall. Suzie had never been this way before. All she remembered, suddenly and irrelevantly, was a large man in a black leather coat with a shaved head. '*Sorry, darling.*' Striding away from her in this direction, as though he owned the place.

The corridor ended in the far corner of this wing. To her right, another led along the range of buildings at the back of the courtyard. To the left, a much shorter one. Mrs Hereward crossed this and opened a panelled door.

The room seemed startlingly full. It appeared to be some sort of office. There were shelves like those in the library, but these were stacked with box files, folders, ledgers. A large mahogany desk filled most of the floor. It, too, was piled with paperwork. A computer rose like a grey battleship out of a sea of scattered documents.

There were three men standing behind it. Floridus Hereward, upright and poker-faced, like a Guards officer on parade. A man she had never seen before, in a battered green Barbour, with a ferret-like face under a flat tweed cap. And Nick, looking pale and wretched, but at least standing and apparently unhurt. He gave her a small, wan smile.

Mr Hereward's face flickered momentarily. He cleared his throat. 'Bad business.'

'Yes,' Suzie said tentatively. 'I'm sorry.'

What had Nick said? She turned her eyes back to him in desperate appeal.

But before Nick could come to her rescue, Floridus Hereward went on, 'Could have turned out nastily. Luckily Marchant thought he was a fox and aimed low.'

'I've been out to get that varmint three nights now.' The voice of the man in the Barbour surprised her. She was used to these rich, West Country vowels from red-faced farmers. She had expected this sharp-featured man to sound more urban, despite, or even because of, his stereotypically rural clothes. Who was he? A Hereward employee? A tenant farmer? Did it mean anything that Floridus had called him only by his surname? Probably not.

'I didn't fancy getting shot, so I gave myself up,' Nick said shamefacedly, apologizing as much to Suzie as to the Herewards. 'I didn't know it was a case of mistaken identity, or I might have just lain low.'

'Lucky you didn't. Marchant would have been within his rights, you know, if he'd put a bullet through you. He'd no reason to think there were trespassers on our land.'

'No. I understand that. I'm sorry.'

'Publicity wouldn't have looked good, though,' Alianor put in. 'Lucky for us, as well as you, he didn't make a clean kill.'

Suzie sensed unease in the room. It was not just the awful embarrassment of the situation, made a hundred times worse by the fact that the Herewards knew her, had been generous to her. There was something none of them were saying. How much had Nick told them? Did they know about Tom and Paul trying to spy on the camp? There had been other men with guns in those woods. And not looking for foxes.

But it had not been them. They had seemed as startled as she was, and Marchant had said that the shot came from him. He had taken up his rifle again, nursing it over his arm, so that he was now standing armed guard over Nick.

Suzie Fewings, descended from a thief, married to a trespasser who had come close to being shot. And the Herewards were like that indignant farmer, the rightful owners of a property that been violated by her family.

'I . . . The car's outside. I'll take him home now, shall I? I'm terribly sorry.'

For what? What had Nick *said*?

Nick looked questioningly at Marchant with his rifle. The ferret-faced man moved back, very slightly, as though unwilling to let his prisoner go. Nick had to edge past him, out from behind the desk.

The Herewards stood in silence, their faces unreadable. There were no farewells. Even the Labradors seemed subdued.

The corridor seemed endless, their steps echoing from the stone flags. The door creaked open. This time, the cold night air was welcome on Suzie's flaming cheeks.

ELEVEN

Nick drove. A guilty silence pressed down upon them, except for Suzie's murmured instructions as he negotiated the unlit track to the lane. Only when they were out on the main road at Eastcott St George did she let out a long sigh that was only partly relief.

'Well. That's that. I won't be going back *there* again.'

'Aren't you going to ask what happened to me? I thought you might be the tiniest bit interested.'

'Of course I am. But he said, didn't he? That Marchant man. He thought you were a fox and shot at you. So you gave yourself up and he marched you up to the house. Then you asked them to ring me.'

'I did not. What do you take me for? I knew you were desperate to keep your name out of this.'

'So how did she know to contact me?'

'I'll tell you, if you'll listen. I belted around the edge of the woods as fast as I could, till I was above the camp. Then I went down into the trees. As I got lower, I began to see the lights again. And then the trees thinned out and I was just above a track through the wood.'

'I know. I saw it too.'

'Just then a man came walking along this track from the camp. I could just about make out that he had a gun, and he was sighting into the wood, left and right, as he went. I crouched down behind a tree, but I must have put my hand on a dead branch. There was an almighty crack. I heard him swear, and next thing that gun went off. It was pretty close too. It hit the tree trunk I was sheltering behind. And he called out, "Who's there?" Well, I gave myself up. You don't argue with a man who's got a rifle with night sights.'

'He said he was shooting foxes.'

'I don't think so. You don't ask a fox, "Who's there?"'

Suzie digested this in silence, while the road rolled past.

'What happened then?'

'Tried a bit of the upper-class accent, you know.' Nick did a fair imitation. 'Not your average poacher.'

'What did you say? How did you explain what you were doing there?'

'I lied. Naturally. I thought I did rather well, under the circumstances. Do you remember that bit on local television the other night? About that white stag which was found dead? It was the second one in a few weeks. I said I'd been driving along the lane and thought I saw another one of them crossing the road ahead of me and leaping the wall. So I'd stopped the car and gone after it, to see if I could get a better view.'

'Did he believe you?'

'Hard to say. He wasn't giving much away. Said I could tell that to Mr Hereward. So there I was, under armed guard, quick-marched up to Hereward Court. It didn't feel like my finest hour.'

'And they'll have wanted to know who you were.'

'Yes, of course. I tried to stall, but I was on shaky ground. I gave them a false name, but they wanted some sort of ID. I'd left my wallet in the car, but it didn't look good, me coming up with the innocent story about stalking a white stag, and then refusing to confirm who I was. In the end, I had to tell them where I'd left the car. They rang someone at the lodge . . .'

The lodge among the dark rhododendrons. A light in the back window. A stone seemed to weight Suzie's stomach.

'. . . but thank heavens you'd gone. Then they wanted a telephone number. I made one up, and just hoped whoever it was would be out. When that didn't work, they turned a bit nasty. They locked me up in some sort of pantry. Freezing cold. And left me to consider my options, in the dark.'

'They didn't call the police?'

'They threatened to. But no, they never did.'

'So how did they get our number?'

'That was Mrs Hereward. After I'd spent an hour or so in the cold and the dark, she came back with Marchant. Told him to search me. He found my mobile. It didn't take her long to discover my home number. Of course, I had to tell her then. I said I knew how embarrassed you'd be, and that was why I hadn't wanted to tell them who I was. Well, that bit was true.'

'And did she believe your story about the white stag.'

'Who knows? That sort don't exactly wear their emotions written all over their faces, do they? Your Floridus in particular. You'd think his face was carved out of the same oak as his wood panelling. Do they give lessons in public schools about how to control your cheek muscles and talking without moving your lips?'

'And when you told them? That it was me?'

'She did raise her eyebrows then, to quite a height. But she didn't say anything. Just took the phone back and rang you. You know the rest. She wasn't exactly chatty, was she?'

'No. You can hardly blame her. The Herewards trusted me.

They left me alone with that chest full of priceless documents. They even let me take things home to copy. And this is how I repay them.'

'Hang on.' Nick's voice had changed. 'That man shot at me. If it hadn't been for the tree trunk, he could have killed me. He knew what he was doing. And I'll swear he wasn't out after foxes.'

'Oh, no. You're not getting like Tom? Conspiracy theory. Big bad Nazis in the woods.'

'Look, I know what I saw. I'm sorry if it's upset your family history, but all I want to do is to get home and down a stiff whisky. I was hoping for some sympathy.'

'I didn't mean it like that. And thanks for trying to protect me.' She put her hand on his thigh. 'I'm sorry. It's just . . . we haven't a clue about people like that, have we? The Herewards, I mean. It may be perfectly normal for their staff to walk around at night with rifles. It doesn't have to mean anything.'

'No, except that he was coming from that camp.'

She knew it would be dangerous to reopen the argument. To say that Marchant could have gone there on some innocent estate business.

They were entering the city. Late-night taxis were ferrying clubbers home. Tom and Millie would be waiting impatiently for news.

'A white stag?' Millie said incredulously. 'Who did you think you were, Dad? King Arthur?'

Nick leaned back on the sofa and half closed his eyes. 'Sorry. You've lost me.'

'I was reading this story, and there's King Arthur and his men hunting in the forest, and they see this white stag. So, of course, Arthur thinks I've got to bag that one, and off he goes, charging through the trees after it. And he and two others get separated from the rest. And all of a sudden they come to a river, and there's the stag, with the hounds biting its throat. So Arthur blows his horn for the kill.

'And then along comes this ship, with sails of silk, and gold on the decks, and nobody steering it. And it stops right in front of them. So, of course, being just thick men, they get on board. And there are these fairy women bringing them gorgeous food and leading them to comfy beds. In the morning, one of the men is lying in the arms of the sorceress Morgan le Fay, but Arthur wakes up in prison, and Morgan is plotting for the third man to kill him.'

'Thanks.'

'Nothing personal, Dad. Just that white stags are always bad news. You wake up in fairyland and you can't get out.'

'That's not quite true,' said Suzie, twisting her whisky glass in her hand. 'If the fairy loves you, she can give you great riches, a wonderful life. You just have to be careful not to get on the wrong side of her.'

'Never trust a fairy. Lay off white stags in future, Dad.'

'Well, I did escape. By the width of a tree trunk. That guy had a night sight on his rifle.'

'There wouldn't be much point going out after foxes in the dark without one,' Suzie objected.

'Foxes!' Tom almost spat.

'I know, Tom, I know. But how could he tell Dad wasn't a poacher?'

'So it's OK to shoot poachers dead, is it?'

'William the Conqueror thought it was . . . Sorry. No, of course it's not. But just suppose for a moment your theory was true, and there's some fascist camp at Hereward Court training to take over the country by violence. What good would it do them to murder Dad? There'd be a lot of explaining to do. It'd bring the police down on them. Your whole scenario depends on them operating in secrecy. And Floridus Hereward made no attempt to deny those men were camping on his land.'

'He had a cover story, though, didn't he?'

'Tom,' she sighed. 'You're never going to see reason, are you? Thanks to you, Dad's been shot at, imprisoned and humiliated. And I've lost the most exciting chance of research I'm ever likely to get. Just because you and Paul went charging off on some wild goose chase.'

'White stag chase,' put in Millie. 'I forgot to say. Arthur escaped with his life, just, but the third knight Morgan le Fay set up to kill him ended up dead.'

There was a silence in the room. Nick stood up.

'It's been a long evening. I'm going to bed.'

Suzie followed him. As she passed Tom, she put her hand on his arm. 'Millie's right. Be careful, Tom. Stay out of this one.

Whatever those people are doing in the woods, keep away from them. Never mind King Arthur, think of *Lord of the Flies*. Put a whole lot of overgrown boys together, away from the normal restrictions, and you never know what may happen. They scared me.'

She kissed him goodnight.

'Yeah, yeah, Mum. No white stags.'

'Time you were in bed, Millie. Turn the lights out behind you.'

She knew as she walked up the stairs that she had not convinced Tom.

Suzie walked into the Record Office and instantly knew that it had been a mistake to come here. This was her self-indulgence every Tuesday afternoon, to make a research trip to the Record Office or the local studies library and extend the reach of her family tree that little bit further.

But all she had in her hand was the sheaf of notes on which she had copied what she knew about her own Dobles of Romanswell and the more prestigious Dobles from whom Alianor Hereward was descended. It had been Suzie's hope that she could bridge this gap and prove that they shared a common ancestry.

Now her cheeks grew hot again, remembering that curt summons to Hereward Court, the sight of Nick guarded by a man with a rifle, their humiliating exit, not even able to offer a credible story for Nick's trespassing at night.

What was the point of proving she was descended from the same family which had intermarried with the Herewards? She would never see Alianor Hereward *née* Doble again. She would never have a chance to tell Floridus Hereward, laughingly, that she was a relative by marriage. Would he really have been impressed? Wasn't she also the descendant of George Arscott, whom a Hereward had sentenced to whipping and imprisonment? That at least she had documentary evidence for. It was the most startling thing she had got out of the Hereward document chest, on a personal level. It was not what she had been hoping for.

She sat down at a table and spread out her papers in front of her. Too late she knew this was the wrong line of research for today. Even seeing the name Doble knotted her stomach.

She would not be going back to Hereward Court now. She could not.

Yesterday had been Monday, her usual day for a visit to Eastcott St George, to return the latest documents she had been transcribing and collect others. She felt a pang of bitter regret. There was so much more she could have done. So many fascinating papers and notebooks listing not only the well-recorded gentry, like the Herewards and Dobles, but the humbler names of estate workers, tenants, petty criminals, victims of their crimes, witnesses. The essential stuff of family history. There were so many people whose research she could have helped, added colourful stories or personal information to their bare family trees, if only, if only Tom had not been so stupid and she and Nick had not tried to stop him.

Marchant with his rifle. If Nick had not been there . . . If it had been Tom he had heard . . . If there had been no sheltering tree trunk between her teenage son and the night sight of that rifle . . .

She shuddered, goosefleshed.

It was useless to think like that. What had happened had happened. Tom was safe. Nick's pride had been wounded, but nothing else. And she herself must now go back to the less glamorous routine of research she had followed before that unexpected invitation to Hereward Court.

The notebook of the magistrate Floridus Hereward was still on her desk at home. She must parcel it up and post it back to the Herewards. It would be difficult to phrase the note which must accompany it. But it had to be done. She would hand the package over at the post office and watch it disappear, taking with it the hopes of any more discoveries.

She sat on, staring at the handwritten pages in front of her. It was no good. She should have looked through her files at home and chosen a different line to investigate. But without those files she did not know where to begin. She could not remember the dates, the right names of people and parishes.

At last she sighed, picked up her things and retreated to the common room. She helped herself to a coffee from the machine, thought of comforting herself with a chocolate biscuit and decided against it.

There were public access computers in this room. A woman got up from one and walked out. Suzie went to the reception desk, booked herself in for a half-hour session and sat down in front of the screen. Nick had never seemed curious about his own family history, but she knew that his father's people were from Lancashire, that his grandparents had worked in the cotton mills. The name of a village at the foot of the Pennines came to mind. She opened up Ancestry.co.uk and clicked on the census collection. The 1901 census was the most recent available. She typed in the surname, the place of residence.

There they were. Only one family of Fewings in the village. Probably Nick's great-grandparents. A smile began to warm her face. She printed off a copy of the handwritten census return. She would study the details later. 1891? 1881? How far back could she trace them before her half-hour ran out?

Anything, rather than think about the Herewards and the Dobles.

It was as painful as she thought it would be, sealing the last Hereward notebook in a padded envelope. The note had been difficult to write. In the end, she had kept it short, courteous and to the point.

> Dear Mr and Mrs Hereward,
>
> I am returning the notebook I borrowed, with a copy of my transcript for your records.
>
> Many thanks for your kindness in allowing me access to these documents. A number of people across the world have already thanked me for the family information they have found from these transcripts on the website.
>
> Yours sincerely,
> Suzie Fewings

No mention of that appalling night. No useless reiteration of apologies. The matter was over, sealed up like the notebook in its envelope. There was nothing to be gained by referring to it. She would have to try and banish it from her mind.

All the same, it was a sadness to reach the front of the queue at the post office. She placed the package on the scales, handed it under the screen with her money. It was gone.

Another week passed. Another Monday afternoon. Freed from the pressure of her morning in the office, Suzie busied herself with housework, determinedly emptying out and washing kitchen cupboards. She must not let herself think where she should have been, could have been, this afternoon. But she found it would have been better to choose something other than manual work. It left her imagination too free to wander. She wrung out a cloth in the soapy water unnecessarily hard. She was only making herself miserable.

The phone rang. Suzie sat back on her heels. Then she clambered to her feet and went to answer it.

'Hello. Suzie Fewings.'

That familiar voice. Brusque, self-assured. 'Thank you for the notebook, my dear. Not ill, I hope. I was expecting you this afternoon.'

Suzie stared at the phone, as if the instrument could explain what she was hearing.

'I . . . No. I'm well, thank you.'

'So we shan't be seeing you again? Had all you wanted out of the old document chest?'

'I . . . I didn't think . . . you'd want to see me again.'

'Why ever not? Flo's been tickled pink about all those folk in New Zealand and whatnot, wanting to read about the stuff in his family papers. Never thought it would interest anybody but us.'

'You mean, you'd let me come back? Do some more transcripts?'

'Don't let me press you, my dear. I realize it must have been taking up a lot of your time. Coming out here every week and then copying it all up. You'll have lots of other things to do. And all your own family history, of course. I know we're only one little bit of it.'

'I . . . yes . . . Thank you.' Her brain was struggling to catch up. 'Yes, I would like to. No, really, I enjoy doing it, whether it's my own family I find out about or not. If I could come again . . . If you're really sure you don't mind . . .'

'Never could read those court notebooks myself, what with the old boy's appalling scribble and no punctuation. I'm glad you've managed to make sense of them.'

'It was fun, really. And all those colourful stories, even what people said when they were arrested.'

'It's a hoot, isn't it? Gives you a real eye-opener about what it was like being a Victorian bobby. Good stuff for the novels. Yes, come and do some more.'

'Could I? Next week?'

'Two o'clock, same as normal.'

The Herewards' phone went down with that same decisive abruptness.

Suzie was left with a smile of wonder, that seemed to start somewhere down by her feet and spread through her whole body.

TWELVE

She borrowed the car again. It boosted her flagging self-confidence. Her muscles were tight with nervousness as she rang the bell.

Alianor Hereward greeted her, above the Labradors' joyful welcome, as though nothing had happened.

'Come in, my dear. Nasty weather, isn't it? I hate it when the clocks go back. It's practically dark by the time I have to fetch the brats home from school.'

'Is it a good school?' Suzie remembered her surprise that the Herewards sent their younger children to the village primary, even though their eldest son had been at Harrow.

Alianor snorted. 'Dreadful. They had a good headmistress, but she left. The chap they've got now is hopeless. Doesn't believe in homework. Luckily Freddie's already got a place at a good boarding school for next year.'

'Harrow?'

'Hardly. He's only eleven. He's too thick anyway.'

Once again, Suzie had betrayed her ignorance of what the Herewards took for granted. Harrow must be one of those public schools you didn't go to until you were thirteen.

Alianor was leading the way along the familiar corridor to the great hall. From behind, Suzie watched the stomping gait that threw her weight from one short leg to the other. Not, she smiled to herself, the readers' image of a romantic novelist.

Mrs Hereward threw open the heavy door. Suzie checked in surprise. She was used to negotiating the intricate layout of the model railway, stepping over its tracks, sidings, stations, undulating landscape.

Today, a boy was playing with the trains. He turned a red-cheeked face to them, black-haired, bold-eyed. Genetically Alianor's son, not Floridus Hereward's. With a sharp sorrow, Suzie thought of the dead son and heir, the boy who should have continued the family pattern of names . . . Mark, Floridus, Mark . . . This must be Freddie. The one Alianor had said stoically was more suited to the job than the artistic Mark would have been. *A feel for the land.*

His nasal voice suggested the flush in his cheeks was more than normal. 'Don't let the Labs in, you idiot.'

'Stay!' his mother roared at the dogs, and slammed the door on their eager muzzles. 'Don't mind us. Mrs Fewings has just come to look out a few more papers.'

'Watch where you're putting your feet. I've just made a loop line round the lake.'

'Good oh. I'm sure Mrs Fewings will be very careful.'

Suzie picked her way with even more circumspection than usual over to the document chest beside the fireplace. There was, as ever, no fire lit. The room was punishingly cold. She was glad she had remembered to put on a heavy Aran sweater.

'Freddie's got a stinking cold. Had to keep him home from school, drat him.'

He looked, Suzie thought, with his over-bright eyes and hot cheeks, as though he should be tucked up warm in bed. She supposed he belonged in a world of cold baths, long days in the hunting field, draughty mansions. The Herewards' priorities were different from the Fewings'.

Again she felt that sense of alienation. She was here merely as a scribe. The family which had generated these documents she was copying were of another class, with other mores.

'Got everything you want? I'll leave you to it, then. If you're frozen stiff, come through to the kitchen. You can make yourself tea if no one's around, can't you?' She did not say where she would be.

Suzie was left alone with the unsettling presence of the belligerent Freddie.

'Hello,' she tried. 'Your cold sounds rotten.'

The boy leaned over the track on all fours, presenting his rump to her. He did not answer.

She began her usual methodical task of unpacking the upper layers of documents. She laid neat piles on the floor in the

same order she had found them. She would replace them just
so. Some she was already familiar with: the census notebooks,
the rent books, the bundles of nineteenth-century letters. Life
was too short to transcribe everything which was here. She
must be selective. What papers were most likely to contain
details of the ordinary people living on the Hereward manors?
The Herewards themselves did not need her to act as their
chronicler.

Alianor had expressed gratitude for her transcriptions of
the court notebooks, which were indeed difficult to read. In
return for her generosity in allowing Suzie back, she should
do some more of those. She picked out two more of the exercise books in their marbled covers and laid them aside. But
she was curious to know what might lie deeper.

Freddie was sniffing maddeningly. Would he be offended
if she offered him a tissue? She was just fishing one out of
her handbag when he produced a man-sized cotton handker-
chief from his pocket and blew an elephantine snort into it.
She put the tissue back. Were paper handkerchiefs a bour-
geois solecism? She didn't know.

Bending over the chest again, her attention was caught by
a brown leather cover, half exposed. A much slimmer note-
book than the magistrate's exercise book, narrower than A5.
She opened it. In a curling, confident script she read: 'An
Account of the Felonious Sacking of Hereward Court by
Rebels. Mark Hereward.'

There was no date. A shiver of excitement ran through her.
Hereward Court had been looted in the Civil War of the 1640s.
It had not been General Fairfax's disciplined Roundheads who
did it. They had placed their cannons up on the ridge where
she and Nick had parked the car. From this commanding height
they had quickly subdued the defiant Court. What was it the
Parliamentarians called Royalist strongholds? *A malignant
house.* It was afterwards that the villagers, not of Eastcott St
George, but from the more distant Moorfield, Sandton and
Southcombe had descended on the place and carried away its
furnishings.

'Southcombe,' Mrs Hereward had snorted of Suzie's ancestors. 'They'll have been Parliamentarians, then.'

Did she have to add some looters to her thieving ancestor
who had made off with a sack of corn?

She began to turn the pages of Mark Hereward's account. Impossible for her to know how close to the event he had written this, since almost every alternate lord of the manor had been called Mark. An expert might, she supposed, be able to tell from the handwriting. She could not.

'Are you a peasant, or one of us?' The boy's sudden challenge was disturbingly close to her own thoughts.

'I'm not sure. I may be both. I've certainly got peasants, well, agricultural labourers, on my family tree. But I'm researching another line. I think I may be related to your mother.'

Freddie sniffed loudly. She could not be sure whether it was his cold or contempt. 'One of them, then. If you were one of us, you wouldn't have any peasants on your tree. *Our* pedigree goes back to the Battle of Hastings.'

'I know. I've seen it. It must be very exciting to know so much about your history.'

'It's not history. That's in books.'

A quiver of realization shook Suzie. This was what Alianor Hereward had meant. *A feel for the land.* For Freddie Hereward, his genealogy wasn't the written records here in this chest. They were there, it was true, a validation for others to check. For him, his family descent was in the soil of this estate he walked over, the stones of this house, the girth of the oaks in the park, the supreme self-confidence of centuries of unquestioned superiority over everyone else he met.

Once again she felt diminished by the gap between them. It was not just Floridus, with his soldierly bearing, or Alianor's commanding cordiality. Even this Hereward child could make her feel inferior.

She gathered up the two court notebooks. After a moment's hesitation, she added the brown leather book. She was setting herself a considerable task to transcribe all three. But there was just a chance that Mark Hereward's account of the sacking of this house might shed more light on the Puritan rabble who had been responsible. Perhaps her people.

'I'm going to get myself a cup of tea. Would you like me to bring you a hot drink?'

'No, thanks. I'm very particular about the way my cocoa is made.'

She had to stifle a wry smile as she made her careful way to the door.

There was no one about in the kitchen. Suzie stood indecisively with her coat over her arm. Were the Herewards avoiding her? She needed to see Alianor to show her the notebooks she was taking away for transcription. Where was she? Writing her latest novel somewhere? Exercising a horse? It was still too early for her to be collecting the younger children from school. Floridus might be in his office at the far end of the corridor, or out on the estate somewhere, doing whatever it was that country landowners did. There was no sign of the Labradors.

She wondered whether she should go in search of one of them, but she was conscious of having trespassed enough already. Alianor had told her to help herself to a cup of tea. She had clearly foreseen this eventuality.

A kettle was simmering on the side of the Aga. Suzie shifted it to one of the hotter plates and concentrated on remembering which wall cupboards held the mugs and tea bags. Earl Grey, Darjeeling?

She was caught by that sudden memory of her first encounter with Floridus. A stiff, seemingly shy man, but with an old-fashioned courtesy. Nothing to warrant the reputation for eccentricity, '*a bit of a character*', she had heard given to him at the village hall exhibition. Apart, that is, from letting his Labradors jump on the dining table.

She felt a profound regret that she had lowered herself in his eyes.

She drank her tea in an oppressive silence. Tearing a leaf from her notebook, she wrote a message of thanks to the Herewards and listed the court notebooks and the account of the sacking of Hereward Court which she had selected for this week's homework. There was nothing else to linger for. She must drive home.

She was crossing the cobbled yard to the car when she saw him. He was striding in under the archway, his dark, burly form blocking out the light over the lake.

The same man she had met before. Broad-shouldered, shaven-headed, with that long, flapping black leather overcoat.

He checked when he saw her. This time there was no

half-jeering, 'Sorry, darling.' He looked almost alarmed to see her. Angry?

It was only a moment. Then he strode on towards the door near the kitchen, which she had just left. He did not look at her again as he passed.

As before, he did not tug the bell pull to send the announcement of his arrival pealing down the corridors. He just walked in and shut the door loudly behind him. She could hear the faint sound of dogs barking.

The house swallowed him up. He had entered as confidently as if he owned it, or at least had an established and trusted place in it. She could not think what it might be. She recalled Marchant in his flat cap and Barbour, easy to believe as a gamekeeper. This man's appearance spoke of cities, of a type she would have thought alien to Floridus Hereward. It made no sense.

There was something comforting about settling herself into the driving seat and pulling the door shut. It armoured her against a world which, if only because she did not understand it, seemed now vaguely hostile. She had re-established her routine, but she knew obscurely that things were not the same.

As she drove up the slope towards the road she had a strong sense that she would meet that truck again, the one that had been full of men in combat gear, hooting and whistling at her, fired with a macho energy that had left her feeling vulnerable and scared. What should she do if it came careering down the drive towards her? Should she veer off on to the grass? Or would the driver want to show off his off-road skills by circumventing her with a screeching turn?

It didn't happen. Fool, she told herself. That was a few weeks ago. The camp's over. All those city types will be back at their desks, white collars, neat ties, intent on the movement of the stock exchange or commodity futures, or whatever else had funded their excursion into the countryside for team bonding and leadership skills.

She emerged on to the lane. It would be simple to turn right to the village, pick up the main road, seat herself at her desk to begin her transcriptions.

She did not know what insistent impulse made her turn left, away from the village.

The trees were thinning with the onset of winter. A wet

wind was driving the last reluctant leaves sideways. Some of them plastered themselves against her windscreen.

She reached the first crossroads and turned left again, still following the wall. Somewhere along here, Fairfax had positioned the cannons which brought the Royalist Hereward Court to its knees and sent the Floridus Hereward of those times to prison. *A notorious malignant.*

What had been the name of his wife, who was left behind in the mansion? Had she fled for safety with her children? Was she still here when the Roundheads had moved on and the rabble descended to loot the house? What might she have suffered at their hands? The thought of that careering truck full of jeering men sprang back at her.

She was getting mixed up. Those twenty-first century men were guests of the Herewards. Paying guests, but needed and welcomed.

She was startled back to her surroundings by the sight of the lodge-keeper's house. It looked no more welcoming than it had the first time she saw it, with the dark trees and rhododendrons pressed closely around it. One thing was different, though. The tall, wrought-iron gates were no longer padlocked. One wing stood slightly open. Water stood in the tyre tracks beyond.

Nothing odd about that, she told herself. This had once been the main entrance to the house. You could see the cart track, where a road opposite had led down to the village of Quinton Bishop in the valley below. It must still sometimes be more convenient for the Herewards to use this gate than the one near Eastcott St George. And surely whoever lived in the lodge would have a car. She could make out a lower roof, back among the trees, which might be a garage.

She drove on, and stopped again by the gap in the wall. She had no reason to get out, but she did. She stood for a while, looking down at the misty blur of Hereward Court through the drizzle. Then she allowed her eyes to travel sideways along the woods below her, where she had had that frightening encounter.

For a while, the gradient made it impossible to see more than the tree tops, greyer than they had been before without their leaves. Then, as the hillside curved around the hollow, she began to get a fuller view of its slopes.

Oddly, she was not as surprised as she should have been. Even through the murk of a winter afternoon she could see it. There was something red, which might be a car. The same long brown hut. And another one? Was it her imagination that the camp looked more substantial than it had been when she had seen it first?

She shook herself back into common sense. There might be no one staying there. Floridus could be building more permanent accommodation in preparation for next year. Or there might even be a different set of city executives exchanging their centrally heated offices for the cold and wet of these woods.

'He could be planning to let it out to school parties for environmental field trips,' she argued to Nick later.

'All the same,' he replied, 'I don't think we'll mention this to Tom.'

THIRTEEN

'Where are we off to today?'
'Siderleigh. It's north-west from here.'
Nick eased the car out of the drive. 'I suppose you've turned up another bunch of ancestors there.'

'Actually, no, not yet.'

'So why are we going there?'

'There *were* Dobles there, in the sixteenth century. And I've got Dobles fifteen miles away in Romanswell in the seventeenth century.'

'And . . .?'

'And I'd like to make the connection.'

'Bit of a long shot, isn't it? Your agricultural labourers don't seem to move very far. You always say if you can't pick them up in the parish where you were expecting them, you've only got to trawl around the adjacent ones to find them.'

'The Dobles weren't agricultural labourers. Don't you remember that memorial in the church at Romanswell? My Humphrey Doble was a gent, and Mrs Hereward was a Doble before she married. She can trace *her* line right back to the fourteenth century, when another Doble woman married a Hereward.'

'I see.'

They were heading out of town, against the flow of Saturday traffic bound citywards for shopping and football. A long ridge of hills marched blue across the skyline.

After a pause, Suzie asked, 'What do you mean, you see?'

'It's really got to you, hasn't it, this Hereward business? You always used to pour scorn on people who set out to prove they had a duke on their family tree. Now you're determined to prove you're related to that family, come hell or high water.'

'It's not snobbishness. At the other end of the scale, I found it incredibly moving when I discovered Mary Arscott died in the workhouse. It's just curiosity. Now that I know more than I'd ever have believed possible about the Herewards, and seen that family tree with all their wives on it, well, it's natural to wonder if I might be part of that story. And it is the right surname.'

'So don't the Dobles have a family tree like the Herewards? Can't you prove it one way or the other?'

'No. I think my Romanswell Dobles must have been a cadet branch of the family, from a younger son. Humphrey's descendants were gents for a while, then just farmers. They owned land in Romanswell, but none of them as far back as I've got was a lord of the manor.'

'Still, if you keep going back a generation at a time, you'll find out, won't you?'

'I can't. That's the problem. I'm stuck. Romanswell's early registers have been lost. I found some wills which led me back to Robert Doble, gent, of Romanswell in the mid-sixteen hundreds.'

'So where does Humphrey fit in?'

'Robert's the only Doble in the Protestation Returns of 1641 for the parish, when you had to swear an oath of loyalty to the Protestant religion. He must have been a bigwig, because he presented the names for Romanswell. And then, on the Internet, I found a deed naming Humphrey and Anne Doble of Romanswell as the owners of a farm there in 1616. You know, Higher Wampton. I took you there.'

'Or I took you.' Nick grinned over the steering wheel. 'A pretty-posh place now. Riding stables, wasn't it?'

'That's the one. I'm pretty certain Humphrey must be Robert's father. There's a baptism for Robert, son of Humphrey, in the next parish. And Wampton Farm's very close to the parish boundary, so it might have been easier for them to use that church.'

'So what's the problem?'

'I found an older Robert Doble in the Romanswell Muster Roll for 1569. He's probably Humphrey's father. Men often gave their father's name to their eldest son. But he doesn't show up in the 1581 Subsidy Roll for the parish. He might have died or moved. But there *is* a Robert Doble in the Siderleigh Subsidy Roll, and he wasn't there in 1569. He said in a witness statement later that he'd lived in Siderleigh for twenty-seven years. So if he moved there soon after that 1569 Muster Roll, it would all fit.'

'But?'

'But plausible isn't proof. Unfortunately, Robert doesn't say where he moved *from*. And the early Romanswell baptismal registers got destroyed in a fire. I'm probably never going to find proof that Robert Doble of Siderleigh is the father of Humphrey Doble of Romanswell.'

'And is that really so important?'

'Very. Robert of Siderleigh is what you call a "gateway ancestor". When his father died, he became lord of half a dozen manors. There are family trees for most of the lords of the manor, going back to the Middle Ages. It's something you just can't get with agricultural labourers. If I can *prove* I'm related to Robert Doble of Siderleigh, I'm away. I might even get back to the Norman Conquest. And his pedigree will give the women who married the Dobles. They'll all be from the same sort of family. So I can trace their pedigrees too. It opens up a huge new field. I might even find I'm related to the Herewards by blood as well as by marriage, besides being one of Alianor's Dobles.'

'Ah. It all comes back to that, does it? I've humiliated you, getting caught on their land like a poacher. You want to prove you've got the right to come in by the front door. "*One of u*s . . ." Is this where I turn off the dual carriageway?'

Suzie gave him directions. She was fighting back the urge to protest that he was being unfair. It was the thrill of the detective investigation, the desire for that joyful moment when a hunch was confirmed, which drove her, not the shallower wish for social status based on ancestors long dead. But she knew Nick was right, in part at least. She had felt damaged, cheapened, by what had happened that night. She wanted to raise herself in Alianor and Floridus Hereward's eyes, and not be merely the recipient of their unexpected forgiveness.

They were in a steep-sided, wooded valley, on a winding country road. Suzie studied the map.

'There should be a turning somewhere along here. It goes off at quite a sharp angle, up the hillside.'

'I get the picture. Just wide enough for one car, and no room to pass if you see anything coming.'

'Siderleigh's a very little place. Just a cluster of buildings round the church.'

'Not a manor house?'

'No. This is where Robert Doble spent his middle years. Once his father died, he got the ancestral home in Great Thorry, and half a dozen other manors in several counties.'

'So why didn't your Humphrey get them too?'

'I told you. Assuming he *was* Robert's son, he must have been a younger one . . . Left!'

Nick braked beyond the turning. He backed the car to the signpost and Suzie squinted up at the signpost.

'St Andrew's Church. Siderleigh. That's the one. I wasn't exaggerating, was I?'

Nick nosed the car into the steep lane. Tall hedge banks crowded close and grass grew between the tyre tracks. Cautiously they climbed the gradient. They met no other cars.

'I've a nasty feeling we're driving into a farmyard.'

Nick stopped the car. They were indeed surrounded on three sides by farm buildings. To their left, poultry rooted in the bare earth in front of a substantial farmhouse, part thatched, part slated. In front of the car, an open linhay gave shelter to a tractor and some wicked-looking farm machinery. Away to their right, across an expanse of hardcore, more barns and cowsheds.

'I don't understand. The signpost definitely pointed to St Andrew's Church, and we didn't pass any turnings.'

'It looks as though you can drive on round the corner of

that barn over there. Only I'd feel a bit conspicuous doing it, in case it's private land.'

'Shall I get out and look?'

Suzie opened the car door and stepped out. She felt even more self-conscious, afraid of trespassing, out here in the open with the windows of the farmhouse like black eyes upon her. There was no one about.

She started to walk towards the gap between the sheds in the far right-hand corner of the yard. Almost immediately she saw it, its little wooden bell tower just showing over the galvanized iron roof of a barn. She turned back to Nick, with a smile and a thumbs-up sign.

The yard continued round the barn and then funnelled into a cart track leading out on to a lane even narrower than the one they had driven up. She walked to the far end and saw, past the tiny church, a cluster of cottages. She returned to the corner of the yard and beckoned Nick.

He parked the car behind the barn.

The stones of the little church glowed faintly golden in the afternoon light. There was no stone tower, just the tiny wooden projection Suzie had seen from the farmyard.

Nick laughed. 'Is that the bell tower? I've seen bigger hen coops.'

'I bet the church is locked. A lot of these little, out-of-the-way ones only have a service once a month.'

'The signpost pointed to the church, not just Siderleigh. That sounds as if they expect visitors.'

Suzie turned the iron ring of the handle and pushed. The door opened. She caught her breath in delight.

'It's lovely.'

The nave was smaller than the choir of many churches. There were pews for perhaps thirty people, at most, with hat pegs on the wall beside some of them. An ancient-looking pulpit dominated this unseen congregation. The choir beyond might have held another dozen people. Paintings of sun and moon and stars adorned its ceiling.

Suzie sat down in one of the box-like pews and drank in the atmosphere. She felt her spirit connecting with the centuries of worshippers who had once prayed here.

'Wonderful,' said Nick. 'The silence. You can't hear a single vehicle.'

As if on cue, a tractor roared into life in the farmyard bordering the churchyard. They both laughed.

Suzie got up and began to walk around, studying the interior more closely.

'Of course, much of this will be later than the sixteenth century, when Robert Doble lived here. Things like those ten commandments, behind the altar.'

'There's a booklet here,' called Nick from the back of the church. 'That should tell you.'

On a little table, with copies of the parish magazine and postcards of the church, was a small pile of black-and-white publications.

'*St Andrew's Church, Siderleigh: Parish and People.*' He handed her one. 'Sounds promising. Not just a tour of the architecture.' Nick grinned, as the architect part of him shared the joke with her.

She took the booklet half-heartedly. 'I know what it will be. Just a couple of paragraphs about the early history, and then loads about Victorian benefactors.'

'You might just try it and see.'

'"Font thought to be Saxon . . . mention of a church here in King Alfred's time . . . List of rectors from 1265 . . ." No. Listen to this. "This church lies in the former manor of Siderleigh, which for centuries was in the hands of the Hale family. There were Hales at Siderleigh Barton until the early twentieth century, when the last male heir was killed in the First World War."' She raised an excited face to Nick. 'It was a court case about Dorothy Hale's will in 1597 where I found Robert Doble's witness statement – the one that said that he'd lived here for twenty-seven years. That was my dating evidence to prove that he *could* have come here from Romanswell.'

'Anything there about the Dobles?'

'No – Yes! "The fine carved pulpit is thought to be Elizabethan and reputed to be a gift from Robert Doble, a wealthy parishioner."'

'Nice pulpit,' said Nick, admiring the entwined eagles, bears and sea monsters that enlivened its exterior. 'But it doesn't tell you more than you already knew. Robert Doble lived here in the sixteenth century and he had money.'

'No,' she sighed. 'You're right. It doesn't prove that he was *my* Doble. All the same . . .' She came to stand beside him at the pulpit, fondling the deep-cut carving in the oak. 'I sort of feel . . . you know . . . that it's real. If he *was* Humphrey's father, then probably Humphrey lived here as a boy. He'd have sat in one of these pews.'

'If they had seats then.'

'The book says some of the bench ends are fourteenth century. The Hales would have sat at the front, of course. Do you suppose that farm we drove through was their manor house?'

'Siderleigh Barton? I don't see why not.'

'And the Dobles would maybe sit behind them. Or across the aisle. Right *here*, perhaps.'

'Definitely the big nobs. You like that, don't you?'

She flushed. 'Don't keep on about that. I like whatever I find. It's *all* interesting. And just now I'm pursuing a line of gentry. Next month, I could be back to the workhouse.'

He threw up his hands in mock surrender. 'All right. Point taken.'

Suzie walked back down the nave, fingering the bench ends. 'All the same, I feel that Siderleigh's the key. If only I could find the evidence.'

They left the church and walked up to the common on the ridge above the village. As they drove home, a late afternoon light was turning the last leaves of the woods the same mellow gold as the photograph of Siderleigh's church.

The house was quiet that Saturday evening. When Suzie and Nick returned from Siderleigh, Tom was out. He did not come home for tea. There was nothing unusual about that. He was probably at Paul's. Millie set off to spend the evening with friends, grudgingly promising that, yeah, yeah, she would ring Nick to bring her home before ten.

Nick and Suzie sat companionably watching the sea coast of Britain scroll past them on the television screen. A pleasant ache of physical weariness settled Suzie's limbs deeper into the cushions. The walk they had taken had been a brisk climb. It was a good tiredness, a feeling of being satisfied, relaxed.

The hall was suddenly full of noise. The door burst open. The room was filled with young men. It took a moment for Suzie to realize that it was only Tom and Paul. The electricity of excitement crackled off them, bringing Tom's parents upright in alarm.

'We've got them! We were right!'

Tom was waving something in front of their faces. It was several moments more before Suzie identified it as a camera.

'Got whom? Right about what?'

'Those guys at Hereward Court.'

Nick was on his feet, blazing with anger. 'Hereward Court? You've been back there? I *told* you, Tom. They shot at me. I made it clear you were never to try that again.'

Suzie felt the blood leave her face. She knew guiltily that it should be the physical danger to the boys she, too, was afraid of, and in one way it was. But there was another dread, causing her stomach to sink. Alianor Hereward, and presumably Floridus too, had overlooked the awful, gut-churning embarrassment of catching Nick trespassing on Hereward land at night. Things seemed, on the surface at least, to be back to normal. And now this. She was appalled that Tom could have started it all over again.

She looked past him, his rumpled black hair, his face alight with shining eyes, to Paul. For all the trauma of his recent history, she had looked to the Matoposan boy as the steadier, more sensible one. They were the same age, but Paul had a maturity that cooled Tom's wilder excesses.

He looked, she thought, shocked. There was no flashing grin, no crinkling smile in his eyes. His lips were tight. He looked scared.

She glanced from one to the other, her excitable son, his friend stricken into silence.

Tom was arguing with Nick. 'Dad, we couldn't just leave it. There had to be something going on. It was obvious, wasn't it?'

'I told you to stay away.'

'We were really careful. We're not complete idiots. There was no one about. And guess what? It's not just tents now. They're putting up some sort of permanent camp in the wood. Huts or Portakabins or something.'

'I know.'

'You know?' Tom looked from Nick to Suzie. 'How?'

'Your mother saw them.'

'And you didn't tell me?' He swung round on Suzie, blazing accusation.

'We didn't want you to do anything silly.'

'You think unmasking a Fascist terrorist group is silly?'

'Tom,' she sighed. 'It's all in your imagination.'

'Oh, it is, is it? Then how do you explain this?' He waved the camera in front of her face, grabbed a handful of the leaflets that Paul had taken from his pocket and threw them on the coffee table.

'What's "this"?'

Paul quietly took the camera from Tom. He walked over to the television set, inserted a cord in the camera and plugged it in. The picture changed. An array of thumbnail photographs. Paul selected one.

The image suddenly filled the screen, making Nick and Suzie gasp. A grotesque caricature of a man of African origin. The lips blubbery fat. The nose splayed across the black cheeks. The eyes round and rolled back to show the whites. Arms hanging, ape-like. It would have been shocking in any circumstance. It was an acute embarrassment to look at it in Paul's presence. There was silence in the room.

'What is it?' said Suzie at last in a small voice.

But she knew. Enough of the background against which it had been photographed was visible to show that this was a life-size cardboard figure, crudely and cruelly painted. It was punctured with small circular holes, especially over the chest and head.

'Target practice,' Tom said, defiantly triumphant.

Again that tense silence.

Then Nick said quietly, 'OK, so it's a nasty piece of vicious racism. It's a long way from that to what you're suggesting.'

'Read this, then.' Paul picked up one of the leaflets and handed it to Nick.

Suzie took another.

She read the title: *BRIGADE OF BRITONS*. Her eye ran down the columns of hate-filled print, finding expected phrases: *'Our houses, our jobs . . . your sisters and daughters . . . moronic half-breeds . . . our national heritage . . .'* More coded incitement: *'Cleanse this land of ours . . . one less, one victory . . . final solution.'*

You had only to read it alongside that bullet-riddled figure still haunting the screen to know what form that solution would take. She put it down with an unsteady hand.

'And just where did you find this?' asked Nick.

'In one of the huts. Honestly, Dad, there was no one about. The place was deserted. There's no one camping there now. But there was, and there will be again. It's all set up.'

Nick looked ruefully across at Suzie. 'Somehow this doesn't look like a field studies centre for school kids.'

She could not trust herself to say anything.

'Well,' Tom said belligerently to his father. 'Are you going to go to the police now?'

Nick sighed. 'I guess we have to.'

'No.' Suzie's stifled protest brought her to her feet. 'I mean . . . they'd want to question the Herewards. How would you explain what you were doing there?'

The three of them turned on her in incomprehension.

'Does it matter now? We were looking for evidence, and we found it. OK, we were trespassing, but we had a bloody good reason.'

She could not argue, but nor could she help her heart sinking in despair. She did not know how she could cope with this situation.

FOURTEEN

She was haunted by Paul's face, that round, friendly face, of which the cardboard target in the photograph was such a vicious parody. She struggled with the knowledge that the Herewards must be behind this, must at least be colluding with this. Did Alianor know? Was it just something between Floridus and those men in the truck? Could it be a signal for help Alianor was sending out when she insisted that Suzie came back? Did she need a friend?

What was she to do on Monday afternoon?

But before that, she had to face the police.

Four of them went to the police station on Sunday morning: Tom, Paul, Nick, Suzie, all of them witnesses to some degree. Millie complained bitterly about being left behind.

The officer who received them in one of the interview rooms looked disturbingly young. Smooth fair hair, smooth fair face, almost as if he did not yet need a razor. Constable Martin Erdingham. His smile seemed eager.

'I understand you want us to bring a charge of incitement to racial hatred.'

Simultaneously Tom and Paul cried, 'Yes.'

Put like that, it sounded more clear-cut and final than Suzie was ready for.

'I'm not sure we've got that far yet. My son and his friend have got some worrying evidence . . .'

Tom threw the print of his photograph and the leaflets on the table. The constable picked them up and examined them. His baby face made an expression of disgust. But when he looked up, his grey eyes were sharper.

'They're using guns? This is the target for a firing range, isn't it?'

'Yes,' all of them answered, surprising each other.

'You go first, Suzie,' Nick told her.

She had not wanted to take the lead, had hoped she could remain in the background, merely supporting what the others said. Instead, she had to spell out her involvement with Hereward Court, the men in the truck careering down the drive, Floridus's explanation for the camp in the wood. Even her part on that night expedition, when they had come so near to catching her at the edge of the track. Tom and Paul heard that part of her story with astonishment.

'You never said!' Tom ejaculated.

'I was trying to keep you out of trouble.'

She was aware of the tape recorder smoothly spinning beside them on the table.

Nick went next, flushing as he explained his attempt to intercept Paul and Tom, the gunshot in the dark, his capture by Marchant.

'They imprisoned you at the Court, and they didn't call us?' The constable was leaning forward, scenting another issue for his charge sheet.

'I doubt if they believed my story about the stag, but I rather think they hoped they'd scared me off sticking my nose in any further.'

'Although,' Suzie said, 'the funny thing is they invited me back. At least, Mrs Hereward did. As if nothing had happened . . . Unless she wanted my support.'

'And those guys were still there? Did you get another look?'

She dropped her eyes. She felt shamed, somehow, by having to confess that she had spied on the Herewards. 'I drove along the lane where I'd seen the camp before, only this time there seemed to be more huts.'

'There were. That's where we . . .'

The constable held up his hand, cutting off Tom's eager flow. 'All in good time, son. We'll get around to you.'

'That's all,' Suzie confessed. 'I told Nick, but we agreed not to tell Tom. We didn't want to start them off again.'

'So why did you go back?' Now the constable did turn to the boys.

'We didn't believe it,' Tom said confidently. 'Time's money to those city types. They might do that sort of backwoods stuff for a day out or a weekend, but they're not going to give up a week or two, just for team bonding, are they? It didn't make sense.'

Constable Erdingham nodded. 'Sharp thinking, lads. You've got a point. If they're not city slickers, the question is, who are they?'

Paul pushed a leaflet forward. 'It says here. The Brigade of Britons.'

'Never heard of them.'

'I tried Googling them,' Tom cut in eagerly. 'There's loads of stuff. All like this. Hate propaganda. How blacks are going to take over the country. Don't just throw them out. Kill them. The sort of lies that make you sick even to read it. Why don't they stop it?'

'It's not so easy. The Internet was designed to avoid central control.'

'Yeah,' Tom said. 'So that the USA could keep running even after a major strike on the Pentagon.'

'Lack of control is the downside of freedom. Do you have the URLs?'

Paul passed across a sheet of paper on which a list of website addresses was printed in a neat column of underlined blue type.

The constable studied it. 'New ones on me.'

'You've seen this sort of thing before?' Nick asked.

'We get all sorts. You wouldn't believe. May I keep this?'

'Of course,' Paul said. 'That's why I brought it.'

'So –' Constable Erdingham pushed the evidence aside – 'what happened when you went back?'

Suzie's stomach clenched as she heard, for the second time, the boys telling of creeping through the woods, the eerie silence, the feeling that the camp was deserted now, and then the discovery of what Suzie had concealed from them, the newly built huts.

'Just open. Nobody there, but they were unlocked. We just walked in.'

And found . . . that.' Paul gestured to the photograph.

'Must have given you a funny turn.' The constable looked directly at the Matoposan boy.

Paul nodded. A silence hung over the room.

Constable Erdingham swept the papers together and stacked them in a neat pile. 'Anything else?'

Tom handed him more photographs. 'Shots of the camp. So you can see the set-up.'

'Thanks. Right, leave it with me. I'll check out those websites. Have to consult my superiors, but I think you're on to something rather nasty here. Well done, lads. I shouldn't be encouraging trespassing, let alone breaking and entering, but in this case . . .'

'What are you going to do? Will you see the Herewards?' Anxiety drove the words from Suzie's mouth.

'Not up to me. But under the circumstances, I'd be very surprised if we didn't. If that camp's still under construction, they can hardly claim they didn't know what was happening on their land.'

It was over. What happened next was out of their hands. She had done her civic duty. An indignant voice shouted at her that it was much more than that. Could she have watched that obscene photograph on the screen in Paul's company, and not acted? But why, why did it have to be Hereward Court?

Tomorrow was Monday. Would the police get to the Herewards before she did?

She tried a hesitant question. 'I'm due back at Hereward Court tomorrow, to return some documents. Do you think I should still go?'

The police constable stood up. Seeing his height, she revised her opinion of his babyish appearance. He considered her question for a moment. 'I'd say yes. Might be useful to have someone inside. Keep your eyes open. Let us know if you see or hear anything interesting. I'll give you a ring beforehand if we do anything on our side which might make that not a good idea.'

Suzie walked out into the fresh air in a daze. So she was to be, not just an informant, but a spy. Her return for the Herewards' generosity.

Suzie was half out of her seat before she realized that the ringing of the telephone came from the television set and not from the hall.

'It's Sunday,' Nick explained patiently, as she settled back again with a frustrated sigh. 'That PC probably won't be reporting back to his bosses until they're at full strength on Monday morning.'

'But he seemed excited about it. He was taking it very seriously.'

'Still, it's not as if it was an emergency. OK, we could be on to something important, but one day here or there's not going to make a difference. Not if the thugs aren't at the camp now.'

'But the Herewards are expecting me tomorrow. I have to know whether it's still safe to go. Imagine walking in there, if the police have been to interview them, and them knowing it was us who told on them.'

'I'm not sure if I'm keen on you going back there under any circumstances. It was bad enough that night I got caught.'

'They thought you were a fox, or a poacher. It was understandable.'

'That guy had night sights on his rifle. He was aiming to do more than scare me. And what the boys found out makes it much worse. Those sort of thugs wouldn't think twice about getting blood on their hands. It's part of the adrenalin rush. They're the lone heroes, saving Britain from catastrophe. They'll justify anything to themselves. And you're a hostile witness.'

'It's not them I'm seeing. It's the Herewards.'

'What's the difference?'

'Nick! Just because some far-out group have hired a bit of their estate for their war games, it doesn't mean the Herewards are in on it.'

'No? Your Floridus must be in and out of that campsite while they're putting up the huts. Tom and Paul just walked into one of the cabins and found that stuff. Don't tell me Hereward hasn't done the same. He must know what's going on. And if he doesn't approve of it, why hasn't he cleared their filth out? Told them not to come back?'

'How do I know? Perhaps he left it there so he can confront them with it next time they come.'

'Suzie! Get real.'

'I'm just trying to be fair.'

'But you do think they're coming back?'

There was an uncomfortable pause.

'I suppose so.'

'And you still want to go there? Suzie, it's not worth it. Just for a bit of local history.'

'It's not that.' Suzie frowned, staring unseeingly at the television drama unfolding in front of her. 'I'm not sure why. I think it's Alianor.' She lifted her eyes to meet Nick's concerned face. 'What if you're right? What if Floridus is behind it and Alianor knows about it, but doesn't want to be part of it? It would explain several things. Why she invited me back after they caught you, when I thought they'd just show me the door. Something she said once about Floridus being out killing things. And the way she seems to be hoping that I'll discover something about my Dobles which will prove we're related. I think she needs a friend, Nick. I'm sure she wants me back.'

Nick looked at her in silence, his expression unreadable. At last he said, 'Our young policeman is hoping you might come back with more evidence. I don't think he saw you acting as marriage guidance counsellor for Mrs Hereward. I'd be happier if you didn't go.'

'I'll be all right, as long as the police haven't been on to them by then. That's why I keep listening for the phone.'

'All I'm saying, love, is be very careful. These are seriously nasty guys. One wrong step and you could be out of your depth.' On a sudden impulse he crossed the room and hugged her hard. 'I never thought I'd say it, but stick to family history, this time, won't you?'

She kissed him back. 'I promise.'

*   *   *

She was on foot again. Nick needed the car today. It was a day of bare skies and sunshine and near-naked trees. The leaves were still wet underfoot. As Suzie walked along the lane from the bus stop she felt exposed, her guilty knowledge too obvious. When she saw the row of wheelie bins at the Herewards' gateway it did not bring the former lift of her spirits, the sense that she was entering a privileged area. There had been no call from the police, but she turned into the drive with a feeling of nervousness. She could only hope that the Herewards knew nothing yet of Tom and Paul's discovery.

The onset of winter had made no difference to the rhododendron shrubbery. Its leathery evergreen leaves rose above and around her as she started down the drive towards the bend.

She was unprepared. As she turned the curve which would bring her in sight of the house, he was almost upon her. Tall, burly, swift-striding. He was dressed as before in that flowing black leather coat. The sunshine glinted on his shaved head.

He checked, visibly as surprised as she was. There was no mocking greeting. His eyes were hard, shrewd, assessing her up and down.

'You here again?' The Estuary vowels were aggressive, lacking the slow warmth of the West Country.

'Yes,' she said, feeling the need to justify herself, in answer to his sharp, accusing tone. 'I'm on my way to see Mrs Hereward. She invited me.'

'Did she now? After she caught you trespassing on her husband's property in the middle of the night. Rather odd that, wouldn't you say?'

His use of pronouns disconcerted her. 'It wasn't me; it was my husband. And it wasn't Mrs Hereward who caught him; it was a man called Marchant. A gamekeeper, or something. Anyway, Nick had a perfectly good reason. He'd seen a—'

'A white stag. Go on, pull the other one. It's got bells on it.'

She flushed, angry with herself, as well as with him. How did he know all this? Who was he, to hold her and Nick to account?

'If you'll excuse me, it's none of your business. We've apologized to the Herewards and they've kindly agreed to overlook it. I've been invited back. So if you wouldn't mind letting me pass . . .'

He stood too close, too big, looming in front of her.

'Oh, but I think it *is* my business. I don't think I want you here, Mrs Nosey-Parker. I think you'd better give back those papers and go home and stay there.'

He knew why she'd come. She hadn't told him.

'That's a matter for Mrs Hereward.'

He looked around him slowly, at the grounds of Hereward Court, with exaggerated surprise. 'I didn't know Mrs Hereward owned this. That's news to me.'

It was on the tip of her tongue to say, 'And you don't own it, either.' But prudence – no, if she was honest, fear – held her silent.

She sidestepped to get past him. He moved his bulk to block her. She heard the creaking of his leather coat. He smiled, but said nothing.

She dug her nails into the palms of her hands. She would not turn back. 'Excuse me. I need to return these documents. I have an appointment at two o'clock.'

He looked down at her reflectively, for what felt like a long time. Then, 'Make this the last time. Don't say I didn't warn you.'

She knew from his shrug that he was releasing her, giving her grudging permission to proceed. He did not move. She had to walk round him. She must not look back, but she heard no sound of his footsteps striding on up the drive. He was still watching her.

She wanted to run down the hill, under the archway and into the sheltering courtyard. If she had been nervous before, she was afraid now. She was not sure of what. He had no name, no function here that she could identify. But his physical presence loomed far too strong for anonymity. It was like the shock and horror of fairy tales. Beauty coming upon the Beast, Red Riding Hood finding the wolf in her grandmother's bed, Bluebeard's bride discovered by him in the forbidden chamber.

That, she knew, was how he had meant her to feel. To scare her off.

Which meant he knew what there was to conceal.

Did Alianor Hereward?

The courtyard was shadowed from the low afternoon sun. It did not feel quite like the refuge that she had hoped it would be.

The bell clanged, shivering down stone passages. The barking of the dogs brought a welcome note of normality. She allowed herself to be engulfed in their leaping warmth and enthusiasm.

'Down, Dizzy! Get off her, Gladstone!' Alianor's roar sounded as genial as ever.

She was inside. The door shut on the cold exterior.

'How did you get on with your Dobles? Any luck yet?'

Suzie was taken aback by the directness of the question. Mrs Hereward was not one for preliminary small talk.

'We went to Siderleigh on Saturday.' That seemed an age ago, before Tom and Paul had come bursting in with their finds. Could it only be two days? She struggled to remember Siderleigh's significance. 'It's where Robert Doble lived in the late-sixteenth century, before his father died and he became lord of the manor of Great Thorry. I'm fairly sure my Humphrey Doble must be Robert's son, but I can't find proof of it.'

'Humphrey? Hmm. That rings a bell.' Alianor swept Suzie into the cold, north-facing library and pulled a scroll from one of the shelves. When she spread it out on the mahogany table, Suzie saw that it was another pedigree. This time it was her own Doble family.

'Thought so. Look here. *Robert Doble, b. 1533. Humphrey, 1535.* What date was your man?'

'He and his wife owned a farm in Romanswell in 1616.'

'If they were the same man, that would make him eighty-one in 1616. Not many people lived that long in those days. And if his wife was alive as well . . . No, my dear, you're barking up the wrong tree there.'

'I think he was Robert's son, not his brother.'

'Humph.' Another derisive snort. 'What else have we got? Robert's eldest son, James. Inherited the manors, of course. Daughter Elaine, married Thomas Huccaby. *Other issue.*'

'One of them could have been a Humphrey. Names were passed down in families, weren't they?'

'Not proof, is it? Could be wishful thinking. Now, what have you got to show me today?'

She took Suzie's proffered transcripts and ran her eye over them. She gave occasional snorts of laughter at the colourful exchanges of the court cases. 'Spiffing stuff. I can see I shall have to move from my colonials to Victorian low-life. Got to be some good chapters here, wouldn't you think? Now, my dear, do you want some more? Not fed with up with us yet?'

'No,' said Suzie. 'It's fascinating. If you don't mind me carrying on . . .'

'Nobody else is going to do it.'

She led the way to the great hall. It was deserted today. Suzie was relieved not to have to sort through the papers under the supercilious gaze of Freddie.

Alianor met her again in the kitchen. They shared mugs of hot tea and ginger biscuits. The shadows were lengthening early as the days grew shorter. Ahead of Suzie was the long, solitary walk up the drive. She wished she had been able to bring the car.

'I can give you a lift,' Mrs Hereward said unexpectedly. 'I need to deliver some leaflets in the village before I meet the brats from school.'

Was it coincidence? Could she have seen that encounter high on the drive? Did she know how much Suzie had been dreading the walk back? Or did she have her own reasons for not wanting Suzie to risk meeting that man again?

FIFTEEN

As soon as Suzie got home she checked the answerphone. The green light was steady; there had been no calls. Several times as she prepared the meal she paused, knife or spoon in hand, thinking she had heard the phone start to ring in the hall. It was always a false alarm.

Millie came in from school, trailing her bag. 'French *and* Biology,' she said gloomily, humping it on to the kitchen table.

Suzie rescued the uncooked pie just in time.

Tom breezed into the kitchen half an hour later. His vivid blue eyes were alive with anticipation. 'Did you go? Are the police on to them?'

'I went. The police haven't rung.'

The light died out of Tom's eyes. He shrugged. 'It figures,

I suppose. Guess they'll want to ferret out as much of the Herewards' dastardly dealings as they can before those guys know anyone's on to them. And check out this Brigade of Britons lot on the web. It makes sense to stack up the evidence before they go in mob-handed. Pity. I can't wait to see that scum get their comeuppance.'

'I feel a bit like that myself. I mean, I keep waiting for the phone to ring and wondering why it doesn't.'

Just then it rang.

Suzie dashed for the kitchen door, but Tom was nearer. He sped down the hall and grabbed the receiver.

'Yes, Fewings.' There was a short pause, while Suzie stood expectantly, wiping the flour from her hands on her apron. 'No bloody thanks. We've got one.' He turned to her, the eagerness of his face now downturned with disappointment. 'Double glazing. Do we want a conservatory?'

'I don't suppose they'll ring now.' Suzie sighed. 'It's gone five.'

'You reckon the police work office hours?'

'As you said, it's early yet. They've probably got a lot of digging to do first.'

'How was your visit to the Reichstag? Did you spot anything else sinister?'

A shadow passed over Suzie's mind. She found herself reluctant to tell him about the leather-coated stranger who had barred her way to Hereward Court and warned her not to come back.

'Mrs Hereward and I discussed my family tree. I'm getting closer, but I still can't prove I'm related to her.'

His voice took on a tone of incredulity. 'Do you *want* to be?'

'Look, whatever's going on, we don't know how much the Herewards are involved in it. Mrs Hereward in particular. This isn't the French Revolution. Nowadays we don't guillotine people just because of their family tree. She's a perfectly nice woman. Well, a bit odd by our standards. But she's been very kind to me.'

'Touch your forelock and know your place, do you? That lot are brought up to be perfectly polite to their servants and tenants, as long as they don't put a foot out of line. I bet you if there's a pro-hunting march in London, not one of the Herewards' tenants would dare to stay home.'

Suzie remembered that exhibition in the village hall. The warning from Mr Beaman to keep quiet about the hunting ban if she wanted permission to use the old census. The young man who'd said you couldn't fart in Eastcott St George without Mr Hereward's permission.

She said reluctantly, 'You're making assumptions. I'm not even sure where Alianor Hereward stands on hunting. You're probably right about Floridus, though. I should think he lives for blood sports.'

Though she hated the thought of killing animals for fun, there was something comforting in imagining Floridus and the Barbour-coated Marchant stalking through the woods with guns, intent on pheasants, rabbits, deer, or whatever else they shot. Not deer, perhaps. The Herewards would rather give chase on horseback. Make their terrified quarry flee for its life. She doubted if the anti-hunting legislation had made much difference.

She pulled herself up short. She was letting her imagination wander to traditional country pursuits, however much she disliked them, because it was so much better than picturing what else they might train their guns on. She had a sudden vision of the flesh and blood reality caricatured by that painted target in the hut. Someone like Paul.

She could not imagine that shaven-headed man with the leather overcoat riding to hounds with the local hunt.

She should have told Nick about that man. She wanted to. She lay in bed beside Nick, needing the warmth of his arms around her, his sharing of fear on her behalf, his sharp insistence that she must never go back there, that she was running into too much danger. Or did she want him to laugh off her terror, make her see it as no more than a distasteful encounter with a lout, not something more sinister, more threatening?

Though she longed to tell him, she found it difficult to put it into words. Just as it was impossible to convey to someone else why the commonplace imagery of certain nightmares was so terrifying, so she could not explain the degree of dread she had felt from a few stereotypical details of terror: the swing of the skirt of his leather overcoat, the sheen of his shaved skull, the stubble on his heavy jowls. She did not want ever to find herself alone with him again. Yet how could she communicate that to Nick? The man had done nothing. He had not touched her. (She shivered at the thought that he might have.) In the end he had let her go on her way. Yes, his tone had been threatening. But an aggressive style of talking was normal for some people. She probably ought not to take it seriously.

Yet she did.

She rolled away from Nick. She hugged the hostility of that encounter to herself, because if Nick were to find it as menacing as she had, it would make her fear worse still. It would mean she was not exaggerating.

In any case, it could not be long now. The police would arrive at Hereward Court. They would search the estate, make a thorough investigation. Whatever that man's part in what was going on there, they would discover it. They would put an end to it. She could go back to the innocent pursuit of family history by other means.

She would tell Nick about it one day, when the memory had become less sickening and she could laugh it off. She was definitely not going to tell Tom about him.

The week crawled past. Every day when she returned from her morning's work in the charity office, the first thing she did was to check the answerphone. There was never a message from DC Erdingham. No information about when they would visit the Herewards. When the phone rang it was always someone else.

Suzie continued to work on her transcripts with a feeling of unreality. Would she ever be going back to Hereward Court again? She had thought her visits were over once before, but Alianor, and presumably Floridus, had forgiven her. But her association with them – she hesitated to call it friendship – could surely not survive a police investigation. It was out of her hands. She was in limbo, waiting for someone else to make a move.

By next Monday morning she could bear it no longer. She phoned DC Erdingham from the office at the back of the charity shop in her coffee break. It took some time to be connected, while she struggled to explain her business. At last he answered, his voice a little high-pitched, reminding her of his youthful appearance.

'It's Mrs Fewings,' she said. 'Suzie Fewings. You were going to warn me if you'd been to Hereward Court, so that I wouldn't just walk in there without knowing.'

'I remember.'

'It's Monday again. I went last week and it was all right. You hadn't been. What about now?'

A little pause. 'You'll be all right. No need to worry.'

'Nobody's been to interview the Herewards?'

'The matter is under investigation.'

'But you haven't actually gone out there?'

'No.'

'Oh . . . all right then. Thank you.'

She put the phone down, feeling oddly dissatisfied, in spite of his reassurance.

She was free to go. The Herewards did not realize yet what Tom and Paul had discovered on their property. She could go back there as though nothing had changed.

She was not sure now whether she wanted to.

She was glad that she had been able to borrow the car this week. She felt a little safer than on foot. Despite her misgivings, she did not pass the man on the drive this time. There was, she supposed, no reason why she should. In all her weekly visits she had only seen him three times.

This afternoon's visit to Hereward Court passed in an aura of undefined strangeness. Alianor seemed a little subdued from her usual genially domineering self. She barely rebuked the Labradors as they leaped around Suzie. The dogs' enthusiasm, at least, was normal.

Suzie herself was almost tongue-tied. She had unleashed something on the Hereward family which could prove catastrophic for them. She felt an urgent need to warn Alianor, to apologize in advance. She fought it down.

It was an elegiac feeling, sorting carefully through the Hereward papers in the document chest. This was, she reflected, almost certainly her last visit. The police had had the information for over a week now. Surely they must move in soon? If they left it much later, the situation might have changed, evidence could have been removed.

She went back to the kitchen with a deed from Elizabethan times giving the details of church land in Eastcott St George which included a record of which villagers lived where.

It offered another rare and precious insight into the lives of people's ancestors, this time five hundred years ago. The information was older than anything she had found yet. It gave her a shiver of exquisite pleasure to be handling it, even if this was a nineteenth-century copy of the original.

At the kitchen door she checked with an unreasonable alarm at the sight of Floridus Hereward. He was drinking tea and staring out at the sombre woods.

He turned at the sound of her entry. His stiffly held back gave him almost the movements of an automaton. He looked at her without a smile or a frown, as though he did not remember who she was, and was not much interested.

'I'm Suzie Fewings,' she reminded him. 'I've been copying documents from your wonderful collection. I came to tell Mrs Hereward what I'm taking this week . . . if that's all right.'

He glanced down at the pages in her hand. He would not be able to read from across the room what they were, but he did not ask.

'Yes. It's perfectly all right if Allie says so.'

'She hasn't seen them yet. I usually take them to her, in case it's anything too valuable for me to take away.'

'Tea?' he said, as though she had not spoken. 'There are some biscuits in the tin.'

She found she did not want to stay in the kitchen with him, trying to make polite conversation and not mention the enormity of what she was about to bring on him. Despite Tom's passionate condemnation, she found it hard to cast this rather tongue-tied yet courteous man as a racist villain. Then she thought of Paul's African mother. If she were standing here in Suzie's place, how different would her reception be? Would she meet abuse? Cold rejection? Would he cover up prejudice with a veneer of civility? Suzie had no idea.

'Do you know where Mrs Hereward is?' Like Floridus, she was avoiding his contribution to the conversation, his offer of tea.

'Got a sick horse. No need to bother her. You can take the stuff, if it amuses you.'

'I'll . . . let you have it back next week.'

Though she might well have to post it.

She turned away in relief. She had done nothing to find out

more information for the police. She would just go home now and leave it to them.

There was no reason for her to turn left at the gate, away from the village.

She drove to the crossroads and made another left turn, following the narrow lane along the ridge above the Hereward estate. She was not looking for anything in particular today. It was like picking at a half-healed scab.

The lodge had that same grey, forbidding look, with its close surround of trees. She found herself slowing the car. The gate was partially open.

He came striding around the bend of the unkempt drive, still in the same dark trench coat. She revved too loudly in her haste to accelerate away. Too late; he must have seen her. Through her rear mirror she saw him almost run to the gate and stare after her.

So he was living at the lodge. She thought of the two black shirts she had seen flapping dismally on the clothes line the first time she came this way. He was not an occasional visitor. In some way she did not yet understand, he belonged to Hereward Court.

He had seen her slowing to look at the lodge. He had recognized her, she was sure of it. He had stared after her car long enough to memorize the number plate.

SIXTEEN

Suzie carried the milk bottles from the doorstep into the kitchen. Nick and Tom were enjoying a relaxed Saturday morning breakfast. At seventeen, Tom, she realized with renewed wonder, was now as big as Nick, perhaps even taller. Sprawled across the kitchen table, one arm cradling his cereal bowl, he seemed to take twice as much as room as his father. Nick sat more neatly, knife and fork deftly dissecting his bacon and toast.

She eased the armful of plastic bottles on to a corner of the table.

Tom grinned at her. 'You and Dad going somewhere nice today? Stack up some more evidence that you're related to the fascist aristocracy?'

'I thought we might take a walk on the moor. We could go past a farm where one of my great-grandfathers was an agricultural apprentice.'

'That's not exactly going to impress them when you go back to the Herewards next Monday.'

She had her back to them, storing the milk in the fridge door. 'I'm not going back.'

'Come again.'

Suzie turned round to face him. Nick, she could sense, was also alert with interest now.

'I've decided I don't want to go to Hereward Court any more. Any day now, the police are going to raid it. I know they have to, but I feel responsible. If it hadn't been for me, none of this would have happened.'

'Come on, Mum. If it hadn't been for you, people like him would still be amusing themselves using black guys for target practice.'

'We don't know that it was Floridus.'

Tom spluttered into his cornflakes. 'Mum, get real! He *owns* the place. That hut was wide open. He has to know what's going on.'

'I expect you're right. All the more reason why I should stay away.'

'But you heard what the police said. They want you to keep your eyes open. You might see some more evidence. Suspicious types coming to the house, or in the grounds. You can't drop out now.'

'She can if she wants to,' put in Nick. 'If half of what you're assuming is true, some of the guys she saw could be very ugly characters. If might be best to give them a wide berth.'

'Even without that,' said Suzie, 'I can't go on making these raids on the document chest indefinitely. Mrs Hereward's been very tolerant, but she must be beginning to wonder how long I'm going to keep turning up on her doorstep.'

'I thought you said she seemed to want you to do the transcripts,' Nick said.

'Yes. But it might be just politeness. And it takes a lot of my time copying them. I'm probably spending more hours on it than I can really justify.'

'What about the family history community you keep telling me about? Your contribution to research? All the same, if you're not happy about going, don't.'

Should she tell them now about the man at the lodge?

'Pig,' said Millie's voice from the doorway.

She was leaning her slight frame against the doorpost, as though her legs did not have the strength to support her. Her fair hair was tousled, falling over bleary eyes. She was dressed in a tee shirt which just covered her bottom and a long, baggy cardigan. Her feet were bare.

'I beg your pardon,' said Suzie. She surveyed her daughter. 'Don't you need a pair of trousers?'

'Pig,' said Millie again, straightening herself precariously from the doorpost. 'We've got a day off school on Monday. I was going to ask if you'd take me to Hereward Court.'

'You?'

'Why not? You and Dad have been there, and Tom has, sort of. I'm the only one who hasn't seen it. The rest of you go on talking about this great adventure you're having. Plots and guns and calling in the police and stuff. All I get to do is sit at home by the telephone.'

'It's not a rock concert,' put in Nick. 'You don't buy tickets to watch it. This is for real.'

'I know that. I'm not a complete moron. But if Mum's supposed to be noticing what goes on, two pairs of eyes have got to be better. I might spot things she doesn't. *I* don't need to have my head buried in an old document chest, do I?'

There was silence in the kitchen. Tom broke it. 'I could come too.'

'No!' cried Nick and Suzie simultaneously.

Nick went on, 'We've done our best to keep you out of this, Tom. I nearly got shot for my pains. The last thing we want is you getting caught up in it again. You've already done your bit, and more. You were lucky to get away with that.'

'What about Millie, then? Why's it OK for her to go?'

'I never said it was,' Suzie countered quickly. 'I said I wasn't going back, let alone taking her.'

'But you will, won't you, Mumsie?' Millie said coaxingly. She shuffled across the kitchen floor to put her arms round

Suzie. 'Just this once. If your precious policeman hasn't fouled it up by Monday. You could go one more time, couldn't you?'

A tempting voice was telling Suzie that she might not feel so bad if she had someone with her. The frail-seeming figure of her thirteen-year-old daughter might not appear to be much of a defence against a man who looked like, and almost certainly was, a racist thug. But already her spirits felt lighter as she imagined the two of them joking together on their way down the drive. Surely Mrs Hereward wouldn't mind? She had children of her own. Suzie remembered the flushed face of Freddie dismissively refusing her offer to make him cocoa.

'It can't be much longer, can it?' she said, weakening. 'It's a fortnight now since we gave Tom's evidence to the police. I know they'll want to get as much background stuff on this Brigade of Britons as they can, before they move in. But it has to happen sometime soon. I won't be able to go after that, will I?'

'Does that mean yes?' Millie turned a wheedling smile up at her.

'You'll need to be on your best behaviour. There's a lot of valuable stuff around.'

'Trust me. I'll be the sort of daughter you could take to a royal garden party.'

Suzie knew that, if this was the dramatic role Millie had to cast herself in, then she would.

Mist cloaked the tors. It was not so thick that it was imprudent to walk on the moor, but it cast a dull December shadow over the landscape. Grey mist, not white.

'I keep looking overhead,' Suzie sighed to Nick. 'I can just about convince myself that I can see blue sky through the cloud and that the sun's about to break through, but somehow it never happens.'

'It's not going to now.' Nick dug his gloved hands deeper into his pockets. 'It's perishing cold too, the sort of damp cold that gets into your bones.'

'You should try working at Hereward Court. Mrs Hereward was right to warn me that it would be freezing, and that was back in the autumn. I don't know how they can bear to live there without central heating. And I'm sure it can't be good for the building. You can see the damp on the inside walls and the plaster's peeling.'

'Perhaps they should open it up to the public. Bring some money in.'

'I don't think Floridus would like people tramping over his home. He seems quite a private person. He does have paying guests sometimes, shooting parties. But they'll be a better class of clientele.'

'If he wants to hang on to a house that size for one family, he'd better start thinking about sharing it with the hoi polloi.'

'That's why his story to me about letting city types camp in his woods sounded so convincing. He needs the money and he wouldn't have to have them in the house. But if Tom's right about the Brigade of Britons, I'm not sure they're the sort who would pay all that well. They might not even pay at all.'

'If Tom's right? You mean you're not convinced by those leaflets? The photographs?'

'I suppose they were pretty damning.'

For a moment a light wind tugged the mist away from the tor in front of them. The granite rocks loomed dark, the topmost just balanced upon a pile of others.

'Damning? I should say they were. It wasn't just the general "immigrants out" stuff. The hard core was seriously sick. I felt ashamed to be reading them in the same room as Paul.'

The cloud was closing down again. Suzie could barely see the rocks.

'Why do you think the police haven't done anything yet?'

'We don't know that they haven't. Just because they haven't confronted the Herewards doesn't mean they're not on the case. They could be keeping the place under surveillance. See who visits it.'

'I do.' She laughed nervously. 'Do you think I'm on a police file somewhere?'

'Very suspicious.' He squeezed her arm. 'Hobnobbing with some pretty unsavoury characters.'

'Floridus doesn't *seem* unsavoury. Not when you meet him.'

'I have, remember? With the business end of a rifle in my back. Anyway, murderers don't make it easy for the police by going around with horns on their heads and cloven hoofs.'

'A murderer? Is that what you think he is?'

'You read the leaflets.'

It silenced her. She walked through the wet-beaded heather, which had long turned from purple to black. She had been afraid at Hereward Court, but it was not of the Herewards.

She knew she should tell Nick now about the burly man in the leather overcoat, who walked into Hereward Court as though he owned it and had stood over her menacingly, warning her not to come back. She had taken the decision not to go there again. She should have stuck to it. How had she come to let herself be committed to taking Millie too?

She was being ridiculous. She wasn't Paul, was she, with his obvious African heritage? She was a middle-aged, middle-class, white woman. She had a family history going back in this part of England for centuries. She needn't feel personally threatened by those leaflets, need she? Not once she was inside the house?

All the same . . .

'There was a man,' she said. 'I've seen him three times now. I think he lives in the lodge. You know, by those gates we passed near the broken wall.'

'I remember it.' He broke off with a change in his voice. 'Look, I think this mist is closing in. If it's all the same to you, I think we should head down to the road, while we still know where it is. I haven't brought a compass.'

It was already getting hard to see ahead. In a frighteningly short time the road below them was lost behind a wall of grey. They picked their way over the rough ground, where water trickled between stones. There had been a small trail they were following towards the tor, but now there was not enough light to pick out a similarly slender thread leading down through the heather.

'If we just keep heading downhill, we should hit it,' Nick said.

Suzie gave a cry of alarm as a dark boulder rose up in front of her. A sheep staggered disconsolately away into the murk. She laughed nervously.

They did not see the road until they stumbled on to its level surface.

'Which way is the car?' Suzie asked.

'Right, I think.'

Should she open that difficult subject again, now they were

safely on the road? The man had threatened her. With what? She wasn't sure now. But he had wanted to stop her going to Hereward Court again.

Or had she just imagined the menace? Could he be some sort of steward of the estate, just trying to deter unwanted visitors from entering? When she had told him about Alianor's invitation, he had grudgingly let her pass. It was some while ago now. She could not recreate for Nick the depth of the fear she had felt, standing so close in front of him.

Nothing can happen to me, she thought. I'll have Millie with me. And this really will be the last time I go.

SEVENTEEN

'Not exactly Buckingham Palace, is it?' Millie observed as Suzie turned the car off the road by the wheelie bins.

'I did warn you. The Herewards may own a big house, but they're hard up. At least, by their standards.'

She thought of the fees for Mark at Harrow before he died.

'I like it!' Millie's tone changed as they rounded the bend and the house lay four-square below them, nestled in its parkland beside the small lake. 'Look at those dinky towers. Tom used to have a wooden fort like that.'

Suzie felt a surge of inappropriate pride, as though it were her own house Millie was approving. She had become so bound up with Hereward Court these past weeks, its history, its family. Whatever evil was happening in the woods, whoever the man was who occupied the lodge, she still found it hard to associate them with the house itself, with good-natured Alianor, even with the distant but courteous Floridus.

'They're not for real,' she told Millie. 'There was probably a fortified manor house here once, but this one was built later. The battlements are just for show.'

'All the same, I fancy a bedroom in one of those towers. Only how do you arrange a fitted wardrobe if the walls are circular?'

'If you're planning on doing the Rapunzel bit, you'll have to grow your hair a lot longer than that.'

She felt amazingly light-hearted, bowling down the drive while she chattered to Millie. The truck full of jeering men in combat gear, the menacing one in the leather coat standing over her, even Nick, pale-faced, guarded by a man with a rifle, drifted on the edge of her consciousness like a half-remembered bad dream.

'Cool,' said Millie, as Suzie eased the car through the archway. 'Though it would have been better with four white horses and a carriage.'

Only when she switched off the engine and stepped out of the car did Suzie's misgivings return. Should she have rung Alianor to ask if it was all right to bring Millie? Was she assuming too much familiarity? Millie couldn't really wander off while Suzie explored the document chest, could she? And if she did, what could she expect to learn?

Millie was still unfolding her thin body from the passenger seat when Suzie's worries were interrupted. Several figures erupted into the courtyard from a door in the far corner. Shrieking, a girl with brown plaits dashed across the cobbles, followed by a smaller fair-haired boy, with a larger dark-haired one in pursuit. The older one stopped when he saw them.

The Hereward children. Suzie could not remember the names of the younger ones, but she recognized Freddie. She had an uncomfortable memory of the lordly way he had questioned her about her ancestry as he lifted his flushed face from the railway set in the great hall.

'Hello,' she said, putting on a determinedly cheerful voice. 'I'm glad to see your cold is better.'

He did not return her smile. 'Mummy's in the library.' His dark gaze went past her. 'Who's that?'

'My daughter Millie. She's got a day off school.'

Millie stood taller than Freddie, but he somehow managed to look her up and down as if from a superior height. 'I know that. So have we.'

The girl with plaits and the younger boy were giggling under the archway. Suddenly the girl called out, 'Bags I first with the canoe!' and raced away.

'No, you don't!' cried Freddie, and broke into a gallop after her.

Millie pulled a face at his retreating back.

'Freddie,' explained Suzie. 'Heir to all this.'

'Does that excuse him for looking at me as if I was something the cat brought in?'

'He can be a bit intimidating for an eleven-year-old, can't he? That effortless superiority.'

'I thought being one of the aristocracy was all about minding your manners.'

'I told you, the Herewards aren't aristocrats. And I'm sure Freddie's perfectly polite to people he considers his equals. Though you're right, a real gentleman is courteous to everyone. Like Floridus, in fact. In the few times I've talked to him, he's always been scrupulously polite to me, even though he's probably written me off as one of the peasants.'

They were walking towards the oak door in the nearer corner.

'I thought you were related to Mrs Hereward?'

'Only possibly. I've got Dobles on my family tree, and that's her maiden name. But I still haven't proved the link.'

Suzie hesitated at the door. Should she ring the bell, as she usually did? Or did Freddie's information about his mother being in the library give her leave to walk in and find Alianor?

She hedged her bets by opening the door and calling, 'Hello?' as she stepped inside.

There was a moment's silence, while Millie avidly took in the portraits on the stairs. Then they heard a skidding of claws on flagstones, a gulping bark, and Dizzy and Gladstone tore round the corner of the corridor to greet Suzie like a long-lost friend. She was stroking their heads and fending off their welcome at the same time. She felt gathered into the pattern of the house, at home here. With a start of surprise she realized that she felt she belonged.

She turned to find Millie backed several steps up the staircase in alarm.

'Do they bite?'

'In my experience, they're a couple of softies. They're bred for retrieving game. They're supposed to have soft mouths, not to mark the birds.'

'I'd rather not think of myself as a dead pheasant, thank you very much.'

Suzie led the way down the echoing corridor. It still felt a little daring to be coming in uninvited, unless Freddie's remark counted as permission. And yet it seemed not wholly out of place.

The door to the library was ajar. Alianor Hereward sat at the vast table, surrounded by books and a few parchments. She looked up, a little distractedly, as Suzie knocked gently on the open door.

'Thought there must be somebody there when the dogs went shooting off.'

Then she saw Suzie. She pushed back the chair clumsily and jumped to her feet.

'It's you, my dear! I'd forgotten it was Monday. I'm so glad to see you again.'

She strode across the floor. For a few astonished seconds, Suzie thought the other woman was going to throw her arms around her and kiss her. But Alianor checked at the last moment, as though years of conditioning had reasserted control.

'Who's this?' she asked, but with a warmer tone than her eldest son. 'Your daughter?'

'Millie,' Suzie introduced her. 'I hope you don't mind me bringing her. The school have got a day off, and I didn't want to leave her on her own.'

Even as she spoke, she was aware that it sounded thin. She had not said that Millie, at thirteen, was perfectly capable of meeting up with her friends, but had wanted to come here.

'Don't I know it? It's the devil, isn't it? I've got my three brats under my feet too.'

Suzie looked past her, out of the library window. There seemed to be some sort of fight going on between Freddie and his sister over the red and white canoe at the water's edge. Should she draw Alianor's attention to it?

But Mrs Hereward was shepherding them towards the great hall. 'No, perfectly all right. I'm sure you've brought her up to be careful with other people's property. It's my own I have trouble with. Knocked a piece off a perfectly good marble fireplace playing cricket in the dining room this morning.' She flung open the door of the great hall. 'There you are. Help yourselves.'

Millie gasped, as Suzie had done, at the train layout filling the immense space. With extreme care she followed Suzie across it to the document chest by the fireplace.

Belatedly, Suzie reached into her shoulder bag and handed the latest batch of transcripts to her hostess.

'More court cases.'

'Thanks. Right, well, I'll leave you to it.' But Alianor stood beside them, as though there were more things she would like to say.

Suzie, kneeling by the chest, looked up at her. 'Is everything all right?'

Alianor started. 'What?' Then her habitual mask of cheerfulness came over her face. 'Oh, of course it is, my dear. Just a bit busy. Doing some of my own research. Don't mind me.'

Still she hovered. 'Seen Flo, have you?'

It was a second before Suzie remembered that this was her nickname for Floridus. 'No. Just your children in the courtyard.'

'Not with that man who lives up at the lodge? Big fellow, shaved on top, like one of these lager louts? I think you met him.'

So he had told the Herewards again, about that.

'No. I mean, yes, I've met that man. But I haven't seen him today.'

'Good-oh . . . I mean, good hunting. Thanks for these.' She waved the transcripts and picked her way over the tracks. She stopped by the door. 'Your husband all right, my dear? No more chasing after white stags?'

'No,' said Suzie, crimsoning at the memory. 'Nothing like that. He's fine.'

'Good-oh,' said Mrs Hereward again, but without enthusiasm. 'You never know what you're going to find in these woods.'

She stumped away.

Suzie and Millie looked at each other.

'What was all that about?' Millie queried.

'I don't know. She's always been a bit odd, by our standards at least. But not like that.'

'It sounded almost as if she was trying to tell you something.'

'Or warn me off.'

'I think she's scared.'

'What *exactly* did he say?' Nick demanded.

They were all hanging on Millie's words. Suzie, Tom and Paul, too, were crowded around the kitchen table. There was no thought of the evening meal, which Suzie had not even started to prepare.

'I *told* you.' Millie was enjoying being for once the centre of attention in a drama in which, until now, her parents and the boys had played the principal roles. 'I thought I'd have a look around outside, while Mum was busy with her old papers. You lot keep going on about the woods, and I'd never even seen them.'

'You weren't thinking of going into them, I hope,' cut in her father.

'Dad! I'd only got about twenty minutes, and Mrs Hereward could have seen me from the window.'

'Yeah, right,' Tom defended his sister. 'Let her get on with it, Dad. Paul and I haven't heard it all yet.'

Millie flashed him a look of astonishment for his unexpected support.

'Well, like I said, I went back to this courtyard and out under the arch, and there's, like, this little lake opposite and then big grassy fields, and the woods are quite a long way away, so you can't see much from there. Only I didn't get any further because there were these Hereward kids mucking about with a canoe. The big boy was paddling it . . .'

'Freddie,' said Suzie.

'Yeah, fat Freddie. And the girl was arguing with him and saying it was her turn.'

'Sisters! So what's new?' said Tom. 'Sorry!'

She glared at him. 'And I was just heading off in the other direction to see if I could spot that camp thing you all keep talking about.'

'You can't see it from the house.'

'Shut *up*, Mum. Anyway, I'd hardly gone any distance before this boy, Freddie, shouts after me, "Where do you think you're going?" Well, I turned round and he's got out of the canoe and the girl and the little boy have grabbed it, and he's standing on the drive with his hands on his hips and sort of red in the face.'

Suzie had a flash of memory: red-faced Freddie challenging her over his train set.

'So I said, "Just getting a bit of fresh air, thank you very much." "Well, you're on my land," he says, very hoity-toity. "You can't just walk where you like here. You have to have permission." Well, I'm not having a kid his age talking to me like that, so I said, "It's not *your* land. It's your father's, and your mother said it was OK for me to be here, so there!"

He didn't like that. He screwed up his eyes, sort of piggy-like, and his voice got all pompous. "My mother has some very funny friends. But they'd better watch out. I know who you are now. It was your father Marchant caught spying in our woods that night, wasn't it?" "He wasn't spying," I said. Well, all right, Dad, I know you were, really.'

'I wasn't spying. I was just trying to stop Tom and Paul.'

'Whatever. Anyway, he's a really nasty piece of work, that Freddie. He said, "Marchant should have shot him. I would have done." "Charming," I said.'

'Get to the point, kid,' begged Paul.

'I *am*. Dad asked me exactly what he said. Well, I'm telling you, aren't I?'

Paul held up his yellow-faced palms in surrender.

'"You wait," he said. "It won't be long now. My dad's got a plan. He's got hundreds of people helping him. They're training with guns and things. Better than the SAS. One day, people like you are going to wake up and find there's been a coup. That's what you call it when you wipe out a bad government and put the right sort of people in their place. People like us." "Who are you kidding?" I told him. "A handful of blokes playing boys' games in the woods, against the whole British army?" "That's all you know," he says, looking sort of crafty. "What if it's not just us? What if there're loads of places like this. I've heard my dad talking . . . First, you get all the nig-nogs up in arms . . ."'

Suzie shot an anxious look at Paul.

'"Then everybody will come over to our side. Especially the Army. They know this government's too soft on the riff-raff: nig-nogs, scroungers, lefties, greens. Well, one day you're all going to get a big surprise. Soon." And there's his little sister, and she's tugging his arm and telling him to shut up. Only he'd got himself so worked up I thought he was going to hit her. Then he seemed to catch his breath and go sort of quiet. He turned back and, like, glared at me and you could see he didn't know what to say, 'cos he'd already said too much. In the end, he, like, tossed his head and said, "Well, that's what *I'd* do, anyway." And then he went back to the pond and grabbed the boat off the little one and started paddling across the water as hard as he could go.'

There was silence round the kitchen table.

Paul shook his head. 'It could happen, man. Someone attacks the black community. Does something *really* nasty. They get fired up and hit back. It can escalate. Before you know where you are, you've got full-scale riots everywhere. If they make sure enough white people get hurt – and this Brigade of Britons would see to that themselves – you'll have the tabloid papers baying for tougher government. But little Freddie's right; there's not one of the current parties would fit the bill. And here's Herr Hereward and his like, waiting in the wings. New right-wing party. Landslide election. Blacks out.'

The Fewings family heard him and had no answer.

'We've got to take this to the police, Dad,' Tom said at last.

Suzie knew she couldn't argue. She no longer wanted to.

'Hearsay evidence,' said Nick. 'An eleven-year-old boy. They'd never get Floridus Hereward to admit it.'

'Come on, Dad. It won't stand up in court, but at least the police would know the score. They don't seem to have lifted a finger on this one yet, but if they knew it was just one part of a national network, with a real agenda, and planning something soon, they'd *have* to do something. Get the names off Hereward. Hold them on some sort charge or other. If they search the house they might find contact numbers, email addresses. Get on to the other cells. For heaven's sake, we've got to *do* something about this.'

Suzie had a vision of the man in the black leather coat who had not wanted her to visit Hereward Court. He had been right to fear her coming.

She levered herself up from the kitchen table she had been leaning on. 'Tom's right. We have to report this. We can't keep it to ourselves.'

EIGHTEEN

It was Nick who rang to arrange a meeting with DC Erdingham. He came back bristling with indignation.

'Wednesday afternoon. It took some time getting through to him, and then he said he was busy tomorrow. To be honest, he didn't sound that eager to see us at all.'

'Did you tell him what it was about? That we think they may be planning something awful soon?'

'I tried. But it wasn't the same as us hearing it from Millie herself. I could tell what he was thinking. I might have been the same in his place. One kid reporting on what another kid had said.'

'I'm not a kid!' Millie flared. 'I'm a teenager.'

'Yes, well. We'll have to get you time off school. Wednesday, three o'clock. I'll pick you up.'

'I'm coming too,' said Suzie. 'I know more about the situation than you do.'

This time Tom would be left behind, to his fury.

As they drove into town Suzie said, 'It's odd. They *still* haven't been to Hereward Court. It's been weeks since we showed them what the boys found. I don't understand what they're playing at.'

'Don't want to frighten the horses until they've got the information they want on them.'

'But a lot of that information may be at Hereward Court.'

'I'm sure they know what they're doing.'

'I hope so. It was a bit scary on Monday, even before Freddie let the cat out of the bag. I couldn't help feeling Mrs Hereward was trying to tell me something. A cry for help. I wish now I'd followed her back to the library and made her tell me properly.'

'This man who lives at the lodge. Why didn't you tell me about him before?'

'I did start to once. On the moor. Only then the mist came down and you were more concerned about getting back to the road.'

'So it's my fault? It wasn't exactly the only time you could have mentioned him.'

'I know. I . . . I didn't *want* to talk about him. I'm frightened of him. It sounds silly, but I was the first time I met him, and he was quite cheerful to me then. Maybe it was the black leather coat, sort of Nazi style. And the shaved head.'

'Lots of perfectly gorgeous guys shave their heads,' objected Millie.

'I know, I know. But this one . . . He sort of strides about

as though he owns the world, well, Hereward Court, anyway.
And yet he's not a bit the Herewards' type. Essex man, maybe
. . . know warra mean?'

Nick drove into the police station car park in silence.

As he locked the car he said, 'Maybe your Floridus is scared
of him too.'

DC Erdingham looked younger even than Suzie remembered.
He ushered them courteously into an interview room and
folded his long limbs into a chair on the opposite side of the
table. He laid a notepad in front of him.

'Well, now. Who's going to start? Millie?'

'Perhaps I should give you the context first,' Suzie interjected.

'Go ahead, then.'

She waited. Then, 'Aren't you going to switch on the tape
recorder?'

He looked startled. 'Oh . . . yes.'

He pressed a knob. The tape started to spin.

'Mrs Fewings,' said the DC into the microphone.

Suzie explained about the day off school, and Millie
wanting to see Hereward Court. About finding the Hereward
children also had a holiday. She dwelt with emphasis on
their greeting by Mrs Hereward and her strangely pointed
questions about whether they had seen Floridus and the man
from the lodge.

'I thought she seemed frightened of him. Not obviously.
She's the sort of bluff, no-nonsense type. But I think she was.'

'And, like, she was really glad to see Mum,' put in Millie.

The constable sat impassively listening. He had the writing
pad and a pen in front of him, but Suzie noticed that he was
not making notes. I suppose he doesn't need to, with the tape
recorder, she told herself.

'After she'd gone, I started to sort through the papers, to
see what else I could take home to transcribe. At first Millie
was interested in looking at them, especially the really old
ones with big wax seals attached.'

'Henry the Eighth, would you believe?' said Millie. 'Cool.
I told my history teacher and she got really excited.'

'And then she asked if it would be all right if she went
outside. I told her not to go too far. Especially not into the

woods. Mr Hereward warned me about that the first time I met him. Because of the shooting.'

'It's the pheasant season,' said the DC.

'Some pheasants!' said Millie, not quite under her breath.

'Right, Millie,' said the constable. He was smiling, Suzie realized, for the first time. 'What happened?'

Millie told her story once more. Suzie noticed how it became clearer, more coherent, with each telling. As though she had crystallized the memory into a form which, even if not accurate in every detail, was now the received version.

Constable Erdingham waited until she had finished and then switched the tape recorder off.

'Thank you.'

Millie and Suzie gasped simultaneously.

'Is that it? Aren't you going to ask me any questions?' Millie exclaimed.

'You gave a very clear account. I think we've got all we need.' He rose from his chair.

Nick had sat silent until now. 'What are you going to do about it? I know this Freddie's only a child, but we've already seen that something's going on. Something quite nasty, judging by the stuff Tom and Paul found. And if the boy's overheard more, about their planning a big push pretty soon . . .'

'Your information will be passed to the relevant quarter.'

'But I thought *you* were the relevant quarter,' Suzie said. 'You're the CID. You said race crimes were your responsibility. You seemed really concerned the first time. You told us to let you know if we found anything else. And why haven't you been to Hereward Court yet?'

The policeman's fair face flushed. 'I'm just a lowly detective constable, I'm afraid. You can be sure the matter's in safe hands.'

'Then who's in charge?' Nick demanded. 'Who do we need to talk to?'

'You were right to come to me. I'll pass it on.'

'And will whoever you pass it on to want to talk to Millie, or Suzie?'

'I can't answer that.'

His hands were busy, stacking the unused notepaper. They watched him, baffled. He coughed nervously, then led the way to the door.

'Thank you for coming,' he said.

The words rang hollowly down the corridor.

'What was the point of *that*?' Millie exploded on the steps outside. 'He wasn't interested!'

'He's got it all on tape,' Suzie reminded her. 'He'll pass it higher up the chain. After all, he's only a constable, and this is getting really serious.'

'He asked plenty of questions when we took Tom and Paul to see him,' Nick said. 'You could see his eyes light up. Like, "*I'm on to a really interesting case here. I can make my mark with this one.*" And today, just deadpan. "*I'll pass it up to my superiors.*" I don't understand what's going on.'

'Typical!' snorted Millie. 'Tom finds something out, and everyone's all over him. When I do, nobody wants to know.'

'I'm sure they do,' Suzie soothed her. 'Maybe it's above his pay grade. It's probably being handled by someone more important.'

'Says you. So why didn't somebody more senior interview me? And anyway, nothing ever happened about what Tom told them, did it?'

'We don't know that.'

'Millie's right,' said Nick, opening the car door. 'I wish I knew what their game was.'

'Perhaps he thought Freddie was making it up,' attempted Suzie on the way home. 'After all, it's possible.'

'Mum, I was *there*. Do you think I can't tell when some kid is just boasting? He was for real.'

'Well, exaggerating, then.'

'For heaven's sake, how many kids do you know who know the word "coup"? I had to stop and think what it meant myself, until he went on and told me. He's got to have heard it from some grown-up.'

'You've got a point there, love,' Nick said from the driving seat. 'Well spotted. The question is, who was Floridus Hereward talking to, for Freddie to overhear the word? From what you say, that camp's been empty for weeks now. If they were the Brigade of Britons, it couldn't be them. There was that rat-faced Marchant, who did a citizen's arrest on me, after he'd nearly topped me with his rifle.'

'I'm not sure it would be him,' Suzie said slowly. 'He seemed more like a gamekeeper, didn't he?'

'He was coming away from the camp the night he caught me. He's got to be in on it.'

'Somehow, I can't see Floridus discussing top-secret policy with him.'

'Appearances can be deceptive. Just because he speaks with a country accent doesn't mean he's a mutton-headed yokel.'

'All the same, my money's on that man in the leather coat. He seems, sort of . . . *powerful*.'

'Could be. None of us have seen him except you.'

'I've met him three times now. He's definitely more than a tenant. He's in and out of Hereward Court all the time. And he certainly doesn't want me around the place.'

'You didn't tell DC Erdingham about him, did you?'

The realization jolted Suzie into silence. It was several moments before she said, 'I should have, shouldn't I? I never thought. I was so shocked when he just switched off the tape without asking Millie any questions, it drove everything else out of my head.'

'Want to go back?' Nick's grin was only half-heartedly teasing.

'Some hope,' Millie interjected from the back seat. 'Like, he really didn't want to know, did he?'

'You're right,' said Suzie. 'I could ring him after we get back, but somehow I don't think he'll be interested.'

It was a cold thought. She felt a private shudder. It had been impossible to explain, even to Nick, just how frightened that man made her feel. She could sense him now, close in front of her. The creaking of his stiff leather coat, the jowly face, the dome of his shaved head, too big, too shiny, lowering over her. There had been nothing explicit in his threat, but he had made her feel like a mouse, helpless under the shadow of a hawk. A body too muscular, a will too strong, for her to escape.

And yet she had. She had pleaded Alianor's invitation and he had let her walk on.

She was confused. It was difficult to think that she had talked to people who could be plotting the deliberate incitement of racial violence, violence that could lead to deaths. A stronger shudder this time, as she thought that death was what these

people wanted. Many deaths. If the coup was to bring down
the government, it had to take more than a few broken heads.
Could the old-fashioned, courteous Floridus Hereward, with
his upright military bearing, really be plotting mob slaughter?
She could more easily believe it of the shaven-headed man
with the Estuary vowels, which had so jarred in a West Country
manor house. Or was that just prejudice?

How involved was Alianor?

Tom was home before them, his face avid for news.

'Nothing,' Millie vented her anger on him. 'Zilch. He just
taped what I said and waved us goodbye. It was a complete
waste of time.' She stomped past him up the stairs.

'You're joking!' Tom swung round on Nick and Suzie. 'You
tell him there's a gang of racists set to start a civil war, and
the police aren't going to do anything?'

'Maybe they are,' said Nick. 'Maybe they're just not
telling us. But if so, that detective constable was putting on
a pretty good performance of a man who's been warned off
the case.'

'Thanks! I really enjoyed that outing.'

Suzie carried her knapsack from the car to the front door,
calling back to Nick as he closed the garage. He overtook her
with a grin.

'Any time. I'll say that for your ancestors: they picked some
pretty stunning places to live.'

They had spent an energetic afternoon in a village perched
on a hillside close to the county border. After checking out
the parish church, which had revealed little of interest to
Suzie, they had climbed to the Iron Age hill fort which dominated the skyline for miles around. Up there, in the clear winter
sunshine, they had been able to see for a vast distance across
two counties. To the east, plains stretched out towards the
sea, silvered with watercourses. To the west, the land was
more rugged: steep cliffs, sudden valleys, secret woodland,
with church towers standing up here and there, waymarks of
civilization.

She was tired but happy.

She had hardly opened the door before a tide of movement
surged down the hall towards her. Tom was waving a newspaper in her face, with burly Paul filling the space behind

him. The Matoposan boy's face was uncharacteristically solemn. Tom's was alight with anger.

'Get an eyeful of this! No wonder your little policeman hasn't done anything. It's the same the whole world over. Scratch the back of the right people and you can get away with murder. And I mean that literally.'

'Calm down,' said Nick from behind Suzie. He took off his jacket and hung it on the hook. 'At least let us get inside the door before you bawl us out.'

Suzie took the newspaper from Tom, while she unknotted her scarf. It was the local evening paper. The Fewings didn't have it delivered, though they might occasionally buy a copy in the local shop.

'Paul saw it,' Tom said, looking round at his friend.

'Yeah. My folks take the rag. My mom likes looking at the house adverts, even though she can never afford to buy one.'

He grinned self-consciously. Suzie felt a pang of guilt. She and her family had this beautiful detached house with its large garden, while Paul's father, who had been a university lecturer before he fled Matoposa, now cleaned aeroplanes for a living. Paul's home was a small rented flat in the upstairs of a terraced house.

'Let's sit down and look at it properly, if it's so important.' Nick pushed open the sitting-room door and led the way to the sofa. Suzie sat beside him. She spread out the page Tom was pointing at.

The photograph leaped out at her.

Floridus Hereward, smiling more broadly than she had ever seen him do in the few meetings she had had with him, was raising a glass to a heavy-jowled man in a uniform decorated with badges and braid. The photograph was in black and white, somewhat grainy, but it was easy enough to recognize it as the uniform of a very senior police officer.

'Get this.' Tom read the caption aloud from behind her. '"Chief Constable Hugh Denning and Mr Floridus Hereward celebrate the opening of the new clubhouse at the Moor Grange Golf Club. The Chief Constable is president of the club and Mr Hereward, who owns land adjoining the course, donated the site for the clubhouse." Look! They're best mates. Of course he's not going to let some little detective constable embarrass his friend Mr Hereward, is he? That's why you haven't heard anything. He's told him to stick our evidence in a filing cabinet and forget it. Same with Millie's tape.'

Millie had joined them, a pouting wraith hovering in the doorway. 'I might have known that if I found out something important, nobody would take any notice.'

Suzie looked from one to the other, struggling to adjust her thoughts. 'Don't you think you're jumping to conclusions? Just because Floridus meets the Chief Constable socially, and does his club a favour, it needn't mean there's some sort of conspiracy. It's not surprising they know each other. After all, I expect he's a JP. That sort usually are, aren't they? It sort of goes with owning the manor. I've been transcribing the notes of one of them who was a magistrate in the nineteenth century. Family tradition.'

'Yes, and it's a family tradition that if you own x-thousand acres you can bloody well do what you like to the peasants,' Tom retorted.

'Hold on. Mum's right,' Nick defended her. 'One photograph of them together at a society do doesn't prove there's a right-wing cover-up. The British police force doesn't operate like that.'

'Oh, no? Look at the grins on their faces. Don't tell me they're not muckers. They don't want people like us stirring things up on the Hereward patch, do they? And I thought you told us the Herewards were hard up? So what's he doing *giving* away land? Does he even play golf? Oh, no, he's seeing to it that Mr Chief Constable will make sure nothing happens to him.'

'Look at the facts,' Paul said quietly. 'How long is it since we went to see them, Suzie? We had hard evidence, didn't we? Photographs, pamphlets. And what's happened since? Nothing.'

'We don't know that. True, they haven't raided Hereward Court, or questioned the Herewards. I can't believe Alianor wouldn't have let something slip if they had. Or that they'd have let me go on visiting. They'd have to know it was us put them on to it.'

'So? And you said yourselves that guy didn't really want to know what Millie heard. Just taped it and gave you the brush off.'

'It will be undercover stuff,' said Nick slowly. 'If they *are* investigating some sort of racist network, they'll want to keep a low profile. I can understand that. All the same . . . You're right, Paul. It's been a long time. Something should have happened by now.'

'And it's not going to, is it?' said Tom. 'Not unless we make it happen.'

'Tom!' exclaimed Suzie and Nick together.

'No.' Nick laid on his sternest emphasis. 'Tom and Paul, you are *not*, definitely and absolutely *not*, to get involved in this again. If you're right, you could run up against some very dangerous men. And if the police *are* investigating, despite what it looks like, then you could foul things up.'

'How?' demanded Tom. 'By finding more evidence?'

'Stay out of it. That's an order. Just imagine for a moment the consequences if those men got their hands on Paul.'

The Fewings turned to look at the troubled face of the Matoposan boy.

'Yeah. See what you mean,' muttered Tom. 'Still . . .'

Nick picked up the newspaper and sighed. 'I wish I didn't believe you, son. But I have a nasty feeling some things may not have changed as much as I wish they had.'

'That's it, then?' said Millie's thin voice from the doorway. 'And are you going to keep on hobnobbing with the enemy, Mum?'

Suzie twisted her hands in her lap. 'I'm not sure now.'

NINETEEN

Nick switched off the bedside light. 'I know what I think. I think you're not going back to that place. The only reason I agreed to you going on doing it was because that DC thought you might be able to come up with some more information. Only when you do, suddenly he doesn't want to know. Not even when Millie says they may be nearing a flashpoint. What's the point? If that guy at the lodge is the ugly character you say he is, you're well out of there.'

He dropped a kiss on her forehead and settled down to sleep.

Suzie lay back on the pillows, staring up at the darkened ceiling. 'There's Alianor, though. She didn't exactly say that there was something wrong about him and Floridus. But she was dropping some pretty heavy hints. I'm sure she was upset. I don't like the thought of leaving her alone there. What if she's working herself up to telling me something important?'

Nick rolled over to face her. 'Suzie, love. How long have you known her? Less than three months? Don't you think she'll have friends going years back? Blood relations? Surely there are people she's much more likely to confide in? Why does it have to be you?'

Suzie hesitated. 'Because I'm there? Because I keep turning up on Monday afternoons. She knows she can rely on me. Look what happened after they caught you in the woods. She actually rang up and *asked* me to come back. How strange was that? And anyway, she doesn't look like the girlie type who meets her old school mates for a gossip in a wine bar. Maybe she doesn't have anyone else to talk to. After all, she can hardly chat to the next-door neighbours over the garden fence, can she? The nearest house must be a mile away, apart from the home farm and the lodge.'

'All the same, this is serious, whatever the police seem to think. Ring Alianor if you want to talk to her. But you stay away.'

She knew that she should. She ought to parcel up the documents she still held, as she had done before, and post them back to Hereward Court. She should have done with this.

But they stayed on a shelf in the study, with the transcripts she had printed out for the Herewards stacked neatly on top. By Sunday she was still keeping her options open, though she was sure that Nick was right. It was not as if she really wanted to go back. She had already gone way beyond what anyone could reasonably expect in making the contents of the document chest available on the Internet.

More chillingly, she thought often of that man in the leather coat, confronting her like a barrier across the drive, preventing her from getting to the house. She was not sure she would have the courage to get past him a second time. She didn't even want to risk meeting him.

Nick dropped the Sunday paper he had been reading after lunch. 'Have you rung her?'

'Who?' asked Suzie, though she knew.

'Mrs Hereward. You were going to tell her you wouldn't be coming again. And you were worried about her.'

'Oh . . . yes. I mean, no. I haven't rung her.'

'Don't you think you should? Or are you just going to send her a note?'

'I'll have to post the documents back, if . . .'

'If? You're not changing your mind, are you? Suzie, I'm not joking. I don't want you anywhere near that place again.'

She found Nick's masculine concern for her comforting, even, in an odd way, sexually exciting. She got up obediently. 'All right, I'll tell her.'

Alone in the study, she was less sure. Hereward Court and its document chest had been such a big part of her life these past weeks. She remembered the physical thrill that ran through her, handling those centuries-old papers. The handwriting of long-dead people, not seen through the blurred screen of a microfiche reader, but with the ink under her fingertips. The ponderous wax seals attached to ribbons, bearing the insignia of Tudor monarchs. The lifelong obligation of humble tenants in pence or capons, the trivia of parties at the big house. She would miss it. She would miss all the people she had discovered. There would be no more excitement of seeing a new transcript flash up on the family history website, with her own name recorded as the contributor, no grateful emails from the far side of the globe.

She checked the Herewards' phone number and lifted the receiver. As it started to ring, she prepared herself for a long wait. She imagined those echoing corridors, the time it would take anyone to reach the phone . . . if there was even someone indoors. Wouldn't their sort of people be out on a Sunday afternoon? Doing something with horses, perhaps?

She was startled when a voice answered at the second ring.

'Hereward.'

The voice was so masculine she was almost deceived. But then she realized that the abruptness must be Alianor's.

'Mrs Hereward?' she checked to be sure. 'It's Suzie Fewings.'

'Hello, my dear. What can we do for you?'

This was going to be difficult. Alianor . . . No, both the Herewards had been so generous to her.

'I . . . I just wanted to tell you I'm putting your documents in the post. It's that bundle on the parish lands, showing where people lived in Queen Elizabeth's reign. It's getting near Christmas, and what with one thing and another, I don't think I can manage to keep up the visits. So I'm ringing to say an enormous thank you to you for letting me come as often as you have. Everybody's so grateful for all the information you've made available to us.'

There was a short silence. 'You mean you're not coming back?'

Before Suzie could frame her answer, the voice receded, as though Mrs Hereward had turned her head away. But her stentorian tones to someone else were still audible. 'It's Suzie Fewings.'

A sudden chill touched Suzie's skin. Floridus must be in the same room. He had wanted to know whom Alianor was talking to. Her heart sank. There was no possibility now that she could ask Alianor personal questions. If there really was something frightening the other woman, something she had been on the verge of confiding to Suzie, there was no way she could tell it now.

The voice grew fainter still. Suzie strained to hear. 'Says she's finished with our document chest. Won't be coming again.'

It felt like a betrayal. If Floridus really was part of a plan that involved the man at the lodge, he would be glad to see the back of Suzie. Anyone who was not 'one of us' on the estate was a potential threat.

Alianor would be left on her own.

But Mrs Hereward's voice came back as brusque and cheerful as ever. 'Righty-ho, then. Must have taken an awful lot of your time. Flo's been tickled pink that so many people are interested in the old Hereward Court. Send those documents back, won't you?'

'Of course. It's been brilliant of you to let me take them home.'

She ought to put the phone down, finish it. There was nothing more she could do. There was no way she could get through to Alianor with Floridus listening.

'Did you find out what you wanted about your Dobles?'

The unexpected question threw Suzie's mind sideways. All her thoughts about Hereward Court had been dominated now by what was happening in the present. She hadn't given a moment's consideration recently to pursuing the question of whether or not she and Alianor were descended from the same ancestor, five centuries ago. Her brain struggled to recall how far she had got.

'No. I feel they must be related to yours. I've got my Humphrey Doble, son of Robert, in Romanswell. And you have a Robert Doble living at Siderleigh about the right time. But I can't *prove* they're father and son. I don't suppose I'll ever find the evidence.'

'Chin up. Something may turn up. Let me know if it does, won't you? If you think the Hereward stuff is interesting, you should see what I've got on my Dobles. I'd be happy to show you.'

'Right. Thank you. That's very generous of you.'

'Merry Christmas then.' The phone went dead.

Suzie replaced her own receiver more slowly and sat looking at it. It might not be over yet. Alianor had left a door open for Suzie to return. Had that just been well-bred politeness? Or another cry for help?

She knew she should not go, even if she found the evidence. This had become far more deadly than family history.

A little voice in her head told her that family history had been deadly too. Bloody riots and civil war were not twenty-first-century inventions. But there was all the difference in the world between reading about them in the safe pages of history books, or on a website, and finding yourself caught up in violence that was about to happen.

Nick glanced at the clock on the wall behind him and put down the sports pages. 'Do you want to see the news?'

Suzie laughed. 'That means that you do.'

She reached across and flicked the television set on.

The late evening bulletin had already started. Grey-suited figures, shaking hands before settling down around a long table, proved to be ministers at an economic summit in Bruges.

The shot changed to the studio. The presenter had an

abstracted air, as though absorbing new information. He seemed to realize the cameras were on him and sat briskly upright to face them.

'We're getting breaking news of rioting in Bristol. I think we can go over to our reporter there . . . Hang on . . . Yes, we've got a picture . . . What can you tell us, Dipali? What's happening?'

The reporter's wide, dark eyes were luminous against the winter night. Behind her there was a flurry of activity. Police in fluorescent jackets, a hovering crowd, faces caught in the artificial light. A white police van sped past.

'Hugh, details are only just coming through. I'm standing on the edge of the St Paul's district. It's known for its ethnically mixed population. There's been some sort of major disturbance here in the last hour. The police have cordoned off the area, but there are unconfirmed reports that three people are dead. As you can see behind me, there are certainly a lot of emergency vehicles heading that way. The police seem to be going in in force. And I've personally counted three ambulances and a fire crew. But no one from the police is ready to talk to us yet.'

'Do we know what started it?'

The young woman shook her head. 'It's too early yet. People round me are saying that a gang of white youths attacked some black teenagers, but we haven't been able to get into the area to interview eyewitnesses. From the sound of it . . .'

Suddenly she ducked. Suzie and Nick flinched themselves as the air flashed behind her. There was a loud crump. Two policemen manning the barrier spun round to check what had happened.

'As I was saying, Hugh,' the reporter recovered herself with a shaky little laugh, 'we've been hearing what sound like petrol bombs. Whatever's going on, it's clear that the police haven't got control of the situation yet.'

The small crowd was edging in around her. Teenagers in hooded jackets were grinning over her shoulder and gesticulating at the camera for their friends to see. Older men looked hunched and worried. Most of the faces around her were black, but not all of them.

The reporter looked around and picked out a tall boy, standing more quietly than the others.

'Can I ask you, how close were you to where it started?
Did you see how it happened?'

The teenager looked uncomfortable. 'Nah. I wasn't there.'
Then his head snapped up and he burst out, 'It's always us,
innit? They pick on us, and then if we hit back at them, it's
"Oh, look at those fucking blacks, beating up white folks.
Send 'em all home." Home! Like we was all born in Jamaica,
or something. Just because you've got a black face. They piss
me off. I hope those brothers . . .'

He became suddenly aware of the microphone she was
holding out to him, of the television cameras relaying his face
to millions of viewers. He turned away alarmed, pulling too
late at his hood to shield his features.

'That's a true word, son,' said one of the older men, putting
a hand on his shoulder.

'It's just what Freddie said.' Suzie spoke her horror in a
small voice. 'They *want* the blacks to hit back. They *want* it
to escalate.'

The screen had changed again, back to the presenter in the
studio. He promised to give them an update in the next bulletin.
The news moved on to flooding in the Severn Valley.

Suzie switched it off, without asking Nick if he minded.
Silence hung over the room.

'Do you suppose this is what Freddie overheard? Could
this have been what his father and somebody else were plotting?'

'Hard to say. It wouldn't be the first time whites have beaten
up blacks, or vice versa. To say nothing of blacks and Asians.
There's plenty of aggro around without a national conspiracy.
But, yes, it's a coincidence. We haven't had anything on this
scale for a long while.'

'And we *told* the police. We showed them Paul and Tom's
photos. We reported everything Millie heard. And they didn't
do anything.'

'Hold on. You have to admit it was a bit vague. All right,
it gave a general picture, the way they might operate. Inflaming
hostility to the point where it could destabilize the country.
We've shown there's a gang of very nasty thugs out there.
But there was nothing specific. No dates, no places. How
could the police have known it was going to be Bristol on
this particular Sunday in December?'

'They could have raided Hereward Court. They could have searched Floridus's office. Found out who'd been in that camp and gone after them. I've been waiting for them to do it, week after week. If it really is the Brigade of Britons who've started this, there must have been some evidence there.'

'I thought you were the one who wanted to soft pedal? You didn't want Tom upsetting the apple cart. I seem to remember you found Floridus rather charming.'

'That's not fair! As soon as I saw the photo of that target with the bullet holes, I knew it was serious, I said we had to tell the police. I haven't tried to shield Mr Hereward.'

He held up his hands. 'Easy. I was only teasing you.'

'Nick! It's not a joking matter. She said three people may be dead.'

Nick got up and walked across to the patio windows. He drew aside the curtain and looked out into the dark garden. 'And we're asking ourselves, did we do enough to stop it?'

'And what if this is just the beginning?'

'We can only pray it's not.'

TWENTY

The shock waves of the night before rolled on through the Monday morning radio broadcasts. Two people were now known to have been killed, both black. Fifteen people had needed hospital treatment, including two policemen. Three of the other injured were white. At the height of the riot, petrol bombs had been thrown. The police were keeping an open mind about how it had started until they had assessed the evidence. Community leaders appealed for calm and lamented that this should have happened in a district which had done so much good work to build racial harmony.

'People are saying this may have been the work of outsiders, brought in to incite violence in a mixed community,' probed the interviewer.

'I wouldn't know about that,' came back the rich tones of the woman who represented the local ward. 'But there was no word of trouble here before yesterday. Normally, you'd feel something, you know, simmering, waiting for a flash-point. This came out of nowhere.'

Tom brooded over the breakfast table. 'Paul's not going to be happy about this.'

'Are any of us?' retorted Nick.

'Should have listened to me,' said Millie, scowling.

They sat so long listening for more information that they were almost late for work and school. At the last minute, Suzie remembered to pick up the packet of documents she had sealed up for the Herewards. She would take it to the post office in town.

At one o'clock, she locked the office at the back of the charity shop and walked through the rails of second-hand clothes towards the street. She had the packet in her hand. Even now, she felt a reluctance to let it go. Her final link with Hereward Court. It had been a memorable experience. For these last few moments she could remember the inno-cent enjoyment of the first weeks of discovery, before she had become aware of the cloud of menace hanging over the house.

Margery, the shop manager, looked round as her customer headed for the door. She smiled in surprise at Suzie. 'Forgotten your packed lunch? If you're popping out for a sandwich, you'd better be quick. You don't want to miss your bus to Eastcott. Or have you got the car today?'

'I . . . I'm not going.' Suzie found it surprisingly difficult to say she would never be going again.

'Go on. You said that once before. But you were back again next week. It gets you, doesn't it, this family history busi-ness? People seem to get addicted. My nephew's just the same.'

'I haven't really found as much about my own family in the Eastcott papers as I'd hoped.'

Janet, the volunteer who helped Margery part-time, came out from behind a row of coats. 'Lucky you, though, swan-ning it out to Hereward Court, week after week. I bet you could tell us things about how the other half lives.' Her sharp features were avid for gossip. 'What's Lady Hereward like?'

'She's not a lady. Just Mrs Hereward.'

'Still, they're big nobs around here, aren't they? You always seem to be seeing their names in the local rag. He's quite dishy, isn't he? She's a bit of a plain Jane though. You'd think someone with her money could make an effort with her hair.'

'They don't actually have much money. It takes a lot to keep up a place like that.'

'Oh, they always plead poverty, those kind of people, so they don't have to pay tax like the rest of us.'

Suzie edged towards the door. It was uncomfortable to be forced to defend the Herewards, today of all days.

Margery had seen her dilemma. 'Off you go then. Don't let us keep you from your lunch.' She smiled sympathetically at Suzie, before turning away. 'Janet, could you put the kettle on for us while the shop's quiet? I'm dying for a coffee.'

Suzie escaped into the wintry street. She made her way to the post office in the centre of town and joined the queue. It was oddly like waiting in line to pay one's last respects at a funeral. When it was done, she turned from the counter and came away with empty hands.

She felt a great sadness. It was final this time. She realized as she walked away that, in spite of what she had told Margery, the house itself had become a character in her own family history. At least one of her ancestors had started his young working life as a farm apprentice on the estate. An older Floridus Hereward had ridden out from there to try another of her family at the Quarter Sessions. More of her people might well have been among those who descended on Hereward Court in the Civil War to loot it after its capture by the Roundheads. And if her hunch about the Dobles was right, some of her more affluent medieval forebears must have been guests at family feasts in the Herewards' banqueting hall, the very room where she had knelt beside the document chest, reverently unpacking its contents.

It was a lot to lose.

And then she felt shame sweep over her. People had lost their *lives* last night. She had a horrible feeling that Hereward Court must be the malignant house behind that.

She had a late lunch when she got home. She scoured the newspaper, but it had been printed too early for any more details of last night's riots. The main lunchtime news broadcasts were over. She tried a television news channel, but it told her nothing she didn't already know. She switched it off.

The afternoon stretched in front of her. It was not that there weren't plenty of things for her to do. There was always house-work. There were Christmas cards to write. Perhaps she should have stayed in town and occupied her mind with shopping for presents.

But Monday afternoons had become set aside from domes-ticity. And she was in no mood for festive preparations.

She made herself dust the sitting room and vacuum the carpet. She checked the clock. There was still an hour before the children were home from school.

Almost without conscious volition she found her feet taking her to the study. She sat down at the desk. A remembered voice sounded in her head. '*Did you find out what you wanted about your Dobles?*' She tried to push it away. This was defi-nitely not the road to go down. Not today.

What else? She reached up to the shelf and took down her bulky family history file. Her thumb rippled through the alpha-betically arranged contents. Yet it halted at the envelope marked 'Doble'. Guiltily, she drew it out and laid it on the desk. It was like picking at a scab which she knew she should leave alone to heal.

Besides, she had gone as far as she could with this inves-tigation, hadn't she? She was never going to know if she was related to Alianor.

Somehow, the computer seemed to have switched itself on. She accessed the Internet and clicked on 'Favourites'. The National Archives Access to Archives. She gazed at its home page.

What was the point? She had already searched these records for references to the Dobles, used wild cards for variant spellings. She had trawled through the long list of catalogues it offered her and found some interesting documents, including some relating to the farm Humphrey Doble had occupied in Romanswell in the early 1600s. Lots more, of course, for Alianor's lords of the manor of that name. But not that elusive link between them. It was a waste of time to go through all that again.

All the same . . .

She clicked 'Search the Archives' and chose 'Access to Archives'. She typed in *D*b*l**, to cover both Doble and Dobell, selected the South West region, and after some thought entered 1650 as the latest date she was interested in.

She hit 'Search'.

The screen changed. She ran her eye down the summaries of documents. Many of them she had seen before. There were some new entries from Dorset, too far away to be of interest to her. Several documents which a Doble had witnessed in the 1400s, which told her little about him. Then a group of leases in the parish of Kennerton.

She sighed. It was true the dates of these were sixteenth century, but she had no ancestors that she knew of in Kennerton. Alianor's Robert Doble had lived in Siderleigh before becoming lord of the Doble manor at Great Thorry. Kennerton was not far from Siderleigh, but miles from Romanswell, where her own Humphrey and Anne Doble had settled.

But, having got this far, she supposed she should look at the details.

They did not appear to be very promising. In the early 1500s Martin Doble of Great Thorry had leased 'messuages, lands and tenements' at Woodlake in the parish of Kennerton for the lives of George May, his wife Alys and their son James. Great Thorry was even further away from Romanswell. Still, it showed that Dobles who did not live in Kennerton had owned property there.

A generation later, William Doble, presumably Martin's son and heir, had renewed the lease to James May. This deed did not state where William Doble lived.

The third entry in the catalogue was dated 1570. She was getting close in time to the critical period. The lease was for the lives of George and John May, sons of James May of Kennerton, and George's daughter Pascha. But as she read the name of the landlord she stiffened with excitement. *Robert Doble, gent, of Siderleigh*. This had to be Alianor's Robert. The one who might, just might, be the father of her own Humphrey.

Her eye raced down to the fourth entry in the catalogue. The words jumped out at her from the screen. They were too

exact for her to believe what she was reading. The owners of
Woodlake were now:

> Robert Doble of Siderleigh, gent, and Humpfrye Doble
> of Romanswell, gent, his son.

The right names, the right parishes, side by side. And the
incontrovertible words, *his son*. Proof positive of the blood
relationship for which she had thought she would never find
the evidence.

Just wait till she told Alianor this . . .

The cold truth sank in. She was not going back to Hereward
Court. She was never going to see Alianor Hereward again.
This was just a hobby, a game, wiped out by the shocking
reality of what had just happened on those city streets, by the
knowledge that more and worse things would probably be
done yet.

She sat on in front of the screen. From force of habit, she
copied the text from the precious lease and pasted it into her
family history files. There was now so much more she could
have found out. If only she had discovered this a few weeks
earlier. If only those thugs had waited until after Christmas.
If only Alianor could have opened up her ancestral files on
the Dobles to Suzie before she'd found the proof.

'*Something may turn up. Let me know if it does, won't you?*'
She could hear Alianor's invitation in her head.

TWENTY-ONE

Paul was with them. They were all watching the early-
evening news intently. Suzie tore her eyes from the
screen to study the boys' faces. She was aware of an
undercurrent of excitement on Tom's. His breathing was faster.
He pushed back the waves of his black hair impatiently. His
vivid blue eyes were fixed on the shots of the almost-deserted,
devastated streets in Bristol. She sensed uneasily that a part
of him was almost wanting more violence to erupt, so that
he could vent his righteous anger on the people behind it.

He was still too young to put himself fully in the shoes of those who would suffer.

Paul's face beside him, she noted, showed only sorrow. He was the same age as Tom, but a lifetime older in experience. Paul knew what it meant to be threatened with death. He had seen friends of his father silenced by the ruling party. He and the rest of his family had fled for their lives. To Britain. A country where they thought they would be safe.

She turned back to the programme. The lamplit streets were eerily quiet. There was a heavy presence of police officers in body armour. White cars cruised down the silent road, their headlights shining on the wet surface. Christmas decorations hung incongruously over the damaged shopfronts.

'So far,' the reporter was saying, 'the situation seems to be under control. There have been no further outbreaks of violence and the retaliation which everybody here was fearing doesn't seem to have materialized. As usual in these cases, there are conflicting reports about how it started, but the police investigating think it began with an attack by white youths on black. Certainly the two fatalities were young black men.'

'Fatalities!' exclaimed Tom. 'She means they were murdered.'

'Shut up, Tom. I think we've grasped that,' ordered Nick.

'Community leaders here are working overtime to calm things down. The last thing anyone here wants is tit-for-tat action that could inflame the situation.'

'Who's she kidding? That's exactly what the Brigade of Britons wants,' Tom muttered.

The reporter turned to a large Afro-Caribbean woman standing beside her, her figure made bulkier by her padded winter coat. She nodded vigorously.

'That's right. We don't know who did this yet, but the word is that those men who started it weren't from around here. We've had our share of trouble, and we kinda know the fellows you have to look out for. None of our guys recognized them.'

The reporter turned back to face the camera. 'The police made a few arrests last night. They still have four men in custody. But they're all from the local Afro-Caribbean community and their lawyers are claiming they acted in self-defence. None of the white men who allegedly started this have been caught.'

'No, they were clever,' put in the woman with her. 'They just melted away when they saw the police coming. And left our people to pick up the tab.'

The camera moved past the women to show a shattered shop window, now boarded up. It panned to signs of fire on the premises next door. Some people, Suzie reflected, had seized on the opportunity to do a little looting or had got carried away by the violence of the moment.

Paul sat back on the sofa with a sigh. 'It didn't work, did it? They failed.'

Tom stared at him in astonishment. 'What do you mean? Two people dead. Fifteen in hospital. You call that failure? If it is, I don't want to know what success looks like.'

'That's what I mean, man. You *really* don't want to know. If they ever get their way, it'd be revenge attacks, black on white, not just in Bristol but every city. This is only the beginning. It didn't work this time. Those Bristol folk have had the sense to cool it. But these things build up. One community hurts another, and then they hit back. Pretty soon they get to hating each other. There'll be a next time. And a next. If this Brigade of Britons is a national movement, and the agenda is what Millie heard, they won't be satisfied till the whole country is in flames.'

It was a long speech, and all the more sobering because Paul was normally so irrepressibly cheerful. The Fewings sat in silence while the weather forecast globe spun their world before them.

At last Nick said, 'Well, we did all we could. It's out of our hands now.'

Tom hit his hand against his thigh and jumped up. His blue eyes blazed. 'There's got to be *something* we can do.'

The boys had gone upstairs, trailing a wake of agitation. In Tom's case it was fury. To Suzie's concern she sensed that the undercurrent in Paul's emotion was fear. It was impossible for her truly to imagine what it was like to walk around in a white society with a face that was undeniably black. It was something he could do nothing about, might not wish to alter, but for which he would, by racists, be judged and condemned. To *death*?

You're being melodramatic, she scolded herself. But

reason told her she was not. The pamphlets the boys had come home with had reeked of hate. The bullet-ridden target, with its caricature of a black man's face, had been used for practice with weapons which might be used in deadly earnest.

Suzie gazed at the paintings on the sitting-room walls. They were mostly landscapes of places in Britain she and Nick loved. There was a quay of warehouses with tall-masted ships moored alongside, a moorland scene with ponies, a cluster of thatched cottages around a village green, a Norman cathedral. She had traced her forebears to some of these sites. She wanted desperately to believe in the goodness of her country, the common sense of Britons that would never allow such a thing to happen on a large scale. Yet those racists on the Hereward estate had hijacked that very word 'Britons' for their own evil purpose. There was no society so mature, so generous, so warm-hearted that it could never be perverted by hate. Not even her own.

Nick had been drumming his fingertips on the arm of his chair. His frustration was under better control than Tom's, but it was no less real. Suddenly he straightened and turned to face her.

'I'm going to tell our MP.'

'Des Parry?' Suzie called up a vision of the fresh-faced junior minister who looked younger than he really was.

'We've hit a blank wall with the police. I'd been giving them the benefit of the doubt. I told myself they were prob- ably working like mad behind the scenes, and just not telling us anything. But this Bristol tragedy changes things. If it really was the Brigade of Britons behind it, the police should have found out about it by then. They could have stopped it. People are dead. For once in his life, Tom's got it right. This can't go on.'

'And you think telling the MP will . . . what, exactly?'

'I'm not sure myself. Go over the heads of the local police force, I suppose. Take it straight to the Home Secretary. Somebody needs to take this seriously and lean on them hard.'

Nick jumped up, his spirits obviously lightened immedi- ately by the prospect of doing something positive. He strode across the room and into the study.

Minutes later, he came back with a quick grin and a flash

of his deep-blue eyes that made him look so disturbingly like Tom.

'Done. I've sent him an email. Told him it concerned national security. I've asked to meet him as soon as possible.'

When Suzie went upstairs to bed, the boys were still talking in Tom's bedroom. Suzie realized guiltily that she would usually have sent Paul off home before now. She tapped briefly on the door and opened it.

Immediately she was aware of the suddenness with which they broke off talking, the startled looks they turned on her.

She made herself smile more or less normally. 'Would you like a bed for the night, Paul, or do you have a home to go to?'

The boy's grin reasserted itself as he stood up. 'I'm on my way, ma'am.' He ruffled Tom's hair. 'See you, brother.'

She stood aside to let him go downstairs. As the front door closed behind him, she thought of the black teenager walking home alone through the lamplit streets. He would be safe, wouldn't he?

Your imagination's getting the better of you, she told herself. Whatever you're afraid of hasn't happened yet. Not here anyway. This is a West Country cathedral city. Not in the forefront of progress, perhaps, but civilized, friendly people.

Then the feeling she had caught as she opened the door came back with full force. She rounded on Tom.

'What was going on when I came in here? You and Paul. You're up to something, aren't you?'

The blue eyes widened in a semblance of childish innocence. 'Us? You've got to be joking. What could we do, anyway? We raided the place and got all the evidence. Took it to the police. What else do you expect us to do? Burgle Hereward Court?'

'I wouldn't put it past you. Come on, now. What were you talking about, to make you look so guilty?'

His eyes flickered away from hers. 'Oh, you know. Just ideas. Whether it was any use taking some of that stuff to the papers. Not the local rag. They'd be scared stiff of getting across Floridus Hereward and his chum the Chief Constable. But the nationals. The *Guardian, Independent*, that sort of thing. But Paul's worried that publicity might drive that lot underground. At least we know where they are at the moment, or one of their training camps, anyway. If we blow it, they might clear the rest of the evidence out before the police go in. Lists of names, what they're planning. The really important things. They could be anywhere then.'

'Dad's got a better idea. He's going to see our MP. He wants the government to lean on the police from the top.'

'Oh, yeah? I hope it keeps fine for him.'

'It's all we can think of. It's worth a try. . . . Well, goodnight, love.'

'Night, Mum. Sweet dreams.'

The old charm was returning and with it Suzie's suspicion. She stopped at the door and looked back at her son.

'Is that really all you and Paul were discussing?'

Tom threw up his hands. The smile in his eyes for her intensified. 'Mum, you know me. Would I lie to you?'

'I hope not. But you might not be telling me everything.'

She waited. He shrugged.

'You raised hell when we raided their camp. I promised we wouldn't go back there again. What more could I do?'

Suzie stared at him hard, then sighed. 'I'm not sure. But give me your word that you won't.'

'Won't what?'

'I wish I knew.'

Tom got up and kissed her. 'Don't let it get to you, Mum. All this suspicion. It's *their* plots you need to be worrying about, not your own family.'

He released her and stood smiling down at her from his greater height.

She smiled back, still uneasy. 'Stay out of trouble, Tom.'

'Look, Mum, I've promised you we won't go back to that camp. And, hand on heart, we're not going to break and enter Hereward Court. Trust me.'

'I wish I could.'

'You've hurt my feelings.'

She closed the door on his laughter. But her worries would not go away.

Nick came home from work next day and went straight to the study to check his email. Suzie was in the kitchen with Millie when he came to report. Tom hung over the banisters to listen.

'Friday. He holds a surgery in his constituency office then. They've booked us a slot at six thirty.'

Millie snorted. 'Not exactly falling over himself to plug a hole in national security, is he? Friday!'

'He's an MP, love. He only comes down from London at the weekends.'

'Huh.'

'Do you think they really might plan something else straight after Bristol?' Suzie asked Nick.

'I'm not a criminal psychologist. How would I know?'

They were all tense, feeling sure that they had vital information which the rest of the world would not listen to. Are we deluding ourselves, Suzie wondered, making a mountain out of a molehill?

As she turned to the stove and began to prepare a meal she knew in her bones what it was that had really convinced her that this was serious. It was not the hate-filled propaganda, which might have been empty words, nor the men in combat gear with guns, nor Freddie boasting of a coup involving his father. It was the man with the bald head and the leather coat, barring her way on the drive, looming over her, too close, with deliberate menace. He had meant to frighten her off, and now he had. He must have a reason.

She was alone in the house on Wednesday afternoon. Outside the kitchen, a pale December sunshine was catching the dried flower heads of agapanthus, turning them to gold, glinting on the silver bark of the eucalyptus tree, catching the sheen of a blackbird's plumage as it attacked the holly berries.

Suzie was making her Christmas cake. She was enjoying piling the rich ingredients into the bowl. She beat the butter, eggs and sugar until they were pale and fluffy, darkened the mixture with raisins, sultanas and currants, added golden peel and scarlet cherries, a dash of whisky.

The phone rang. She wiped her hands and hurried to the hall.

'Hello?'

'Mrs Fewings?'

Something about the Estuary twang made her heart sink a moment before her mind made the identification.

'Who are you?' The question came out too high and tense.

'You don't need to know my name, darling. But I know yours.'

She was tempted to slam the phone down. She didn't want to talk to him. He might be miles away, but he still had the power to terrify her. Yet his next words froze her, so that she had to listen to him now.

'It's Suzie, isn't it? And you've got a son called Tom. And a daughter Millie.'

What could her children possibly have to do with him?

'I'm afraid Tom's been a very naughty boy. And his friend. Paul, isn't it?'

Her mind was racing. The boys had raided the camp weeks ago. They'd told the police, but nobody, absolutely nobody else. They knew it was vital that the Herewards didn't get warning of any police raid. Suzie caught back the words that would have betrayed that.

'I don't know what you're talking about. Tom's at school.'

'It's a wise mother that knows what her children get up to after dark. Or are you so busy working out who your great-great-granny married that you haven't bothered to ask him where he was last night?'

She scrabbled to remember. Yes, he'd been at Paul's. The two boys were always in and out of each other's houses, sharing notes on homework, or so they claimed.

'He was doing his school work,' she said breathlessly, and hoped it was true.

'Oh, dear, dear, dear. Is that what he told you? Naughty Tom.'

She was trying desperately not to ask the question he was forcing her towards.

His voice taunted her silence. 'Go on. You're gagging to know what he *was* doing, aren't you? Well, I'm going to tell you, because I'm just a teeny bit cross about it, know what I mean? I was out last night, and when I got back, I found I'd had visitors. Not your usual burglars. They weren't even bright enough to take something valuable to cover their tracks. No, it was just my papers they were interested in. *Very* nosy. And my computer. Young Paul's doing an A-level in ICT, isn't he? Sorry, darling, but if they thought they'd find evidence to nail me at the lodge, they'll have been really disappointed. Such a shame, because I know ever such a lot about *them*. I know where they live. I know the route they walk at night. Quite quiet round your way, isn't it? And Paul's family, now. Asylum seekers, weren't they? I've heard they'd get a very warm welcome if they had to go home suddenly. Know what I mean?'

Suzie's blood was chilling. She didn't even have to ask Tom if this was true. He'd promised so cheerfully not to go back to the camp or to the manor house. He'd said nothing about the lodge. And this man knew so much. Their addresses. The boys' movements. Paul's family. She saw with horrifying clarity how vulnerable they were. Her Tom, her beautiful son with the laughing eyes. The Shino family.

The next words shocked her even more. 'And little Millie. That was very careless of you, darling, to bring her to Hereward Court. I warned you to keep away. But no, you had to drag your thirteen-year-old daughter into it. Tsk, tsk. Not a very good mother, are you?'

Suzie's mouth was dry. Her tongue seemed paralysed. With an enormous effort she forced herself to say, 'What do you want?'

'Want?' His laughter mocked her. 'What do you think I am, darling? A blackmailer?'

'Why are you ringing me, then?' She hit back at last. 'Why don't you tell the police?'

A silence then. His voice came back lower, silky with menace. 'I think we both know that, don't we? You already tried it yourself. The police aren't going anywhere with this one. No, Mrs Suzie Fewings, this is between you and me. Or should I say, between me and your children?'

He rang off.

TWENTY-TWO

Suzie came back into the kitchen and stared at the evidence of her cake making. The pilot light told her that she had switched the oven on. It was a long time before she could remember what she had been doing and why.

Christmas? Could they now survive those few short weeks

to open their presents, gather around the festive table, cut this cake, as they had every other year? She was haunted by the fear that there might be, not four of them, but an empty place, a dark shadow of absence at the feast. The menace had been all the more terrifying because he had not been explicit about what form it would take, or on what condition.

Mechanically, she emptied the contents of the bowl into a cake tin and set it on the oven shelf. She even instructed herself to set the timer, conscious that she was in no state of mind to remember to take it out when it was done. When she straightened up she felt giddy with shock.

She willed herself to say nothing to Millie and Tom when they came home from school, though there were no other thoughts in her head she could talk about. Tom galloped upstairs anyway. Millie lingered in the kitchen, looking at Suzie sharply.

'You all right?'

'Yes, of course I am,' she lied.

She busied herself putting away the baking ingredients, though she could hardly remember which cupboard they belonged in. Millie shrugged, selected a biscuit and made off to her bedroom.

As soon as she heard Nick's key in the lock, Suzie ran to meet him. She drew him into the study and closed the door.

'Hey, what's this? You've bought the kids some present you don't want them to see?'

'He phoned me.'

She told him everything she could remember.

'Tom did *what*?' Nick exploded.

'I know. But it wasn't just that that's so frightening. That man *knew* it was Tom and Paul. He knows where we live. He knew I'd be at home alone when he rang. He knows about Tom and Millie, and what they told the police. *How* does he know about it? We haven't told anyone else.'

Nick stared at her as the implication sank in. 'If no one outside the police knows, then . . . he must have got it from them. So nothing we tell them now is safe.'

She watched the fear take hold.

'What are we going to do?'

She could see the struggle inside Nick. Every instinct in

him was wanting to protect his family, but he didn't know how.

'Nothing,' he said slowly, at last. 'I could take the risk for myself, but not the children.'

'You won't talk to our MP now?'

'If I was confident they'd go in fast and get every one of those thugs, yes. But I don't believe it would work like that. And if that guy gets a hint that we haven't kept quiet . . .'

'Should we tell the children?'

'Too true we will. How could Tom be so *stupid*?'

Even Tom looked chastened when Nick had finished venting his fury on him.

'Well, nothing was happening, was it?' Tom tried to defend himself. 'And Mum kept saying how sinister this guy looked. He had to be up to his neck in it. We found evidence in that hut, didn't we? It seemed a good bet there'd be more in his house.'

'And did you stop to think, even for a moment, about Paul? You know the family haven't got full refugee status, only temporary leave to remain. If they blot their copybook, the Home Secretary could put them on the next plane back to Matoposa. Have you thought of what could happen to them then?' He saw Tom's face pale. 'No, you didn't think, did you? This is all a great game to you. This is people's lives you're playing with.'

'It's people's lives they were playing with in Bristol, Dad.' Tom said through tight lips.

Nick was momentarily silenced. Then, 'And what about Millie? Did you think about putting her in danger? You knew that man had threatened Mum. You knew he was dangerous.'

Tom had run out of arguments. Millie was looking scared. Suzie put her arm around her.

With an effort, Nick controlled himself. He sat down on the sofa.

'Sorry, Millie. I don't want to frighten you. But we have to take this seriously. From now on, neither of you is going out alone at night. No, don't argue, Tom. Millie, if you want to go anywhere, like round to Nicola's, or you, Tom, to Paul's, I'll take you in the car. I hope it was just a warning, that so long as we keep our noses out of this, they'll leave us alone. But we won't take any chances.'

'That's it, then, is it?' asked Millie. 'Game over?'

'As far as this family is concerned, definitely yes.'

'What about Paul's family?' Suzie put in. 'Shouldn't we warn them too?'

'You're right. I'll get the car out. We'd better do it now.'

The leafy roads where the Fewings lived gave way to Victorian terraced houses whose front doors opened on to the pavement. It was hard to find a space to park. As Tom led the way to Paul's home, Suzie tried to recall his parents. They had met a couple of times at school functions.

It was Mr Shino who opened the street door. His broad-featured face was unmistakably like Paul's. He looked in surprise at the Fewings family gathered on the pavement behind Tom.

'What's this, Tom? Looks like a social occasion.'

'Can we come in? We've got something important we need to tell you.'

'That sounds serious. Come up.'

They followed him up a narrow staircase, the treads covered in brown vinyl. The door above opened on a small living room. It seemed crowded, with its central table bearing the remains of the evening meal. Mrs Shino, still wearing the blue overall of the care home where she worked, rose from her seat with a slow grace. Her shy smile politely denied the expression of consternation in her eyes at being caught un-prepared by visitors. Paul was not in the room, but a smaller girl and boy looked at all the newcomers with brown eyes stretched wide.

'Good evening, Mrs Fewings.' Paul's mother held out her hand. 'We met at the carol concert, didn't we? Would you like a cup of tea?'

Suzie felt the embarrassment of the unannounced visit. 'I'm sorry to disturb you like this. We should have rung first. But we have something we thought we must share with you. It concerns Tom and Paul.'

There was a sound behind them. Paul had come into the room. He looked in alarm at Tom.

'What's up, man? I wasn't expecting you till seven.'

'Something's come up,' Tom said tightly. 'You need to know.'

'This is all very mysterious.' Mr Shino was trying to lower the tension in the room. 'You'd better sit down and tell us.'

There was some awkward shuffling to accommodate them all. Nick, Suzie and Millie squeezed on to the two-seater mock-leather settee. Mr and Mrs Shino took dining chairs. Paul and Tom remained standing.

Once they were settled, Suzie opened her mouth to tell once more the words of the phone call which had so terrified her. But Tom got in first. He looked straight at Mr Shino.

'It was my fault. I did a crazy thing last night.'

'Me too, man,' Paul objected. 'I was right there with you.'

Tom threw him a grateful look. 'You know that place where we went before, where we found the leaflets and Paul took a photo of that target thing?'

Mr Shino nodded, his face serious now.

'Well, we . . . went back. Not to the huts. We promised we wouldn't. But there's a lodge. A sort of gatehouse where the drive to Hereward Court starts. Mum saw a pretty sinister guy who seems to live there. And he's in and out of the Herewards' place as though he owns it. We figured that whatever this Brigade of Britons is up to, he must be in on it. Maybe running it, even. So Paul and I . . .'

'Thought you'd take a look.' There was none of Nick's outrage in Paul's father's voice. He sounded almost as if he expected it.

'Well, yes. Only we couldn't find anything. Paul practically took his computer apart, but there wasn't anything incriminating.'

'And?'

Suzie knew it was her turn. 'This afternoon . . .'

She launched into her account of the phone call. She tried hard to tell it as factually as she could, to be precise about the words the man had used. But she could not help the dryness in her mouth, the tremble of her voice from betraying her terror.

'That's a nasty experience.' Mrs Shino shook her head in sympathy. 'I know. I've had that sort of call.'

Suzie was surprised out of her remembered panic. Tom had told her the Shinos' history before they fled Matoposa. She had forgotten that her own frightening experience was far from unique. She was joining a community she had known little about.

'That's what so worries us,' Nick put in. 'It's not just the threat to our own children, though that's bad enough. But you've escaped danger once. I hate the thought that we've put you in it again.'

'As I understand it, Paul was right there in this with Tom.'

'Tom should never have allowed it. They shouldn't have gone.'

'And if they *had* found evidence? If there'd been plans to start another riot, like that one in Bristol, and they might have stopped it, would you have still said they were wrong?'

Suzie and Nick stared at him open-mouthed.

Nick found his voice. 'But this lot are deadly dangerous. They're prepared to kill for their twisted creed. We've seen that.'

'So you came here to warn us to be very careful. Not to put a foot out of line. Yes?'

'Yes.'

'Tell me, what were you going to do before you had that phone call? Paul says you'd arranged to see your MP. To ask him to take it higher up the food chain. What are you planning to do now?'

'I don't think there's anything I can do, after those threats. It was bad enough when it was just him menacing Suzie. But Millie . . . Your children . . .'

Paul's father stood up. He was not as tall as Nick, but he looked a big man, drawn up to his full height.

'Mr Fewings, let me tell you a story. One of the times they arrested me in my country, they pushed me into a room not much bigger than a cupboard. No windows, no light. There was only one other thing in that little room: a puff adder, one of our most poisonous snakes. They said I must stay there until I told them what they wanted. When I was ready to talk, I could knock on the door and they would let me out. Then they locked me in and left me in the dark.'

'What did you do?' breathed Suzie.

'When you are in a space that small with a puff adder, there's only one thing you can do. Keep very still. I stood without moving a muscle all night. When they unlocked the door in the morning, I told them they could shut me in there as often as they liked, but I still wouldn't help them.'

There was an awed silence. Then Nick asked, 'What are you trying to tell us?'

Mr Shino moved across the room to put his arm across Paul's shoulders.

'That I'm proud of my son. A chip off the old block. Mr Fewings, if you love your country, you keep that appointment.'

TWENTY-THREE

Des Parry, MP, had a dishevelled look, as though his Friday evening surgery was the last duty in a week which had contained rather too many engagements. He threw Nick and Suzie a professional smile as they entered the room and motioned them to the chairs in front of his table. He picked up Nick's email and studied it. The smile faded. When he looked up at them again his boyish face showed alarm.

He thinks we're nutters, Suzie realized. He must get them all the time. People who are convinced there are reds under the bed or fascists in the woodwork.

'A threat to national security? Would you like to be more specific?'

Nick told him everything that had happened.

'So,' Des Parry said carefully, 'you think you've uncovered a plot to destabilize the country by inciting race riots, in the hopes that this will lead to wholesale violence and demands for a stronger government.'

He's grasped it, Suzie reluctantly acknowledged. He may not believe us, but he can see what this is all about and why it would be important if it were true.

'You people must know these groups exist,' Nick said. 'It's not just al-Qaeda you have to worry about. There can be terrorists nearer at home too.'

'And fantasists, I'm afraid.' He held up his hand. 'Don't misunderstand me. I wasn't referring to you. You look a pair of perfectly sensible citizens. But this . . .' He gestured at the notes he had been diligently writing. 'Don't you think that whatever games they're playing at Hereward Court, that might be a far-right fantasy?'

'I did think that at first.' Suzie asserted her voice into what was, after all, more her story than Nick's. 'When Tom and Paul were getting carried away with conspiracy theories. But once I'd seen that target, and knew that men were practising killing people who looked like Paul . . . And then that man from the lodge . . . It was a horrible phone call. He didn't ring me up just to warn me off messing with a fantasy. He was seriously threatening me.'

'And yet you didn't keep quiet. You're telling me all this. That means that *you're* serious.'

'I know Freddie's only a child. But the Bristol riot came only days after he boasted to Millie about a coup. I couldn't live with myself if there were others, and I'd done nothing to stop it.'

'That goes for both of us,' Nick confirmed.

'Have you told the police about that phone call?'

Suzie looked at Nick. 'No. That's what we've been trying to get across to you. It's not just that we went to them twice before and nothing happened. That man who phoned me knew. He knew it was Tom and Paul who searched his house. He knew about their raid on the camp. He knew about Millie and Freddie. Everything. And the only way he could have got that was from someone in the police.'

The junior minister tapped his fingers slowly on the table. 'That's a very serious accusation.'

'It's the only explanation that makes sense,' said Nick. 'Tom has some thing about Floridus Hereward being in cahoots with the Chief Constable. That may be a bit far-fetched. They're certainly friends, but . . .'

'I sincerely hope he's wrong.' Another silence. 'And what did you hope I could do?'

'We daren't go back to the police, not after that phone call,' Nick said. 'I thought you might be able to take it to a more senior level. The Home Office? Isn't there a Minister for National Security, or something?'

'There is.' He thought for a while longer. 'Leave it with me.'

He got up with a decisive movement and held out his had to shake theirs. The interview was over. Suzie looked back from the door and saw him run his fingers through his rumpled hair. The next constituent was already being ushered in, no doubt with a complaint about rubbish collection or the state of the city's pavements. The usual case load of an MP's surgery.

'At least we'll have added some colour to his evening,' she said to Nick with an attempt at a smile.

'Let's see if anything happens.'

'And if it does, what that means for us.'

The doorbell rang in the middle of a weekday evening. Millie was in the conservatory with Suzie, attempting to watch television and copy a map for geography at the same time. Suzie was trying to ignore the reality show while she embroidered.

'Get that, will you, love?' she said.

Millie sighed and put down her mapping pen. 'Do I have to?'

'Yes, please.'

She was halfway down the hall before Suzie suddenly realized. She shouted, 'No!'

But Nick was there before her. He emerged swiftly from the study and cut in front of his daughter.

'I'll do it.'

Suzie drew Millie back into the kitchen, away from the front door.

'What's with the drama? First you want me to answer the doorbell. Then you don't.'

Nick was opening the door. Suzie did not know what it was she feared. A gunman on the doorstep? A masked man who would seize Millie and haul her into a waiting car before they could stop him? For a few seconds her imagination ran riot.

The reality was not what she was expecting. There was a murmured exchange she could not hear. Then Nick was leading a broad-shouldered, silver-haired police officer into the sitting room.

'Stay there,' Suzie ordered Millie, pointing to the conservatory.

She followed Nick down the hall.

The officer was sitting awkwardly on the edge of the sofa. 'Inspector Worlington,' Nick explained.

'Good evening, ma'am.' The inspector was turning his braided cap in his hands. He did not look directly at her.

Suzie wondered if she should offer him tea or coffee, but decided against it. She did not want to miss what was being said.

Inspector Worlington cleared his throat. 'I've come about a rather delicate matter. I understand you have lodged a couple of complaints with DC Erdingham about some goings on at Eastcott St George.'

'At Hereward Court, yes,' Suzie said.

'Hereward Court, thank you. The home of Mr Floridus Hereward. And I gather you've recently pursued the matter with our Member of Parliament.'

Suzie and Nick looked at each other with dismay.

'I'm here tonight, Mr and Mrs Fewings, to ask you to cease this line of enquiry. You've put the incident in police hands and we have all the information we need from you. I should warn you that any further involvement on your part would be detrimental to our operation.'

Suzie decided to risk a gamble. 'Have you heard about the menacing phone call I had? The man who lives at the lodge on the Hereward estate? He threatened my children.'

The inspector held up his hand authoritatively. He got to his feet. 'I'm not here to answer questions, Mrs Fewings. I'm sure you have found this distressing. The best thing you can do for yourself and your family is to stay well clear of this. It is my duty to warn you to say nothing further about it to anyone. Do I make myself clear?'

'As daylight,' said Nick drily.

'And can you assure me that your children will keep this confidential too?'

'They already understand the need for that.'

'Good. I'm relying on you, in their interests.'

'Is that a threat?'

'The British police force does not threaten law-abiding citizens, sir.'

'Well, you're making it sound as though we're the ones breaking the law.'

'I'm sorry if I have given you that impression. If you go

about your normal business, as though none of this had happened, I'm sure you will have nothing to fear.'

He replaced his cap. Nick moved to open the door. They heard him drive away.

'What was *that* all about?' Suzie asked.

'I wish I knew. But we've now been well and truly warned off.'

She felt her eyes widen as the shock sank in.

'He didn't want to know, did he? So . . . it's just us. Nobody else is going to listen.'

'It looks like it.'

TWENTY-FOUR

'I'm going into town,' Millie said belligerently that Saturday morning. 'All right?'

Suzie shot an anxious look at Nick. He thought for a moment.

'It's probably OK. That inspector seemed to indicate we'd be safe enough if we kept our noses clean. Even His Unpleasantness, your guy at the lodge – does he have a name, by the way?'

Suzie shook her head. 'I've never heard it.'

'William Tooley,' said Tom unexpectedly. 'Didn't I say? It was on some of his papers, what few we found of them.'

'Why didn't you tell us?' Nick exclaimed. 'That's vital information. The police may have a file on him.' His words faded into silence. 'For what that's worth,' he added quietly.

'You didn't ask. How was I supposed to know you didn't know it?' Tom retorted.

William Tooley. Suzie tried to absorb the syllables, un-familiar and yet almost disappointingly ordinary. It made it marginally less frightening to know he had a name.

'Anyway,' Millie said, 'he was only threatening us if you didn't keep quiet.'

'And I haven't, have I?' Suzie answered. 'We told Des Parry.'

'Fat lot of good that did,' said Tom.

Nick shuffled the cereal packets on the kitchen table. 'It looks as if it all comes back to the same thing, whoever we tell. No entry. No unauthorized vehicles beyond this point.'

'So can I go and meet the girls?' Millie demanded.

'I'll walk you to the bus stop. You should be all right in a crowd. Just be careful.'

The next few days had an air of unreality. There was no usual Saturday exploration of a countryside parish. Suzie went to a meeting of the Family History Society. Nick stayed home to wait for Millie to phone him.

They watched the news bulletins in tense silence, fearing the spread of the riot in Bristol to a second city. Suzie spent Monday afternoon Christmas shopping, instead of visiting Hereward Court. Outwardly, life was assuming the rhythms of normality, and yet they were waiting, feeling that something had to happen.

A week after Inspector Worlington had called, Suzie was in the study after lunch. She took down her family history files and started to leaf through them. She took out the printout of that crucial discovery: *Robert Doble of Siderleigh, gent, and Humphrey Doble of Romanswell, gent, his son.* The clinching piece of evidence she had searched so long for.

A disappointment crept over her. It had come too late. Mrs Hereward had promised that, if Suzie ever discovered it, there was a hoard of information she could show her about their medieval forebears. If it was anything like the Herewards' document chest, that would mean a stash of private family papers, unavailable in the Record Office or on any website. And this time, it would not be other people's heritage she would be unfolding, but her own.

It *was* too late, wasn't it? She could not, under any circumstances, go back to Hereward Court.

All the same . . . '*Let me know if you discover anything.*' Alianor had sounded genuinely keen to hear. And Alianor, she felt sure, had no hand in all this, might even be as scared of William Tooley as Suzie was. The least she could do to repay her generosity was to tell her this discovery. If Mrs Hereward invited her over, as she almost certainly would, Suzie could invent some excuse.

She picked up the phone and dialled the Herewards' number.

As it rang, she had an alarming thought that it might be Floridus who picked it up. She would just have to pretend it was a wrong number.

The voice was Alianor's, brusque as ever. 'Hereward Court.'

'Hello. It's Suzie Fewings again. I just thought you'd like to hear that I've found what I was looking for. Proof positive that your Robert Doble and my Humphrey Doble were father and son.'

'Terrific! So we're some sort of cousins, yonks removed. Now you really are in the ancestry business. Why don't you come over to the house? I've got such a lot of super stuff I can show you.'

Suzie thought rapidly.

'That's very kind of you. I'd love to, but I'm afraid things are a bit busy at the moment. Christmas coming up, and so on. I just wanted to tell you, that's all. You'd been so kind.'

'Nonsense. Look here, I'm in town tomorrow afternoon. Why don't we meet for a cup of tea? Don't tell me you can't spare half an hour. You can show me your evidence and I'll bring along the old family tree. Half past two suit you? The cathedral refectory.'

Suzie was, as always, swept off her feet by the other woman's forceful enthusiasm.

'Yes . . . Yes, that would be nice. Half past two?'

She put the phone down, fighting back the feeling of alarm.

There could be no harm, surely, in meeting her on neutral ground in the middle of the city, away from the eye of William Tooley?

Suzie rehearsed the words she would need to tell Nick. '*I'm meeting Mrs Hereward tomorrow.*'

Nick was not going to like it. He would argue that, even in town, in the cathedral refectory surrounded by other customers, she would be putting herself at risk. Mrs Hereward would probably tell Floridus, and he might pass it on to William Tooley. That pair might fear that something would pass between the two women which Suzie should not know.

Could it? How much *did* Alianor know?

And that, she thought, is why I must go. It's not just so that we can swap notes about our medieval and Tudor ancestors, fascinating though that undoubtedly will be. It's because I have this feeling at the back of my mind that Alianor does know something. Something that makes her afraid. Something she wants to tell me, against all her instincts. I have to meet her.

So she let Nick go to work next morning without saying anything. The children had left too, the house was quiet. Before she set off to catch the bus to her own work at the office she wrote a note and left it on the kitchen table.

> Meeting Mrs Hereward for tea at the cathedral coffee shop 2.30 p.m. Should be back before 5. Love, Suzie.

She checked that she had her mobile phone. She told herself she was doing everything sensibly.

She ate her sandwiches in the shop with Margery. There was still an hour to fill. Her Christmas shopping was done. Almost from force of habit she found her feet taking her to the local studies library at the edge of the park.

She asked to see the parish file on Great Thorry, where Alianor's Dobles had held the manor for centuries. She felt the shiver of altered perception. These were *her* Dobles now, Humphrey Doble's forebears. At last she had found her 'gateway ancestor', who would open up the past, perhaps even back to the Norman Conquest.

Great Thorry was new ground for her. The file was substantial. She moved swiftly through piles of newspaper cuttings recording more recent events in the village, looking for older material. Her fingers stopped at a transcript of proceedings at the manorial court, back in the 1400s. It had been made on an ancient typewriter, now an historical relic itself, with handwritten corrections and the circle of its 'b's filled with ink.

This was fascinating stuff:

> The bailiff is in mercy because he has not distrained Walter Greneslade and Ralph Moggeforde to answer to the lord because on Tuesday in the Feast of St Katherine the Virgin they broke into and entered a close of John Doble, lord of this manor called Great Thorry, and then and there killed and took away 12 gooseanders without

the leave of the said lord to the prejudice of the said lord.

With frustration she realized that there was no time to take notes on more than the first pages. Should she photocopy them, or just read them through, so that she would have some common ground to discuss with Alianor?

She could not resist the temptation to read on, making swift notes as she went.

> William retainer of John Doble jun. against the peace attacked Stephen Norris with one cudgel – which he produced – and drew blood. Therefore he is in mercy and let him be distrained.
>
> And because William retainer of John Doble jun. against the peace attacked Thomas Palk with his fist. Therefore he is in mercy. And because the same Thomas Payne against the peace attacked the same William with his fist. Therefore he is in mercy.

What did 'in mercy' mean? Judging by the context, not what it sounded like. Some sort of punishment for a punch-up by her young ancestor's henchman.

She glanced at her watch. Bother. There was no time for more if she was to get to the cathedral in time. Just when it was starting to get interesting. She returned the cardboard box to the desk with a smile, and hurried out into the chilly December afternoon.

She crossed the cathedral green, looking about her for Alianor. The lights were on in the refectory, promising a welcome refuge from the cold wind. Hot tea, a toasted teacake, perhaps.

She hesitated at the door. Would Alianor be inside already? She opened the door to look in.

A familiar voice startled her from behind. Those unmistakably brisk, authoritative tones. 'Hello, my dear. Thought I wasn't coming, did you?'

Suzie turned. She had forgotten how short Mrs Hereward was. She was wearing a woolly hat pulled low over her cropped black hair. Her cheeks and nose were red with cold. Not for the first time, Suzie was struck by what a very unromantic novelist she looked.

Alianor's eyes shone with what seemed like genuine enthusiasm. 'Move along in, then. This wind's bitter, isn't it? I could do with a pot of tea.'

At the counter, she ordered tea and seized two jam doughnuts. 'I can't resist these, can you?' She brushed aside Suzie's attempts to pay.

They found a table. The light fell softly through windows formed of fragments of stained glass, assembled from a variety of shattered panes.

'Well,' Alianor said, beaming at Suzie, 'so you found your evidence.'

The words threw Suzie. There were so many thoughts chasing each other round her head, about the past and the present. Which of these did Alianor mean by 'evidence'? How much did she know?

Silly. They had only met to talk about family history.

She recovered herself enough to stumble, 'You know I had this hunch that my Humphrey Doble was the son of Robert Doble of Siderleigh, who went on to inherit the manor of Great Thorry?'

'And was my ancestor, yes.'

Well, I found my proof at last. Somewhere I'd never have thought of looking for it. The Access to Archives website had this sheaf of deeds about a property in Kennerton, which hadn't featured on my radar. And there it was, the names of the landlords granting a lease in 1579. Robert Doble of Siderleigh, gent, and Humphrey Doble of Romanswell, gent, his son.'

'Terrific! Jolly well done. So you've got it. Robert Doble was your ancestor too. That means you and I are cousins.'

'About thirteenth cousins, by my reckoning.' Suzie laughed, embarrassed that she was claiming too much. 'It's hardly close enough to count.'

'Don't you believe it. Everybody who's anybody knows who's connected to whom. Tell you what, if you're a Doble, then you're connected to Flo as well. I'm not the first Doble to marry a Hereward, you know.'

She bent to fish in her capacious shopping bag. Suzie's blood quickened as she recognized the shape of a scroll, shielded from the weather by a Marks and Spencer plastic bag. It must be the Doble family tree.

Alianor laid it on the table without unwrapping it. She pushed back the bench and jumped to her feet. 'This calls for a celebration.'

She marched back to the counter and returned with two enormous slices of carrot cake.

Suzie hardly protested. She was enjoying herself enormously. Her dark doubts about meeting Mrs Hereward again, even away from the malignant house, dissolved in the warmth of this woman's enthusiasm. Wiping their sticky fingers on their napkins, they unrolled the tree and pinned it down with crockery.

She ran her eyes greedily up the list of the dates. Yes! She was right about the Norman Conquest. And then . . . A shock went through her as she realized that the names went on into Anglo-Saxon England, before the Battle of Hastings. Was that . . . *King Alfred*?

'Here,' said Alianor, jabbing a finger at Gothic lettering lower on the tree. 1461. Douce Doble married another Floridus Hereward. And she was sister to Sir William Doble, who was *our* ancestor.'

Suzie refocused her attention.

So close. A shiver of undefined apprehension replaced the euphoria she had felt. So she was descended from the same blood as the present Floridus Hereward.

It didn't matter, did it? So long ago? It had nothing to do with what Floridus was involved in now.

Alianor was rushing on. 'Tell you what. We've got a family portrait of them at the Court. Floridus and Douce, three or four children, and our William hovering in the background like Banquo's ghost. Quite rare, a painting of a family group that old. Would you like to see it?'

'I . . .' Suzie didn't know what to say. Of course she wanted to see it. A fifteenth-century portrait of her ancestor. Not many researchers got this lucky. But she couldn't, could she? She couldn't go back to Hereward Court.

Mrs Hereward was rolling up the scroll, stuffing it into her bag, getting to her feet. 'Come on, my dear. Got to get back to collect the brats. I'll drop you off at the house and show you the picture first.'

Suzie found herself swept out of the café. She was struggling to find the words to decline the invitation.

'I'm sorry. I've got to . . .'

'Nonsense. It won't take long. You'll catch the four o'clock bus back.'

They rounded the corner of the cathedral. Without warning Suzie found they were in a small car park. She was standing alongside the Polo. Alianor was unlocking the door.

Before she could find a way of apologizing, she was sitting in the passenger seat. Alianor turned the key and roared out into the traffic of the High Street.

TWENTY-FIVE

A s they flew through the outskirts of the town at considerably more than the speed limit, Suzie's thoughts were racing too. Should she get her mobile out of her shoulder-bag and ring Nick to tell him what had happened? He would be horrified. Could she calm his fears in words that would not sound strange to Alianor beside her? Did she even want to calm them? They were her fears too.

Alianor had said that she would leave Suzie to view the portrait while she fetched the children from school. That would give her a quiet space to call Nick.

She felt a renewed start of alarm as the car swung abruptly off the main road. It was not the turning she had expected Alianor to take. She had assumed that they would use the side road at Eastcott St George. She knew this little lane though. Her sense of foreboding deepened. This would take them past the lodge.

It was worse than that. As the wrought-iron gates came into view, Alianor slowed the car and swerved to face them. The gates were not padlocked today. They stood a little apart.

'Be a sport and nip out and open them.'

Suzie could not refuse. She got out on the far side from the lodge and looked apprehensively at its dark, blank windows. Was William Tooley in there? Could he see her? He had warned her never to come back again. He had threatened . . . She felt sick.

Desperate to be back in the car and driving on, she ran to

the gates and pulled them aside. It was too late to undo the harm. If he was there, he would have seen her by now.

She was trembling when she got back into the passenger seat. The car lurched forward down the rutted drive.

The house swung into view below them, the little lake, the backcloth of parkland and trees.

'Funny,' said Alianor. 'I get a lump in my throat every time I see it. I know it's not really mine, but there have been Herewards here for nearly a thousand years. Flo's still scared that someone will take it away from him. And I know Freddie will fight to keep it.'

Fight? Fight whom? And how?

She remembered hearing the sound of petrol bombs in city streets.

As the unmade drive levelled out, the wheels ran on to concrete. They sailed more smoothly past the lake and swung in under the arch.

Suzie stepped out into the courtyard. She had not expected that she would ever come here again.

A crackle of gunfire snapped at her taut nerves. She gave a stifled scream.

Alianor came round the bonnet and stopped, looking shrewdly at her. 'Yes, they're back. Flo's city boys down in the woods.'

Suzie tried to read the other woman's expression. Again she had that feeling that Alianor was trying to tell her something. But with the menace of the dark lodge windows and the sound of guns echoing in her ears, she was no longer so sure what it was. Was Mrs Hereward drawing her attention to what was happening at the Court, pleading with Suzie to do something to stop it?

Or . . . A new thought crawled coldly through her. Did Alianor know what was going on here, and share her husband's ambitions? Was this her way of protecting the Hereward heritage? Could she . . .? Suzie remembered now how she had been lured into meeting Alianor in town, then swept into the car and driven off before she could back out. What if it wasn't Mrs Hereward's impetuous enthusiasm, but a deliberate plot, at Floridus's instigation. . . or William Tooley's? He had warned her and her family not to take their investigation any further. And they had.

Ice seemed to freeze the skin of her face. Too late now to reach for her phone. Impossible to turn back for the other gate and the village, and not be escorted into the house. She thought of the name the Roundheads had called it in the Civil War. *A malignant house.* The house of traitors.

Numbly she let Alianor lead her inside.

'It's up here.'

Alianor dumped her shopping on the hall table. Suzie followed as she started to climb the stairs.

She had never been up here before. She turned her head to see the portraits of past Herewards watching her progress up the dark staircase. She remembered belatedly, through her confusion, that it was a picture she had supposedly come to see. Was it one of these? But the age-darkened oil paintings in their heavy gilt frames looked a far cry from the style of the fifteenth century. Georgian, mostly, she guessed. They stared judgementally at her from under powdered wigs.

The silence of the house oppressed her. Alianor had stopped chattering. There was only the sound of their shoes on the wooden treads. As they reached the half-landing she realized what was missing.

'No Labradors?' she asked, relieved to have found something approaching normal conversation.

'I expect they're with Flo.'

Where was Floridus? Out on the estate? Walking through the woods, with a gun over his arm? Talking to those men in the camp?

They reached the upper floor and started along the corridor.

Suddenly she heard it. That unmistakable sound of claws scrabbling on bare wood. The two black Labradors, Dizzy and Gladstone, came hurtling along the corridor. In the moment before they reached her, Floridus Hereward turned the corner ahead of her.

Suzie stopped dead. At once she was engulfed in what seemed like a pack of leaping dogs, though she knew there were only two of them. There was something comforting about their crazy enthusiasm, their licking tongues, as though she was their long-lost friend. It could not wall off her dread of Mr Hereward advancing towards her.

At a yell from Alianor, the dogs subsided. Suzie could see him clearly now, only a few strides away. The colour was

high in his sharply-planed cheeks. She thought she caught
something wary in his eyes. How much did he know of
William Tooley's phone call to her? Who was really in charge
here?

He shot a questioning glance at his wife.

'Suzie Fewings,' Alianor reminded him. As if he could have
forgotten. 'I invited her back. D'you know what she's found
out, clever girl? She's descended from my Dobles, lords of
the manor of Great Thorry, 1500s. We're cousins. Isn't that
marvellous?'

'The Dobles, eh?' The muscles of Floridus Hereward's face
stretched surprisingly into what looked like a genuine smile.
He stared straight at her, as though appreciating her fully
for the first time. 'Has Allie told you? There was another
Hereward–Doble marriage, back in the fifteenth century.
Daughter of one of your ancestors. Have you shown her?' The
last question was directed at Alianor.

'We're on our way there.'

Floridus swung round to walk with them. 'It's a rather
amazing thing. Fifteenth-century family group. You don't find
many of those, outside the royal family. It shows the Floridus
Hereward of those times dedicating the church he'd built for
the priory in Quinton Bishop.'

Suzie remembered the cart track across the road from the
lodge, leading down to that village. It must once have been
a significant road.

Floridus was sweeping them along the corridor, with Suzie
now caught between the two Herewards. 'The funny thing is,
your own ancestor somehow got himself into the picture.
Douce's brother, Sir William Doble. Nobody knows why he's
there.'

A feeling of unreality took Suzie over. She had been terrified of meeting Mr Hereward. Reason told her that he was
lending his estate to a neo-fascist organization. He had opened
this house to William Tooley. He must know what was going
on. He had to be behind it. How could he not be aware that
the Fewings were on to them, that Tooley had threatened her,
forbidden her to come back?

Yet here he was, talking animatedly about family history,
as if that were the only thing between them.

He stopped at a door. The Labradors panted behind them.

'So,' he said, with that smile transforming his usually distant face. 'You're one of us.'

She stared back at him, uncertain what to say. Could he possibly believe that? That a blood connection – what, sixteen generations back – meant that they shared the same agenda in the twenty-first century? He couldn't really think that, could he?

She forced her nervous lips to smile apologetically. 'I'm afraid the Dobles are only one of an awful lot of lines on my tree, and very much down the female end of it. I had other ancestors from Southcombe, who probably came and looted your house in the Civil War.'

He brushed her protest aside. 'Blood will out.' He flung open the door.

Alianor led the way into a large, light room whose windows looked out over the rose garden at the side of the house. There was hardly any furniture. A delicate settee in worn green velvet stood against one wall. An ornate occasional table bearing a black vase stood against another. A few framed pictures hung on striped wallpaper, which showed ominous damp marks. These portraits looked older than the ones on the stairs. Mostly Tudor, by the style of the clothes.

It was not the pictures she cared about. She was uneasily aware of Floridus's presence at her side.

Alianor was making for a far corner of the room.

'There. What do you think of that, then?'

Suzie was caught unprepared. It was hard to assemble her scattered thoughts and remember what she had come to see. Fear had driven it out of her head.

For a moment, she hardly knew what she was meant to be looking at. She had known, of course, that a fifteenth-century picture would not be a canvas heavy with oil paint. As she followed the direction of Alianor's hand, she found herself looking down at the page of an open book in a glass case.

The freshness of the painting took her by surprise. This was delicate, as if the shapes had been drawn with a fine pen and then washed with colour. It reminded Suzie of the maps Millie carefully drew and coloured in her geography book.

In the foreground, a man in a loose gown was kneeling. His hands were holding up a miniature church. A little behind him knelt a lady in a wimple, and behind her, a line of three children of descending height. They must be children, because of their small size, though their dress and faces were like those of their parents.

She drew a sharper breath at the figure standing in the background, his hands put together in prayer. Where the Hereward family were displayed in finery of green and red and gold, this man wore black, relieved only by a gold chain round his neck. His cap was black. She understood why Mrs Hereward had said he was like Banquo's ghost at the feast.

A shiver of knowledge ran through her. Was this really Sir William Doble, her newly discovered ancestor? Peering closer, she could faintly make out some gold lettering near his head. *Wilelmus Dobell*. It was the strangest feeling to be looking at him across five and a half centuries.

'Of course,' Alianor cut through her awed silence, 'don't imagine he actually looked like that. The artist'll have had a stock pattern of how a gentleman and a lady ought to appear. That's why all the little Herewards look like mum and dad. Individuality didn't come into it. All the same . . .' She grinned at Suzie. 'It touches a nerve, doesn't it? Your forebear, and mine.'

The two women stood gazing at the picture in silence, sharing the moment.

She was suddenly conscious of Floridus Hereward, now standing close behind her, watching silently. Her spine prickled. Was he feeling, as she was feeling, that dark presence of a Doble looming enigmatically over the Hereward family? Suzie's ancestor. Why was he there, in a scene which should belong only to the Herewards? Why did he look so much like a threat to them?

Mr Hereward's clipped voice spoke her thoughts. 'That's your William, all right. Looks a bit sinister, actually, lurking behind, looking down on them, what?'

The crawling fear had reached her scalp.

As *she* was a threat to Hereward Court now. He must see the connection. Why wouldn't he?

Staring at the painting, she allowed her mind to probe one generation back. The parents of Douce and William Doble, whose names she did not yet know. Not just her ancestors and Alianor's, but Floridus Hereward's. She and the man behind her were also cousins.

It doesn't change anything, she told herself wildly. That was hundreds of year ago. We're only remote cousins, a huge distance across our family trees.

And even if they weren't, if they had been first cousins, what would it matter? What was being done here at Hereward Court was stark evil. What blood connection there was between her and Mr Hereward had nothing to do with it. She thought of the Shinos, exiles in that cramped flat, of the bullet-ridden target of a man with the caricature of an African face, of two black men lying dead on the streets of Bristol.

She wanted desperately to be out of this house.

The telephone rang, faintly, somewhere downstairs. Presently there were footsteps coming along the corridor. As the door opened, they all turned.

Suzie recognized the man, though she had only seen him once before. The ferret-faced Marchant, who had shot at Nick. It was Marchant who had been standing guard over him when Suzie came to collect Nick from Hereward Court.

'Excuse me, sir,' he said to Floridus. 'Mr Tooley would like a word.'

Suzie's heart froze. So Tooley had seen her from the lodge. If Floridus did not know yet the danger she represented, he was going to find out in the next few minutes. She ought to leave, now.

Mr Hereward was following Marchant out into the corridor. The dogs stayed behind.

Alianor broke the silence. 'Crumbs! Is that the time? I'm late for the school run.'

Still she didn't make for the door. Her dark eyes looked intently into Suzie's. 'No need for you to rush away. You might want to make some notes, eh?'

She nodded, not at the book, but at another closed door opposite the one to the corridor. 'Flo's inner sanctum. Not like the estate office downstairs. His private stuff . . . Dogs!'

And the three of them were gone, a short, determined woman with sleek black hair, and two sleek black dogs with wagging tails.

TWENTY-SIX

Alianor's heavy footsteps and the scamper of the dogs' paws died away. The bare room with the book fell silent. She must go while she still had the chance.

Her eyes went sideways to the door Alianor had indicated. It was in the middle of the wall, between two hanging portraits. It had every appearance of the entrance to an inner room.

The possibility both excited and frightened her. There was no doubt what Alianor had been trying to tell her. '*His private stuff.*' Suzie's original hunch had been the right one. Mrs Hereward might be too loyal – or afraid? – to report Floridus herself, but she wanted someone to do it. Suzie.

She moved slowly towards the door. She was scared.

Floridus must have been working in there before he met them in the corridor. Working on what?

Her hand was going out towards the door knob almost without her willing it.

She hesitated, feeling the blood pounding in her throat. Mr Hereward would be back at any moment.

Or perhaps not. He had been coming away from this room. She could risk a few minutes.

The brass door handle was cold to the touch. She turned it.

The room was almost as bare as the one she had left, but more plainly furnished. There was a table, which would have looked more at home in a kitchen than the upper salon of a stately home. There was a scatter of paper on it. No shelves of files, no computer, unlike the crowded estate office downstairs. Suzie remembered the boys' ineffective raid on William Tooley's rooms at the lodge. They would be careful. No paper trail. No incriminating files on a hard drive. She noticed a paper shredder on the floor behind the table.

There was an old-fashioned green telephone on the windowsill. Suzie's first thought registered only that it matched the stained wallpaper. Then it struck her as odd.

Marchant had come upstairs to tell Floridus there was a phone call for him. There had been no sound of the phone ringing in this room. It must be a different line. She moved swiftly across the room and made a note of the number in her diary.

She had passed the table. As she turned back, it stood between her and the door. There were only a few sheets of paper on it. Nothing typed or printed. Rough notes in a sprawling handwriting. She moved closer. She was almost too tense to swallow.

Birmingham. Jan 10. The Lotus Curry House? A list of six names, all English. Two of them had phone numbers against them. There were ticks beside these and two of the other names.

It wasn't proof. But she knew beyond question. Knew that in less than a month she would be seeing scenes on the television news like the ones from Bristol. People would be lying dead. Passions would be rising, in Birmingham and elsewhere. Community leaders would be struggling to hold the line. One step nearer disaster.

She added the names to her diary. There was a drawer in the table.

Only pens and pencils. A few dusty paper clips. Sheets of blank paper.

Apart from this one memo, a police raid would have found nothing to incriminate anyone.

Names and plans could be memorized. But where did he keep those telephone numbers? She looked around the bare room.

Through the open door came a sound as startling as gunfire. Footsteps coming back along the corridor.

Suzie flew back to the room with the painting, banging her hip on the corner of the table in her haste. She had almost closed the connecting door behind her when he appeared in the doorway opposite her.

Not Mr Hereward. Marchant. A small man, with a flat cap, breeches and gaiters. Staring at her, and at the door behind her.

His features sharpened, if that were possible, even more. She waited, terrified, for him to demand what she had been doing. Instead, he turned on his heel and went, almost running, back down the corridor. She heard his boots clattering on the stairs.

She ran too. At the door she looked wildly in both directions. Surely there should be another staircase? She took off, the opposite way from Marchant, in search of it. But when she found it, round the far corner, she knew with dismay where it would lead her. Down to that corridor along the back of the house, to the estate office. The very place where Marchant would have gone racing to tell Mr Hereward.

She would have to risk the front stairs. She spun round.

And found herself face to face with William Tooley.

It wasn't possible.

That phone call could not have been from the lodge. He was *here*.

She saw the shock of recognition in his dark eyes. Had he really not known she was in the house? Instantly it was replaced by a blaze of anger. He grabbed her arm so hard it hurt.

'You? I thought I told you never to come back!'

'I'm sorry! Mrs Hereward . . .'

He wasn't listening. His fury seemed to fill the narrow corridor as much as his large physical presence. He whirled around, leather coat flapping, and almost flung her behind him.

'Get out! Fast as you can. And don't stop running till you get to the village. *Now!*'

She ran.

At the end of the corridor she went tumbling down the stairs past the disapproving stares of dead Herewards. She threw a terrified look along the bottom passage that led past the kitchen to the estate office. Which staircase would Marchant and Floridus use to come back and accuse her of spying on his papers? Had William Tooley found out about that yet? Would he have let her go if he had?

She was fumbling with the heavy handle of the oak door. Her movements were clumsy with haste. Suddenly it gave, nearly overbalancing her. She was through the gap, into the cold air of the courtyard.

Too many windows. She could be spied on from all sides. She longed for the car, so that she could leap in and speed away. Even the friendly sight of Alianor's Polo was missing.

She dodged past the solitary Land Rover and ran for the arch.

The greater space of sky and parkland calmed her a little. She had got out of the house undetected. But William Tooley knew she was here. When he heard she had been into that inner sanctum . . .

Birmingham. The Lotus Curry House. Jan 10.

She was the only one who knew.

Every instinct screamed at her to keep on running up the drive. Not to stop until she was safe in the village, at the bus stop. But she looked up the long, exposed slope. The dark voice of reason told her she might not make it.

She flattened herself against the outer wall of the house, where she could not be seen from a window, and delved in her bag for her mobile phone. It was a terrifying gamble, when every moment was precious. Her thumb found Nick's number and pressed it. Mercifully, he picked up straight away.

'Nick Fewings.'

'Nick. Don't interrupt. This is urgent. I'm at Hereward Court. No, listen! Birmingham, January tenth, the Lotus Curry House. Remember that. But they saw me. I'm making for the village . . . No. Change that. I'll try the other gate by the lodge. They may not expect that. I love you.'

She rang off. Then, drawing a deep breath, she sprinted past the windows of the library, past the wall of the rose garden, making for the trees on the further slope.

Too late, she remembered that the windows of the estate office looked out this way.

She was out of breath, climbing as fast as she could. The welcome trees were closing in. They would soon shield her.

This older drive up to the lodge was deeply rutted. She had to watch where she was going. She saw the heavy tread marks of all-terrain vehicles.

She looked back, hoping desperately that Hereward Court would have disappeared behind the branches.

It was still in sight. A cream-coloured square with its mock turrets. A truly malignant house.

She turned to push herself on. And then she heard it.

It was impossible at first to be sure where the roar of the engine was coming from. But she had seen nothing on the drive behind her. The vehicle could only be coming from the direction of the lodge.

For a moment she let herself hope that it might be some tradesman's van, nothing to do with the Brigade of Britons. She pictured a friendly local driver, the protection of normality. At the very least, a witness to say he had seen her running for her life.

Reality hurtled round the bend above.

An open jeep, bristling with men in dark overalls, carrying guns. Today they wore helmets with visors. She tried to leap out of the way, but the jeep slammed to a halt, sending mud flying.

Men leaped from the back to surround her. Their eyes glinted through the slits in their helmets.

There were no jeers and whistles. No ribald stares of male mockery. No one spoke. A jerk of a weapon motioned her into the trees.

They knew who she was. They knew where Marchant had found her. Floridus must have told them that only she had the information about what they were plotting next.

She stared into the barrel of the gun. This could not be happening to her.

But it was. If she went into those trees, she would not come out again.

TWENTY-SEVEN

She had no choice. She could not name the guns they pointed at her. Something more sinister than the shotgun Floridus had carried over his arm. Squat, black, its ammunition-heavy body braced against a dark-blue shoulder. Tom would have known what it was.

Tom. Millie. Nick. Was she really never going to see them again?

She fought for her life in the only way that stood any chance.

'You won't get away with it. My husband knows where I am. If I don't come back, the police will take this place apart. They'll know it was you.'

The mouth below the helmet facing her split into a grin. 'You think we're amateurs? The police can do what they bloody well like. They won't find nothing. Not here.'

Her mouth was dry. 'If you put me in that jeep, if you even touch me, they'll find evidence. Fibres. DNA.'

A voice spoke behind her. 'Assuming he does call the police. Got kids have you?'

The bag was ripped from her shoulder.

'Oh, look. She's got a mobile. Kids' names on it, are they? Oh, no. Your bloke telling the police wouldn't be clever.'

Now she did panic. Tom, Millie? *What if Nick had already told the police?*

She spun round. One of them was waving her phone at her, taunting her.

A deeper voice sounded from her right side.

'Do you know, Bart, I think she's only just thought of that.'

'What a pity.'

It was impossible to tell one grinning visored face from another.

'March, lady. You do *exactly* what we say.'

The muzzle of a gun in her chest prodded her round and pushed her into the wood.

Despair settled over her. What a bitter irony this would be, if she had come to Hereward Court seeking her ancestors, only to bring about the end of her family line. She had tried to do what she could, but the forces of evil were too strong for her.

The shock finally sank in. It left her so exhausted that she could hardly drag one foot in front of another. Several times she stumbled on a tree root hidden deep in fallen leaves.

Where were they taking her? Somewhere away from the house and the camp.

If Nick came after her now, he would never find her. Not in time.

They were working their way uphill now, faster than she wanted to go. Her eyes were on the uneven ground in front of her. She did not have the energy to look up ahead. It was partly the practical need to see where she must put the next foot. Partly, too, a last clinging to the vividness of life.

An oak leaf, decayed to the white gossamer of veins. An earthworm, palely pink, disturbed by the boot of the man in whose steps she was following. A cluster of holly berries, shockingly, festively red.

When the men ahead stopped, she almost walked into one of them. She halted too, grateful for the chance to catch her heaving breath.

Her first look upwards took her by surprise. They must be near the top of the hill. Through the thinning trees she could see the sky above the ridge. Something else, further right. Grey. The back wall of the lodge where Tooley was living.

She was aware, above the pounding in her ears, of men talking. The screen of uniform backs parted. There was someone else facing her.

It was the man she most feared of all of them.

William Tooley had shed his long leather coat. She had never seen him before without it. Black jeans, black sweater, a belt heavy with pouches. There was a sheen of sweat on his fleshy face and shaved head. His breath was laboured. He must have been running.

He spoke as though he was in command.

'Right, lads. Well done. I'll take over from here.'

'Come on, Will. Give us some fun. There's plenty of soft ground here. Dig it deep enough and they'll never find her.'

'Get real, sonny.' His voice grated. 'They have sniffer dogs you wouldn't believe, nowadays. Stuff that tells you if the ground's been disturbed. You're behind the times. They search this place, they'll be on to her in no time. And there you are, camped a few hundred yards away.'

'Can't let her go, though, can we?'

'Listen, lads, we've got *real* work to do soon. We don't want any messing with that. The way I'm going to do it, they can't touch us. She goes missing. What a shame. They're bound to have their suspicions, but they can't pin anything on us. Yes, she was here. Floridus waved her goodbye. End of story.'

One of them chuckled. 'And it sends out a message, dunnit? You don't mess with us.'

'Where you taking her?' demanded the man behind Suzie.

'The less you know when you're questioned the better.'

Would they kill her first? Would they risk the trace of blood from the gunshot for a dog to scent? There were other ways commandos knew. A garrotte. A well-aimed blow to the head.

She would vanish without a trace. Months ahead, perhaps, her decaying body might be found in another part of the country. It was more than the December wind which turned her blood to ice.

Or would William Tooley abduct her alive? Would that only prolong the terror, to be driven off, alone, with him, of all men?

She heard it in the distance. The sound of a vehicle.

Emotions raced through her mind, almost too fast to follow.

Nick had come to rescue her.

It was just an unknown passer-by, who would drive straight past.

It was Nick, but he mustn't find her. What chance would he have against nearly a dozen armed men? Nick must live, for Tom and Millie. Nick must live because she loved him.

If only he could be here with her when she died.

The vehicle was slowing. The sound of the engine was clearer now, from the direction of the lodge. The helmeted heads were turning.

'Back!' snapped Tooley.

Hands pulled Suzie into the thicker cover of the trees. The men around her were exchanging nervous glances. Tooley gestured to calm them. He grabbed Suzie and pulled her roughly in front of him.

A car came into sight, bumping along a track just above the wood. It was not Nick's Vauxhall. This was a car she had never seen before, an ancient, rusty Morris Minor. Two men climbed out. The gamekeeper Marchant from the driving seat, and Floridus Hereward.

There was a hiss of breath in her ear as William Tooley swore.

Floridus had his shotgun, Marchant a more wicked-looking rifle. They advanced towards the trees.

Tooley pushed Suzie forward.

'No panic, squire. The little lady's under control. I'll deal with it. You haven't seen her since she left the house, right?'

Floridus's usually impassive face looked flushed and uneasy.
'Is this really necessary? You won't do anything . . . unpleasant,
will you? Mrs Hereward says . . . Well, we're related.'

'Not to worry, squire. You won't hear anything more about
it. Your wife knows Mrs Fewings was here, but she was off
fetching the kids. The police ask you, you were called away.
When you came back upstairs, she'd gone. Don't want to alarm
the missus, do we? And I was in the lodge, wasn't I? Saw her
go past the window, heading for the main road.'

'Right, then . . . If you're sure. I'll leave it in your hands.'
Mr Hereward turned away, as if relieved. 'Marchant will help
you with the . . . arrangements,' he called over his shoulder.
He started to walk towards the drive.

Marchant winked knowingly at Tooley. 'Got a tarpaulin in
the back, sir. Very useful. Wrap her up in that, she won't leave
any traces. Shall I bring it?'

Horror crept through Suzie. Would she be alive or dead
when they laid her on it and rolled it securely so that no
evidence escaped? Where would they take her? Would her
body ever be found?

She began to struggle against Tooley's grip. She knew it was
useless. There were armed men all around her. There was nothing
she could do. But the will to live was too strong not to try.

His grasp hardened. 'Shut up, you little fool.' He nodded
to Marchant. 'Get it.'

The gamekeeper was coming back from the car, trailing a
stiff grey tarpaulin. She studied it in fascinated horror. Was
this her shroud?

It was not the sound which alerted her this time, but the
sudden stiffening of Tooley's body close behind her. His fingers
dug into her arms.

Then she heard it. More vehicles approaching. On the lane
along the ridge. She heard the screeching turn as they took
the gateway at speed.

All round Suzie the men were exchanging questioning
glances through their visors. The glassy eyes turned to Tooley
for orders.

'Get down!' he shouted. 'Stay low.'

The men threw themselves flat among the leaves. Only
Marchant stood in the open, like a rabbit caught in his own
night-sights.

In an unexpected movement, Tooley threw Suzie sideways, with him, behind an oak tree. He drew from his belt what she at first thought was a mobile, and then saw was a radio handset. In a low voice, he spoke rapid orders into it.

'Turn right off the drive past the lodge. A hundred yards. Top of the wood. But watch out for . . .'

The vehicles surged into sight. Three police cars, followed by – oh joy! – Nick's Vauxhall.

Armed officers leapt out. Suzie tensed in horror. On either side of her was the Brigade of Britons, all armed with lethal weapons, under cover in the trees. She saw them turning to Tooley for a signal.

He was talking urgently into the radio. She no longer heard what he was saying.

The police squad was advancing, warily, guns at the ready.

Didn't they know they were walking into a deadly ambush? Should she shout?

Before she could decide, the shot she had been dreading rang out. A solitary round. And it was not from the men in hiding.

A policeman reeled. The rest dived for cover, on the ground, or back behind the vehicles.

Marchant stood alone, his rifle still braced against his shoulder.

Tooley swore again.

'Lay down your weapon,' someone shouted.

Where was Nick? Suzie couldn't see him. Stay hidden, she pleaded with him silently.

The gamekeeper turned the rifle slowly, this way and that, training it on the scattered officers.

She almost missed the moment. A flicker of movement caught the corner of her eye. The dark-clad figure of Nick was sprinting to take Marchant from the side. No!

He had covered only half the distance when Marchant saw him. The gun swung round.

Suzie tried to leap to her feet, but Tooley pulled her down and held her there.

'Nick!'

Another shot sent the echoes ringing. It seemed to pierce her own heart.

Marchant fell. Instantly he was surrounded by police, his rifle snatched away.

Marchant. Not Tom.

But the rest of the officers were coming forward, fanned out, advancing on the trees.

She couldn't bear what was about to happen.

'Keep back!' she yelled in despair. 'They've got guns too.'

Still the policemen came on, their own weapons readied. Every nerve in Suzie screamed that they should be taking cover behind their vehicles. They would be slaughtered before they reached her. Nick was there, foolishly running to overtake them, to find her.

'Nick! No!'

It would only need one shot.

All around her there was a furtive rustling. She looked round in panic. The Brigade of Britons in their dark overalls were rising, stealthily. They were starting to creep back down through the woods.

The police were running. As they came crashing in among the fallen leaves, one of the helmeted Brigade turned and fired. Suzie screamed.

A fount of yellow burst on the leading officer's shoulder. The rest of the police threw themselves flat.

The one who had been hit clapped his hand to the wound, then brought it away, smeared with yellow, and stared at it.

Yellow? Not red?

One of the officers on the ground started to laugh.

William Tooley let go of Suzie. He wiped his sweating forehead with a hand that shook a little.

'Paint guns?' she asked him incredulously.

He got to his feet and hauled her up beside him. 'They look pretty convincing, don't they? Don't be fooled, though. They're using them to train men who want to kill for real. Just lucky for you that was what they had this morning. But I hadn't bargained on Marchant and his rifle.'

She stared at him stupidly. 'But you . . . the radio . . .? *You* called the police?'

The big man sighed. 'I tried to warn you off before you got in over your heads. But you're a persistent lot, you Fewings. Has your Tom ever considered a career in Special Branch?'

Then Nick had found her. She was in his arms and foolishly crying against his chest.

After a while, Suzie raised her wet face and managed a crooked smile for him.

'Meet William Tooley. He's just saved my life.'

TWENTY-EIGHT

Paul hunched his shoulder in his padded jacket and shuffled his cold feet as the wind sneaked across the cathedral close.

'You're telling me that guy at the lodge was Special Branch all the time?' The Matoposan boy whistled and ran his fingers through his short-cropped hair.

'I'm afraid so,' Nick said. 'All the time we thought he was threatening us, he was just trying to scare us off so we wouldn't queer his investigation. We were getting too close.'

'And did we?' asked Millie. 'Foul it up?'

'A bit,' Suzie admitted. 'He's got this cell nailed, but only partial leads to others. Like the one responsible for the Bristol riot.'

'And would they have killed you if he hadn't been there?'

There was silence on the empty green. Nick put his arm around Suzie.

'Oh, look. Here she comes,' Suzie said brightly. She broke away and waved.

Mrs Hereward was making her way towards the cathedral, with what would have been a determined stride had her legs been longer. She grinned briefly when she saw them, though her eyes were dark.

'Come into the warm,' Suzie invited. 'My treat this time.'

They trooped into the cathedral café. The six of them settled themselves on the benches under the stained glass windows reassembled from shattered pieces. Suzie and Tom fetched coffee and cakes.

A shy silence hung over them. There were things which were difficult to mention.

Alianor took that fence, in an attempt at her usual forth-right self. 'Best way, really, from Flo's point of view. Chapel by the lake. One shot. All over. Still, he didn't think about the rest of us, did he? Shotgun to the head. Messy business.'

'How are the children?' asked Suzie.

'A bit stunned. Freddie's trying to get his head around the fact that Hereward Court is his now.'

'But you'll manage it, won't you? Till he's grown up.'

'You bet your life. Been dying to get my hands on the estate for years. I can run it far better than Flo ever did. It was always the way, you know. Hereward men in prison during the Civil War. Or tearing the country apart in the Wars of the Roses. Off fighting some silly crusade, killing anyone they didn't like the look of, Muslim Saracens, Orthodox Christians, you name it. It was always the women who stayed at home and managed the estate. Wouldn't have stayed in the Hereward family for a thousand years if they hadn't. What d'you think of this, then?'

She drew out of her large handbag a glossy leaflet.

'Proof copy. Hot from the printers.'

Suzie took it from her and studied it.

Hereward Court basked golden in sunshine, framed by oak trees. The lake glinted blue, with the canoe seductively beached on its shore. Inside, more photographs showed the great hall with the document chest, but as Suzie had never seen it, swept clear of the model railway set which had filled the floor. The railway itself reappeared in the long gallery, with the Hereward children engrossed over it. Copper pans gleamed in a huge raftered kitchen that was certainly not the modest one where Floridus had made Earl Grey tea for Suzie.

'You're opening Hereward Court to visitors?'

'Should have done it years ago. Only honest way to make money.'

Suzie gazed at the small woman opposite, with the determined chin. It was less than a week since her husband's funeral. The newspapers had been full of the arrests, of Floridus's suicide. And here she was, taking charge of her future, and her children's. Suzie remembered that first time they had met, at Hereward Court, and her shock at learning that the Herewards' eldest son had only just been buried.

Alianor caught her look and gave her a quick, fierce grin. 'You're in on it too, my dear. All those wonderful transcripts you did for us. I thought of setting out an exhibition in the library. People can come and see if their ancestors are listed there. Rent books and all that. Ought to have it up on a computer there, of course. They tell me that's the best way to search for things these days. Only all that nonsense is a bit beyond me.'

'I could do it for you,' said Paul.

The Fewings and Alianor turned to him with astonishment. Paul's face darkened with embarrassment. He shrugged.

'I like messing about with IT. Any excuse.'

None of them said anything. Suzie was remembering that bullet-ridden target in the woods.

Then Alianor reached out a stubby hand across the table. 'I'll take you up on that, young man, before you change your mind.' They shook hands.

'Something else,' Alianor said. 'I thought I'd get a calligrapher to draw up our family trees, so I can hang them on the wall. The Herewards and Dobles. Right back to the Norman Conquest and before.' She turned to Millie and Tom. 'I don't know if your mother ever told you, amongst all the excitement, but that day it happened, we'd just discovered that we're descended from common ancestors. Mid fourteen-hundreds. William Doble senior and Juliot Prodhome. Their daughter Douce married an earlier Floridus Hereward. Their son William junior was my ancestor and yours. You'll see their portraits next Tuesday.'

'Tuesday?' Nick queried.

'That's right. Boxing Day. Mince pies and mulled wine. Conducted tour. You're all invited. Private preview for family and friends, plus a few reporters and TV cameras, of course. We open to the public sometime in the New Year. Soon as I can get public liability insurance and all that nonsense sorted out.'

Suzie stared at her, speechless. She looked down again at the leaflet in her hands. Hereward Court. She had finished her transcripts. She had promised she would never go there again. She had nearly died there. A malignant house. In the photograph, the sun shone down on its turrets.

Yet, astonishingly, something of her blood flowed in the Hereward veins. Part of her was an enemy to this house. In the villagers who sacked the Court in the Civil War, in the farm labourer caught thieving and tried before a Hereward.

Another part of her was in the feudal landowners, the Royalists, the magistrates, in the man who had offered his estate to the Brigade of Britons. It was a disconcerting thought.

She would have to live with these contradictions.

She smiled at Alianor and got to her feet. 'This calls for a celebration. I seem to remember you telling me you had a weakness for jam doughnuts.'

AUTHOR'S NOTE

The characters, places and institutions in this book are ficti-
tious. The Hereward family, in particular, are creations of my
imagination – except for the Labradors. No resemblance to
real people, living or dead, is intended. Hereward Court
borrows features from a number of stately houses.

But I am indebted to many real-life people and organiza-
tions who have done so much to help my own family history
research in ways which have inspired this book, or have given
me other advice. They include the following:

Exhibition of local history, Tedburn St Mary

South Molton Gazette

John Tapp, for the 1821 census transcription

The Fulford family of Great Fulford, for giving me the
freedom of their document chest

Devon Record Office: www.devon.gov.uk/record_office.htm

Westcountry Studies Library: www.devon.gov.uk/index/
community/libraries/localstudies

Genuki genealogical website: www.genuki.org.uk

The Battle Abbey Roll: www.ancestry.co.uk

The Heralds' Visitations: http://uk-genealogy.org.uk/visitations/
index.html

Burke's Landed Gentry

IGI International Genealogical Index: www.familysearch.org

Diocesan Marriage Licences

Abstracts of Wills

Philip Bhebhe and his family for sharing their experience
in Mugabe's Zimbabwe

The nineteenth-century notebooks of Baldwin Fulford JP

Manorial rent books

Mark Stoyle, *Loyalty and Locality: Popular Allegiance in
Devon during the Civil War*

Lay Subsidy Rolls

Parish church histories

Family pedigrees

Property deeds
Access to Archives: www.nationalarchives.gov.uk/a2a

While I have given free rein to my imagination here, many details owe their inspiration to discoveries in my own family history research. You can find something similar to Suzie's experience in the following:

The threshing machine accident – Francis Davies of Mariansleigh, Devon, died in a similar accident in 1883.

Trial of George Arscott and William Pike – John Edworthy and Thomas Furse of West Worlington, Devon, were caught stealing corn in similar circumstances in 1854.

The holy well at Romanswell – Romansleigh, Devon.

The sculptures on the church wall at Romanswell – Burlescombe, Devon.

The little church at Siderleigh – Satterleigh, Devon.